Home FROM Within

LISA MAGGIORE

For Sam

Chapter 1

• 1999 •

I have secrets that need to be forgiven, Jessica thought, staring into the darkness of her bedroom. She sat with her knees tucked under her chin, tented in bedding that was slowly letting out the warmth. The yellow glow from her bedside clock read 3:06 a.m. Jessica glanced at Matt and noticed that he never flinched when her alarm went off. They had been sharing the same bed for many years, but sometimes she hardly knew he was there.

Wrapping her arms around herself, she shuffled toward the bathroom at the end of the hall, flipping on the night-light next to the sink so she could take a hot shower in relative darkness. Cranking open a small window, she drew a deep breath, allowing the smell of fresh dew, hay, and pine to swirl inside her nose.

A faint glow shone from the bulb above the stove as she ate oatmeal in the kitchen. Various songs from her past kept flooding her consciousness, and Jessica tried to distract herself by focusing on the mundane thoughts of the morning, but that only made the songs louder. And behind the songs were voices that did not want to stay buried under her secret armor any longer.

Jessica had been able to keep her feelings about the death of her first love, Paul, buried deep. And down deeper were the memories of her father holding those damn Colt .45s that had served as judge and jury for young lovers sneaking around. Jessica believed the ache in her chest would go away with time; however, it had been seventeen years.

But last night, while channel surfing, she stumbled upon the classic eighties movie *Purple Rain,* starring Prince. She could not stop herself from watching despite the movie ending at midnight. Caught in a whirlwind of euphoric recall, she remembered the excitement of sneaking out with her best friend, Marilee, and going to see the movie—and how the sex scene jump-started her adolescent hormones. She spent countless hours daydreaming of Paul singing "The Beautiful Ones" to her as an ode to loving her so desperately and not wanting to lose her to another. The intensity at the end of the song made her feel alive.

The songs in the movie evoked feelings in her that were a mixed bag of good and guilt. Usually those memories were ones she could bury, not wanting love and death to overpower her again. But not this time. She allowed herself to remember some of them, resurrecting other memories she could never forget.

Chapter 2

• 1982 •

The insides of Jessica's belly felt like a kamikaze pilot doing nose dives as she struggled to imagine how it would feel to have hundreds, even thousands, of other teenagers around her. Being homeschooled at Ms. Mary Carter's "school for the overprotected," run by her mother's church friend, Jessica had never been exposed to a large school setting. The thought made her smile and feel nauseous at the same time. She grabbed a piece of paper from her nightstand, having spent an hour looking at it the night before. It contained all the after-school activities she could finally try—any excuse to spend hours away from home.

For the first time, Jessica got ready without her mother standing, arms crossed, in her bedroom doorway. She said a little prayer in her head, thanking God for Aunt Lodi talking some sense into her parents and allowing her to attend the neighborhood high school. Aunt Lodi was also responsible for Jessica being able to shop for some trendy clothes with only her best friend Marilee, leaving the judgmental gaze of her mother at home.

Jessica took a quick hot shower, and as she dried off felt comfort in the routine smells of the morning: bacon and eggs for her, pancakes for her six-year-old brother, Jason, and coffee for her mother, who was not a breakfast enthusiast. Jessica brushed her long sandy-blond hair and decided not to blow-dry it, so the natural curls would take over. Many of the girls in the neighborhood had perms, and Jessica was glad she didn't need to perm her hair because she knew her father would say no to such a prospect. As she pushed her long bangs over to look in the mirror at her green eyes, she wondered how they would look with makeup. She retrieved her outfit from under the bed: a pair of Sasson jeans, a purple top with shoulder pads and geometric side cutouts, and a purple dago tee. Jessica was so happy her father was out of town and would not be inspecting her wardrobe choice. Two months of relative freedom. "Yes!" she said out loud, celebrating his absence as well as how she looked in her new outfit. She took one more glance in the full-length mirror and then decided to top off the outfit with a silver necklace that had two charms hanging from the chain: a cross and a mini dream catcher that Aunt Lodi had given her during a visit last spring. Aunt Lodi worked on the Menominee Indian reservation and had asked a tribal member who was a silversmith to make the cross and dream catcher just for her.

"Jason!" her mom yelled as she looked from room to room upstairs. It was the first day of homeschooling at Ms. Mary Carter's for Jason. He was not a fan of entering kindergarten, but was a fan of being able to get away with misbehaving while their dad was out of town.

"You're in big trouble, young man, and I'll personally see to it that your father is made aware of this behavior."

"Okay. Okay, Mom," Jason said as he came out of hiding.

Since Jessica's bedroom door had been removed, she could easily hear all the trouble her brother was giving their mother. She felt relieved that her brother's antics would serve as a distraction so she could get out of the house unnoticed, knowing her mother would protest against any clothing item that looked "cool."

Jessica's father coordinated with Bob, Marilee's father, to make sure the girls would meet at the corner and walk to school together. Marilee was Jessica's only friend. Their fathers were like brothers because they served together in Vietnam and ran a successful private security business. Bob was the reason her father moved to Chicago after Vietnam, rather than returning to his hometown in the Upper Peninsula (UP) of Michigan. It helped that they lived only two blocks from each other since Marilee's house was the only home she was allowed to visit. And her very first sleepover happened just this summer at Marilee's.

Jessica grabbed her backpack and peeked through the oak door-frame. The hallway looked clear, and from the sound of things, Jason and her mother were in his room battling over his wardrobe. His room was at the other end of a long hallway. Unlike hers, his bedroom had a door, and it was closed. Despite her stomach growling, Jessica decided to make a run for it. She rushed down the hall, down the stairs, and to the front door, turning off the alarm; thankfully her father had not changed the code again without telling her. She opened the door and yelled good-bye to her mother, then raced to get her Converse from under the porch, secure them to her feet, and speed down the block. Her plan worked—for about three seconds. Her mom was at the front door in a flash, yelling at Jessica.

"Who do you think you are leaving this house without permission?"

"I have to meet Marilee at the corner and I don't want to be late."

"What are you wearing? Who said you could wear *those* clothes to school?"

Jessica felt heat build in her face.

"Come here," her mother demanded as she looked around. Jessica slowly made her way back to her mother's critical eye. "This will be discussed tonight. You are to come straight home after eighth period. It should take you approximately seven to ten minutes to walk home so I will see you at 3:25 on the dot."

Jessica's face flamed. She had hoped that her aunt Lodi had won her some breathing room. Apparently not.

Her paternal aunt Lodi resided in the UP, and when she made a visit in the spring, Jessica had overheard an argument.

"Look at the girl; she doesn't know shit about life. She's going to be a young woman before you know it. You need to let her go."

"Shhhh," her mother said.

"For Christ's sake, Jim, you're going to lose that girl in a big way. She's going to escape from here—that's right, escape, and never talk to you again."

Her father's voice became hard. "You know why . . ."

"I know," Aunt Lodi said, interrupting him, "But you cannot protect her from everyone, including the unknown. You can still be involved from the sidelines. Let her get in the driver's seat. It's time," she said softly.

When Aunt Lodi went to bed that night, Jessica was surprised to hear her mother suggest to her father that she might be right. Jessica could tell her mother didn't like Aunt Lodi. It was not in how she spoke to her in conversation, but how her face and body looked when Aunt Lodi was around. She looked like someone who had toothpicks stuck all over her. Jessica wondered if it was because her father always listened to Aunt Lodi's opinion and sometimes even followed her suggestions—even if it was opposite to her mother's own wishes. And Jessica's father was not a man to take unsolicited advice from just anyone.

"Ooohhhmigod! You actually got out of the house wearing that?" Marilee said as Jessica walked toward her.

"You have no idea how much crap I just went through. I can't believe that I'm fifteen years old, and they still won't leave me alone."

"Well, it could be worse. I mean, your mom did let you shop with me and that outfit looks kick-ass."

"Thanks," Jessica said, beaming. "My mother had no idea the jeans would look this tight. And thank God I hid the shoes under the porch."

"Well it was worth it cuz you look hot."

"Ohmigod, shut up."

Marilee gave her a slap on the ass, and they both laughed hard. "I snuck Barbara's makeup out. Do you wanna put some on before we get there?"

Jessica wanted to wear makeup, but it was definitely on her father's "don't" list.

"Not yet. I think maybe next week."

As they walked through their neighborhood, they passed Victorians with swings hung on the wraparound porches and huge Colonials with three-car garages. All the lawns were manicured, with decorative landscaping and lush green grass that folded its way around property after property. The in-ground watering systems ran early morning and late evening to keep the lawns looking perfect. But in Jessica's opinion, the best part of the neighborhood was the trees. They looked like giant protectors of the earth, their enormous trunks reaching high into the sky. Branches tucked into the trees next to one another, as if they were in a huddle, and hung over the sidewalk and street. Jessica felt like the maple, elm, and white oak trees were looking down at her today and smiling.

After six blocks, the girls were swiftly approaching Heritage High School—a stately structure built in the late 1930s that was ensconced in the middle of her neighborhood, far from the busy streets of Chicago. The front of the building faced the neighborhood homes and consisted of multiple masses of concrete stairs with small pillars anchoring the sides. The archway above the doors gave the impression of nobility and grandeur; at least that's what Jessica thought when she drove past in the backseat of her parents' car.

Students were converging onto the sidewalk from many other parts of the neighborhood, surrounding Jessica in a sea of youth.

"Hi, Marilee," said a couple of girls.

"Hey," Marilee said as Jessica gave a faint smile, unsure how to make small talk.

Jessica knew neighborhood kids only by a "hello" that was given in passing. Marilee had attended the neighborhood elementary school, Wallace, and was friends with a lot of people, plus she was the youngest of six siblings, all of whom were current or former students of Heritage. Jessica felt less nervous with Marilee because of all the people she knew.

Across from the high school, the girls stopped. Jessica held in a gasp as her eyes scanned over the scene in front of her. Some students were in Firebirds and old Mustangs honking and stopping to talk to their friends in the middle of the street. Others were sitting on the huge cement stairs chatting, laughing, and shouting. Girls greeted each other with shrieks and hugs, and a boy chased a girl across the lawn. Some kids were even smoking. *Smoking at this age in front of everyone*, she thought. She smelled something other than cigarette smoke, a strong pungent odor she did not recognize, and noticed some kids who had the brightest hair color she had ever seen: fuchsia, yellow, purple, and blue. A few of the girls even had Mohawks. The writing on their shirts read "Dead Kennedys" and "Sex Pistols." She had never heard of such things. She felt curious about these kids but intimidated too; they all looked so mad.

"I'm so nervous," Marilee whispered, threading her arm around Jessica's.

"Me too."

"Don't worry about the penny thing. My brother told me they only say that to scare freshmen. He never once got a penny thrown at him."

"That's a relief," Jessica said.

"Plus Eddie said if anyone does mess with us, they'll be in deep shit." Jessica smiled at the idea of having a pseudo big brother at school.

The girls crossed the street, almost getting hit by some kids in a tough-looking Trans Am, and continued to walk toward the massive concrete steps at the entrance of Heritage.

"Is that a *Ripp* I see?" said a boy who looked like a man. He was sitting on top of the concrete stairs in a green ragged army jacket that looked out of place on the warm September day. As he perched above them, the pungent odor Jessica had smelled earlier was making its way from the "man" to her nose.

Marilee met his words quickly. "You're so lame."

"No, I mean it, man. You got a *Ripp* in your jeans. Look." He pointed to the seam that ran in between her butt cheeks.

Marilee did not flinch. "I'm so sure, asshole." The man-boy and his friends started laughing.

"Do you know that guy?" Jessica asked, looking back at him and wondering why he thought it was so funny to make jokes about Marilee's last name.

"One of Julie's stupid friends. Just ignore that butt-wipe."

Jessica's heart was jumping. She saw a few boys that *did* look like boys walking up the steps to the side. They were laughing at what they just heard. One had a small smile but did not look impressed. He was staring right at her. Jessica turned her head quickly and pretended she did not see him looking at her.

Upon entering homeroom, the students were instructed to find their names and take their updated schedules from the alphabetical pile on the teacher's desk, then pick a seat. Jessica, who had a death grip on her piece of paper, made her way to the far corner where only a few people were sitting. The smell of vanilla and honey hung in the air as Jessica's homeroom teacher greeted all the students with an endearing smile.

The teacher was a large black woman who wore traditional African clothing. Her floor-length dress was soft and flowing, which was a nice contrast to the bold orange, brown, and gold patterns running through it. She did, however, hold a very long yardstick in her right hand.

"Welcome, everybody. Glad to see you made it out of bed and on time to see me, Mrs. Daley, your homeroom teacher."

Using the yardstick, she pointed to information she had written on the chalkboard.

"You'll need to copy this down and memorize it."

Every once in a while, she would slam the yardstick on the board, just to make sure they were all awake and had their "listening ears" on.

"I know some of this might sound scary, but if you follow the rules, and ask for help, everything should work out just fine for you all."

Jessica kept her eyes glued on Mrs. Daley, not wanting to miss a thing. She felt impressed by her knowledge of the school and liked that Mrs. Daley gave them her telephone number in case of an emergency.

"Sometimes in life the unexpected happens—things out of your control, others' bad choices. But I have no problem helpin' students who help themselves," Mrs. Daley said, and then shared a few stories about students that she had helped. Jessica felt even more impressed. *I am so lucky to have Mrs. Daley*, she thought. The knot in her gut began to loosen and she started glancing around the classroom. She recognized a few girls she had seen in the neighborhood, walking around or riding their bikes. All of them had perms. One girl had on the exact same top as hers. However, the girl's shirt was yellow, and she didn't have a dago tee underneath it. Then she saw him. The him she was pretending not to see—the one who'd been looking at her earlier. And he was doing it again—looking at her. Jessica turned away quickly. She felt an immediate blast of heat to her cheeks, and her heart lurched toward her throat. Jessica did not want him to see how nervous she was. The only experience she'd had with boys was with her little brother and Marilee's brothers Tommy and Eddie. Tommy was twenty-three and joined the Marines after high school, so she rarely ever saw him anymore. Eddie was seventeen, Julie's twin, and a senior at Heritage. Eddie was always kind but not overly friendly. Jessica was his little sister's friend after all.

"So, anyone have any questions?" Mrs. Daley asked. The room stayed silent. "All right then. The bell will be ringing in about five minutes. I want you to look at your schedules again and we'll each go around real quick and say what class and room we're going to next. Maybe someone in here's going to the same place and you can walk together."

Jessica panicked. She did not have the courage to speak in front of her homeroom, especially around that boy who was already making her feel so off balance. She listened carefully as kids fumbled over their words and struggled to figure out exactly what room they were going to next. She felt a little relieved looking at people's faces; they all looked as red as she felt.

The boy who was staring at Jessica announced clearly he was going to room 231, Freshman Biology. Jessica stared at her schedule. *Ohmigod! We are going to the same place!*

"Anyone else headed to Biology next?" Mrs. Daley asked as the bell rang.

Jessica was unable to speak. She tried really hard, but the words refused to come out.

"Well, too bad. I'm sure the rest of you will be just fine, but if you need help, please come back to this room and I'll point you in the right direction."

Despite a blush that covered her chest and face, Jessica looked up and smiled at Mrs. Daley's angelic face.

As the bell rang, the reality of her foolishness hit her. What would that boy think as he saw her walk into the same classroom as him? Jessica got up slowly and tried to think of all the ways she could get out of Freshman Biology. Maybe she could switch classes. But how would she explain the reason to her parents? Maybe Marilee's brother Tommy could come home on leave from the Marines and pretend to be her father. Yeah, and sign papers to get her out of second period Biology. Or maybe Aunt Lodi.

Jessica stepped out of the safe confines of homeroom and was swept into a current of students. She finally managed to swim upstream and after a few minutes arrived safely in front of room 231. For a brief moment, she thought about hiding in the bathroom, but the image of her parents' faces persuaded her otherwise. She took a deep breath, touched her cross and dream catcher charm with her fingers, and walked into the classroom. The biology teacher was standing by his desk fiddling with something, so Jessica caught only a glimpse of his silhouette—tall and gangly, like a tree along the road they passed on the drive to Aunt Lodi's in the UP. As he turned to address the students, Jessica noticed his large black-rimmed glasses, and he sported tufts of gray hair that stuck out in a mess while papers and other items were falling out of the pockets of his white lab coat.

Mr. Wilberg called each of the students alphabetically and then pointed to where he wanted them to sit. One name was repeated because no owner claimed it: Peterson.

"Jessica Turner," he announced, pointing to the last lab table in the back. A girl named Cassandra Stokle was already sitting there. The table held room for six students and was eventually filled with three more. Mr. Wilberg was double-checking his placement when a student walked into the classroom ten minutes late.

"Sorry," the boy said, "I had to help a student find her classroom."

Jessica looked up to see the boy from her homeroom. Her face blazed again.

"You are late. Do not come to my class late."

The boy looked surprised. "What? You want me to leave a cryin' girl in the hallway just to get to class on time?"

"You will get to class on time, crying or no crying."

The boy was about to say something else but hesitated, gave a cocky smile, and said, "Yes, sir. Where do you want me to sit?"

Mr. Wilberg's eyes narrowed. "What is your name?"

"Paul Peterson."

"Peterson?" Mr. Wilberg looked down at the sheet of paper with all the seating decisions. He rubbed his forehead with one hand and then pointed to one of the lab tables.

"Peterson is supposed to be at *that* table. But as you can see, *that* table is full because we did not know we had a Peterson." Some of the students started chuckling. Jessica was amazed that Paul did not appear flustered by what was happening and stood calmly waiting for the confused biology teacher to figure things out. After about thirty seconds, Mr. Wilberg ordered him to have a seat at the last lab table. Jessica felt light-headed as Paul made his way toward her. He gave her a sheepish grin as he sat down next to her, and she noticed for the first time how gorgeous his eyes were; they reminded her of a blue stained-glass window with the sun shining through from behind. Jessica gave him a small smile and turned her attention back to Mr. Wilberg and all his rules.

Chapter 3

Paul Peterson barely looked at Jessica during Biology. He took notes, listened attentively, and quietly nodded at a few kids he knew. When the bell rang, he got up and walked toward them. The boys grinned and pushed each other when they greeted and Jessica watched them talk for a few seconds, and then follow Paul out of the classroom. Despite the seesaw of emotions she'd experienced earlier, she liked the idea of someone taking an interest in her. She had never been intensely looked at by a boy before.

After attending a few more classes, Jessica found herself being pushed by a mass of bodies in the hallway, trying to edge away from a large, smelly boy, when she felt a gentle tug on her arm. It was Eddie, Marilee's brother. He smiled and calmly asked, "Do you know where you're going?"

"I'm trying to meet Marilee in the lunchroom."

"Come on."

Jessica followed Eddie as he made his way through the crowd of bodies and led Jessica to the lunchroom that housed hundreds of students. It looked as wide and long as a football field with windows lining the walls, which gave it a more open feeling, unlike the classrooms. But the booming sounds of teenage voices piled on top of each other were what drew Jessica's attention, never having experienced the contained loudness of her kind before.

"Hey, I'm over here." Marilee waved her hands above her head while standing in a long line to purchase lunch with her big sister Barbara.

Jessica pointed to Marilee, and Eddie said he would see them later.

"I am sooo hungry," Marilee said, all smiles.

"Me too," Jessica said. "Hi, Barbara."

"Hey, freshie. Are you playing nice with everyone?"

Marilee jumped in. "Maybe that's a question we should be asking you."

Jessica hid her smile and continued to talk to Marilee. As they approached the cashier, Jessica realized she had to purchase her lunch; she'd assumed it was free. She jammed her fingers into her jean pockets to search for money, but Marilee told her not to worry; they would share what she bought. Jessica followed Marilee as she paved a way to a table that only had a few students.

"Is Barbara sitting with us?"

"No way. She wants to sit with her wastoid friends."

Jessica took a bite of Marilee's pizza and quickly realized that smell and taste do not match in a school lunchroom.

"Ohmigod, I have to tell you about my gym class. I have the absolute worst gym teacher ever. I want to gag myself when I look at her."

"Geez, what's wrong with her?"

"She kept saying we *have* to change into our gym uniform. She said she would stand in the locker room and make sure we're all in our shorts and T-shirts. And don't even think about bringing a note to get out of swimming because you have your period."

"Ew, that's gross," Jessica said as she reached for a fry, hoping it would be edible.

The girls continued to fill each other in on details of the day, and Jessica wanted to tell Marilee about Paul, but she ran out of time. Right before the bell rang, Eddie sat down at the girls' table to see how they were doing.

Marilee had an earful to say, especially about the gym teacher. Jessica said she was doing pretty good except in the hallways.

"Just elbow yourself through the crowd," Eddie said.

Jessica smiled, appreciating the advice, and for the first time took notice at how handsome Eddie looked. Being away from the only space she interacted with the Ripps, their home, made her think about them in a different way. Jessica surmised that they were an attractive bunch, despite the boys' slightly crooked noses and the girls' frightfully pale skin. Their athletic bodies allowed them star status on any sports team they played for, and their oldest sister, Kathy, even got a scholarship to play volleyball in college. And all the Ripp children had two distinctive traits: black wavy hair and cornflower-blue eyes.

Before parting ways, Jessica was reminded she would be walking home alone after school. Marilee, following in the footsteps of her older siblings, had signed up for cross-country and would be staying after school for practices. Jessica wondered out loud if she should also sign up but really had no interest in running. In fact, the thought of running made her want to throw up.

"I didn't want to sign up either, but that's the tradition in our family."

Right before walking to their next class, Marilee grimaced. "I was hoping to sign up for drama club but I'm not sure how that would go over." Jessica thought about it for a minute. She imagined Marilee up on stage in makeup and costume, smiling and taking numerous bows with an armful of flowers. It was a perfect fit.

"I think you should go for it."

Marilee looked at her for a couple of seconds and then flashed a mischievous grin. "I think I just may."

*   *   *

The smell of floor wax and worn-out shoes hit Jessica's nose as she pulled open the heavy wooden gym doors. The girls in the class were instructed to sit in a large circle. When more girls entered the gym the circle would, on cue, become wider as girls scooted themselves back to make room for the newcomers.

Jessica looked around the circle and noticed two girls with Mohawks sitting next to each other. She tried not to look their way but could not help but sneak a peek; she was so inquisitive about their hair. *Did their parents really let them do that?* For the first time, she entertained the thought that other families had way different sets of rules. The Ripps were not as domineering as her family, but Mr. Ripp and her father were made of the same cloth—serving as Green Berets did that to a man.

Ms. Rando, a petite blonde, stepped inside the circle and oriented the girls to Gym. Jessica had never attended a gym class before. However, she was forced into physical exercise at a young age. Her father had Jessica running a mile before she was eight years old, along with push-ups, sit-ups, and other types of exercises as a regular part of her wake-up routine. He stopped the regimen when Jessica got her period. She figured her mother must have suggested it was time to end the torture. Now it was Mother Nature's turn.

When Ms. Rando's gym speech was over, she walked them to the locker rooms. Although not as creepy about the gym uniforms, she did emphasize that their grade was affected by what they chose to wear during Gym. The Mohawk girls whispered loud enough for the students around them to hear that "there was no fucking way they were wearing those uniforms." Jessica's eyes widened. As the class exited the locker room and followed Ms. Rando into the pool area, she yelled, "Choices affect grades!"

Upon hearing the bell signaling the last period of the day, Jessica felt like she had been trampled by a stampede of wild animals. She told herself she just had to muster one more burst of energy and finish eighth period, Humanities. As one of the first students to arrive in the classroom, she smiled weakly at Mr. Gambino as he peered at her above his glasses, which perched low on his nose, and decided to sit in the back corner again, where it felt safe. Students trickled in and Jessica was surprised at how many kids she was starting to recognize from previous classes. Cassandra from Biology made her way to the back and sat next to Jessica. After a quick exchange of smiles, Cassandra started to talk when Paul stepped into the classroom. Jessica could not concentrate on what Cassandra was saying as she watched Paul gaze around the room, finally resting his stare on her face. He walked toward her, choosing the seat directly in front of her, and then turned and whispered to those around him that he didn't know Al Capone was still alive. A few kids laughed, but Jessica had no idea what he was talking about. She smiled anyway, not wanting anyone to know how uninformed she was.

Mr. Gambino sat on top of his desk and with a deep voice explained the goals of Humanities. Jessica tried to listen intently but was distracted by Paul sitting in front of her. She started collecting details about him in her head: medium build, auburn feathered hair that lay at his collar, a faded red-and-black flannel shirt but not the type a hunter would wear; it even had slight holes in back of the armpits. The smell of laundry detergent and a slight scent of cigarette smoke. She wondered if he was a smoker. And if so, would that stop her from thinking about him?

"So the group project will count for 50 percent of your grade. It is imperative that you learn to work as a team," said Mr. Gambino.

He gingerly got off his desk and walked with a slight limp to the row all the way to the left. "You two and the two in back of you will form a group. The rest of you follow the pattern. Have one person write down the names of everyone in your group, and put it on my desk at the end of the period."

Paul turned to the boy on his right and then to Jessica and Cassandra. "Looks like we're a group."

The four looked at each other for a few seconds, and then Paul spoke up. "My writing sucks."

The other boy, who was dressed in black and had some sort of markings all over his hands and arms, said he did not have a pen or paper to write with. *Strange,* Jessica thought. It looked like he used up all the ink from a pen on himself. Cassandra spoke up and said she would do it. Jessica leaned her body against the desk and squeezed her hands together underneath so no one would see them shake. She quietly said her name to Cassandra and noticed Paul looking at her.

"Why are you talking so quiet?"

Jessica felt so cowardly but impulsively shrugged. To Jessica's relief, Mr. Gambino's voice broke into Paul asking more questions.

Books were passed out, more notes taken, and information distributed until finally the bell rang. Cassandra looked at Jessica. "I'm so glad to go home."

Jessica wished she felt the same.

And just like Biology, Paul got up without looking back and left the classroom. She wondered if he was someone who liked or disliked going home. And would that make a difference in her thinking about him so much?

Chapter 4

When Jessica stepped outside, she was struck by the brightness of the sun and squinted to adjust to the natural light. The warm breeze of fall swirled around her like a blanket she knew well. It felt refreshing to be out of the school building. However, dreaded thoughts of the conversation she would be having with her mother weighed heavy on her.

As with the beginning of the school day, hundreds of students gathered upon the grounds of Heritage. Cars were again filled with teenagers making their way down the street. Jessica daydreamed about getting into one of those cars with Marilee and driving far away to the deep woods where Aunt Lodi lived. Aunt Lodi had a cabin on ten acres surrounded by paper birch, tamarack, and balsam fir trees. A long narrow driveway made of grass and gravel led to her home off a two-lane country road. Two crab apple trees that looked to be one hundred years old sat pocked and wrinkled alongside the garage; the largest held an old tire swing that Aunt Lodi had Jessica's father hang for her when she was a child. A creek ran along the property line, and in the springtime, smelt gathered and filled the entire width. Standing on either side of the bank, you could dip a net in and have dinner for the next week. Aunt Lodi could panfry smelt like no other; she could feed the whole town with her fish fries. "Peaceful" was how Aunt Lodi described where she lived. "Isolated" was what her mother thought. Jessica saw both sides, but decided she preferred the peacefulness of the UP over the city even at this age.

As Jessica walked home, she spotted two girls from homeroom in front of her. She slowed her pace so she would not catch up to them, but began to worry she may not make it home to her mother's order of "seven to ten minutes." Jessica felt like an amateur socializing with girls her age. When she attended Mary Carter's homeschool in kindergarten, the other students were in sixth, seventh, and eighth grades. Jessica was "cute" and "a little lady" but not a peer. As the older students graduated to high school, Jessica was alone.

The two girls strolled down the sidewalk, making no attempts at being hurried. Jessica forgot to bring her watch and tried to estimate how long she had been walking. Before putting all the calculations in her head, she noticed the two girls stopped and were facing her, saying something she could not hear. Jessica looked behind her. No one was there.

"Aren't you in our homeroom?" one asked as Jessica slinked closer.

"Uh, yes," Jessica said.

The girl with the matching-top-but-in-yellow stated, "You're Marilee Ripp's friend?"

"Uh, yes."

Both girls' eyes lit up. "Cool," they said. The girls started making idle interrogation: How come you didn't go to Wallace? How come we never see you on your bike or at the pool? How come you don't hang out in the neighborhood?

The only answer she could muster up was, "Uh well, I'm not sure."

"So you hang out with Marilee's family?"

Jessica's uneasiness was starting to wear away, or maybe her patience. "Uh, like her parents and siblings?"

Yellow shirt girl smiled. "Yeah, her brother and stuff."

"Sometimes. But mostly it's me and Marilee."

"Cool. We should hang out. I know it's the first day and all, but I heard a senior is throwing a bash on the river bottom at LaBart Woods."

"Tonight?" Jessica questioned, and then wished she could take it back, not wanting to be perceived as a dork.

The yellow shirt girl sneered, "Well yeah, today is the first day of school."

"I don't think I can go."

"What about Marilee and her brother Eddie?"

"Well, maybe," Jessica said, not wanting Marilee and Eddie to look like dorks too.

"Oh shit. I gotta get home," said yellow shirt girl after looking at her watch. "I gotta babysit my brothers till my mom gets home from work."

Before she could stop herself, Jessica asked what time it was.

"Three thirty."

"I have to go," she said and ran the two blocks home, not caring what those girls thought of her anymore.

Her mother was on the front porch. As Jessica got closer, she could see her mother's eyebrows pulled together. "Where have you been?"

Jessica tried to catch her breath. "Talking to some girls from home-room."

"What girls? Where are they?"

"They're back that way. I ran home as soon as I realized I was five minutes late."

Her mother looked unconvinced. "Come in the house and get cleaned up. Then we'll talk."

Jessica stepped in and saw a vase of brightly colored flowers on the dining room table. Walking over to smell them, she noticed a card attached.

"That's from Lodi," her mother said as she zipped past the dining room and into the kitchen. Jessica was about to rip open the tiny envelope but realized it had already been opened.

"You are entering an exciting new chapter of your life. Remember we are cheering you on. I hope your first day of high school is as beautiful as the young woman you are becoming. Love, Aunt Lodi, Mom, and Dad." Jessica smirked; this was all Aunt Lodi.

Jessica placed the flowers on her bedside table, and after washing her hands, changing her clothes, and emptying her backpack, she sat and waited for her mother on the leather couch in the office. The office was where all the "talks" took place. Bookshelves were filled from floor to ceiling and ran the length of one wall. Vietnam-era pictures, awards, and antique weapons hung on the opposite wall. There were also two trophy-winning whitetail and bullheads for all to see. A display of absolute masculinity, Jessica realized as she got older. A large walnut desk was placed alongside the French doors that faced the backyard, that way her father could keep an eye on her and Jason. The only object that creeped her out was the black bearskin rug. She hated that her father killed that glorious animal just for it to be stepped on. They didn't even eat the meat like they did with the deer and elk. Jessica sat up tall upon her mother entering the room. Her mother rolled the brown leather desk chair to the middle of the room, right beside the angry face of the bear.

"We need to discuss the situation that happened this morning. You left the house without permission." Her mother held up her fingers that were finely filed down but never held any polish, to count out just how many bad acts Jessica had committed. "You wore clothing we would never approve of, you did not eat breakfast, and you did not bring your Mace." Jessica was surprised by the last statement. Her father ingrained in her the importance of keeping herself protected against the unknown. She always had her Mace with her. The fact that she forgot it made her feel askew.

"I forgot my Mace?"

"Yes, you left it in your underwear drawer." Jessica was used to the invasion of privacy, but this time felt a twinge in her throat. "Now, I understand you are experiencing new things, but the rules here still apply."

"I'm sorry I forgot my Mace. I won't let that happen again."

"Your clothing is another issue. You cannot wear skintight clothing. Your father would never approve," her mother said, tucking her chin-length brown hair behind her ears.

"So what do you want me to wear?"

"You have plenty of clothes that I bought you, but I will carve out a few hours this week to take you shopping for some warmer items."

Jessica felt heat flood her veins. Her mother was ruining her high school career.

"Do you have any questions?"

"No."

Jessica made her way up to her doorless room, falling onto her bed and burying her face in her pillow. Images of her in the hallways of Heritage with students surrounding her, pointing and laughing at her baggy clothes filled her brain. She shook her head in the pillow to pry out the images while holding in the tears.

At the first sight of Marilee on the corner the next morning, Jessica burst into tears.

"Ohmigod, what's wrong?"

"Look at . . ."

"Your clothes. Your mother got to you." Jessica nodded. Marilee surveyed her up and down. Suddenly her eyes flashed as she grabbed Jessica's hands. "Stay put. I'll be right back."

Marilee ran home and came back in less than three minutes with clothes stuffed in her backpack.

"I pulled out pants that are a little short on me, so they should fit you. And that cute red top you like. You sneak out the clothing your mother hates. I'll keep it at my house and bring you an outfit every day. You can change at school . . . or how 'bout the garage?"

"Ohmigod, I can change in your garage and no one would see me walk to school looking like this."

The girls smiled at the plan.

They jogged to school so Jessica could change before the first bell rang. Marilee's jeans fit perfectly and despite the shoes being a little big, they were way cooler than the penny loafers her mother made her wear.

Still out of breath from jogging, Jessica made her way to algebra with Mrs. Hittenbach. She entered the room and instinctively made a beeline to the safety of the back. However, all of the seats were taken so she made a split-second decision and ended up in the middle of the second row. Sitting perfectly still for a moment she tried to calm down her insides, which felt like a terrible storm, all windblown and tattered, and focused on only the teacher's voice to help set her straight. It worked. Mrs. Hittenbach had the voice of an angel. She sang, in verse, the rules of her class and the goals of Algebra, or at least that's how Jessica heard it. It reminded her of Sunday church hymns. Even though Jessica's voice was not on pitch most of the time, she found solace singing loud in church. It was the only place she felt she could express herself without the critical eye of her parents. At least that of her mother since her father would not step foot in church. He never made them feel like they were doing anything wrong by going every

Sunday, but he made it very clear he wanted nothing to do with organized religion.

"When I die, do not have a church service for me. I want to be cremated and my ashes poured on Lodi's property," he announced one night at dinner.

"Cremated and ashes poured on Lodi's property?" her mother choked out. "How could you not want your exit to be filled with love from your family and God?"

Her father smirked. "Katherine, your God and my God are not one in the same. And you are to do as I wish." And that was the end of that. Jessica knew not to prod or ask more exploratory questions. That led to two responses: none of your business and none of your damn business.

As Jessica immersed herself in the first week at Heritage, she made a conscious effort to say hi to more students. The effort to make friends was a great distraction from how she really felt on the inside—all knotted up. But no matter how much she psyched herself up, she felt self-conscious in front of Paul. In homeroom, she veered away from him, sitting as far away as she could. Her mind and body took over, almost preaching, "This one is out of your league. Stay away!" Mrs. Daley was always a warm presence, asking the students about their week and taking a genuine interest in them as people. Jessica could not help but smile at her thoughtfulness and take refuge in her comfort.

On Friday, Mrs. Daley summoned Jessica to her desk and told her that because of Jessica's respectful manner through the first week of school, Jessica was allotted the most trusted homeroom job position: attendance delivery. Jessica was to bring the attendance card from homeroom to the office each morning. Anyone marked absent in homeroom got a call home. A student only had to attend homeroom and would be counted for being in school all day.

However, in the wrong hands, the attendance sheet could be altered on the way from homeroom to the office, ensuring that kids who cut class could not be detected, at least until report card pickup.

Jessica felt honored and a little embarrassed by the news. She figured out pretty quickly that kids who appeared really smart or highly responsible got made fun of. Not always to their face, but it was another way students pecked out social order in high school. But in Mrs. Daley's classroom, there would be none of that. In that first week alone, she gave looks, had private talking-tos, and if needed, would make someone feel stupid for even thinking about laughing at another student in her presence. And once again, Jessica thanked God she had Mrs. Daley in her life.

Chapter 5

Jessica plodded through the first two months of high school hinged to the only two people who made her feel safe: Marilee and Mrs. Daley. She continued to change her clothes in the Ripp's garage; Julie even donated a few items that did not fit her anymore. Eddie got clued in to what was happening when he was not allowed access to the garage by Marilee. Jessica, sporting her cool hand-me-downs, looked at him with pleading eyes.

"Don't worry. I won't tell anyone," Eddie said. "But make sure Dad doesn't find out. That's one secret he will not keep from Mr. Turner."

Jessica also spent the first two months working on overcoming her shyness with Paul. Despite having no bedroom privacy, she would sneak hours in front of the mirror, practicing how to talk to Paul without trembling, or at least with less redness in her face. And in homeroom it was working. Jessica purposely sat near Paul and a small group of his friends and would push herself to engage in the casual conversation being offered. Often she had nothing to contribute because she did not attend concerts or play video games, and radio or TV time was off-limits in her home. But on a few occasions, topics came up that she could comment on. One day everyone was sharing their favorite color, and Jessica said hers was green. Paul said that was his favorite too.

"What's your favorite dessert?" Paul asked Jessica.

Jessica's mother made the best Baked Alaska, but Jessica thought that would not be something most kids her age knew about, so she quickly thought of a dessert all kids seemed to enjoy.

"Chocolate cake."

"Pudding in the middle or no pudding?" Paul volleyed back.

Jessica never had chocolate cake with pudding in the middle, but it sounded divine so she went with her taste buds.

"Pudding, of course."

Paul's smile reached his eyes as he looked at Jessica and suddenly she felt like she scored some points, so she sat a little taller in her chair.

The time she'd spent with Mary Carter had propelled Jessica into a higher plane. She earned straight A's without much effort and was placed in accelerated classes for math and English. In just the first two months of school, Mrs. Daley invited her to join the Honors Society. Jessica also joined Key Club, an organization that worked on service projects throughout the city. Two excellent reasons not to go home after school.

In October, the Key Club went to a community center in a Chicago neighborhood that had a high concentration of poverty and helped elementary students with a project they were working on. Her community project was focused on how to get kids to stop littering on the flawless lawns of the homes surrounding Heritage. The harsh realism that their community service project differed vastly from hers became highly evident. The other students were concerned with shootings, drug use, and lack of jobs. She felt downright spoiled that she did not have to contend with flying bullets or drugged-out parents. Although her parents were far from relaxed, she could not remember a time when a substance influenced them caring for her. Her mother would enjoy a glass of wine now and then, but her father stayed away from the stuff. He wanted nothing that would dull his senses, although Jessica did remember a time at Aunt Lodi's big birthday bash.

Aunt Lodi loved to celebrate, and even the smallest occasion would make her want to bake a cake. One year she decided to throw herself a birthday bash and insisted that they all come to Cedar Creek for the weekend. Jessica was ecstatic at an additional chance to see Aunt Lodi. Even though Jessica usually saw her three times a year, she wanted more; Aunt Lodi was contagious, making even the most guarded ease themselves into the pool of calm water she offered. Jessica noticed that in the company of his sister, her father's appearance changed. The brow that looked as if it had been frozen with creases loosened, and the harsh lines that framed his green eyes and even the scar below his left eye faded, as if he had used one of her mother's miracle beauty products. His body relaxed, allowing Aunt Lodi to put her arm around it and pull him from person to person. Jessica even heard him laugh out loud. She remembered walking over and looking up at his mass of muscle. He had a beer in hand. As he looked down at her tiny frame with a smile that made his face look inviting, he put his arm around her neck and laughingly introduced her to the other men. Jessica wanted to know more about these men. What were they doing that would make him change into good-time Jim? As she got older, she realized that while the men may have been funny, the beer is what made him human. Once she made that connection, she started asking her mother to buy some beer for Dad because he enjoyed it so much at Aunt Lodi's bash. Her mother met her request with a quick response: "No."

During Biology, a girl at their table tried to convince Jessica to give her the answers to their homework. She had received an F on an earlier assignment and was afraid that her parents would ground her if she did not produce an A. Jessica's pulse quickened, and her voice quivered because she really wanted to fit in, but not at the expense of cheating. So she said no.

"Come on, I need some help," the girl whispered again.

Jessica noticed that Paul was studying the situation, but she shook her head and went back to working on the Biology assignment. Then she heard the girl whisper, "Bitch."

"You're the bitch," Paul said. "Do your own work."

"Peterson, did you swear in my classroom?" Mr. Wilberg announced loudly.

Paul said yes, and Mr. Wilberg kicked him out. Jessica felt horrible and was about to say she was sorry when Paul winked at her as he collected his things and then walked toward the door. Before stepping into the hallway, he looked back toward Jessica and gave her a quick grin.

"Is that your boyfriend?" another girl at their table asked. Jessica quietly said no, but her heart thumped a little harder.

Jessica noticed she was getting more attention from boys. It took her a few weeks, but she eventually figured out that two boys in homeroom, Mike and Jeff, appeared to like her but really wanted to use her. She was, after all, the deliverer. They would try to move closer to her seat in homeroom, be extra nice whenever they saw her in the hallway, and invite her to parties. Jessica took notice when Mrs. Daley would narrow her eyes. The look on Mrs. Daley's face said it all: they were trying to play her for a fool. Jessica, having been raised by a Green Beret, was ingrained with the values of loyalty, duty, and honor. That was one thing she was very clear on: she would never let the integrity of her job suffer because of some boys.

But there was one boy who entered her thoughts often. In the same small group for Humanities, Paul and Jessica spent a lot of time together working on the class project and started to connect on a level that was brand-new to her. At night, she would lie in bed and fantasize that she was his girlfriend. They would go outside for lunch and he would hold her hand. He would look at her with a gentle smile and tell her he liked her a lot. For some reason, she could not shake Marilee from her fantasy. She would be along too, with about five boys dragging behind vying for her attention. And she would jabber away, trying to decide, out loud, which one she should pick. Paul would give an exasperated look and Jessica would just smile.

Jessica believed Paul also enjoyed her company. He always smiled when he saw her, and he would wait for her so they could walk to class together. Paul also made her feel protected. In homeroom, his cool eyes would turn icy when Mike and Jeff pulled their chairs closer to Jessica, trying to worm their way into her good graces. Jessica gave them no reason to continue, but they still tried daily.

As Jessica and Paul walked to Biology one day, she took notice of Jeff, who followed behind them.

"Hey, Jessica. I need to ask you something, *alone.*"

Jessica looked at him confused, but Paul asked, "Why? You gonna ask her out?"

"Yeah."

"Are you fuckin' high?" Paul retorted before Jessica had a chance to respond. "She doesn't want to go out with you." Jeff stepped in front of them and put his arm out so they both had to stop.

"I'm asking her, not *you.*"

Jessica felt feverish. "Well, uh . . . you know, I have to think about it."

Jeff looked surprised and Paul looked pissed.

"Think about it? What's there to think about?"

"Because she knows you ain't nothin' but a dog," Paul said.

"What's your problem, man? I'm just trying to take a nice girl out to McDonalds."

"Eww, high class, McDonalds," Paul retorted. Jessica was surprised by Paul's anger but also felt sorry for him; he could not stop running his mouth. Jessica was thankful Mrs. Daley overheard some of the drama from the homeroom door. She walked over and told them the business of asking someone out was finished for the day.

"Get on to your classrooms before you're marked tardy," she said directly to the boys.

Jeff looked hard at Paul, and Paul met it back with a stare that even Jessica's father would have been proud of.

Paul turned and walked quickly down the hall to Biology, and Jessica almost had to run to keep up, but decided to let him be. She had seen that look on her father and knew the best defense was to fade into the scenery. Paul entered Biology twenty paces in front of her and was sitting in his usual seat. Carefully, Jessica sat down next to him, spreading her books out in a quiet way, so as not to erupt the volcano next to her. He brooded all through class. When the bell rang, he did not say the usual, "see ya at lunch." He just got up and left. Jessica mentally played the tape out from earlier to see if she had done something wrong, but there was nothing she could pinpoint. Except that maybe Paul wanted to ask her out first.

She had no intentions of going on a date with Jeff. First off, she didn't like him like that, and second she was not allowed to date until she turned twenty-one. Although by that time, she surmised, she would be long gone and could date freely. A while back, she mentioned to her father that she would probably be away at college by age twenty-one. He said to check back with him when she turned twenty-one.

At lunchtime, Jessica scanned the lunchroom but there was no sight of Paul. Her stomach started to turn over in a sick way, wishing she had given a different answer when Jeff asked her out. But how was she to know Jeff's intentions when he followed behind them?

"Are you okay?" Marilee asked, cutting off Jessica's anguish.

"Sort of."

"Where's Paul? Isn't he gonna come by our table? Or did Eddie scare him off?"

Jessica didn't know how to answer so she just shrugged, thinking about what happened yesterday. Paul and a couple of his buddies eventually joined Jessica and Marilee at their lunch table. They smelled like the pungent odor that had met her nose that first day of school. Paul was laughing at his buddies as they stuffed chips and whatever else they could get their hands on into their mouths. One guy even poured packets of ketchup in his mouth, which completely grossed Jessica out. Paul kept laughing and calling them "tards." As Eddie approached their table, his face said it all. A few of Paul's buddies who knew Eddie said, "Hey, man. What's up, dude?" Eddie quickly made sure they all knew who his little sister was, and that Jessica was considered a little sister too. The pharmaceutical high they were all on came crashing down. All the boys said, "Yeah sure, man, no problem here. Just hangin' out, ya know." Paul was the only one to open his bullheaded mouth.

"So what are you sayin'? I can't sit at this table and talk to these girls?"

"I'm just letting you know what's up."

"Oh," said Paul, "so what's up is that you don't want us sittin' with your sisters?"

"I guess you could look at it that way."

Paul's friends started to crack under the pressure. They didn't want to be in the frying pan, they just wanted to eat what was in the frying pan.

"Hey, man, that's cool. Come on, the bell's about to ring anyways," said the boy who had ketchup on his lips and cheek.

"Yeah," another one said as he clumsily stood up. "I need to be at my next class or I'm in deep shit."

Paul eyed Eddie for a few seconds. Jessica noticed how glassy and red Paul's eyes looked, and she felt torn. She wanted to be Eddie's little sister, but she also wanted to be Paul's girlfriend, a prospect she knew was out of the question but still loved to daydream about. Jessica was starting to resent Eddie for acting like her father. Paul left the table last, staring Eddie down. "See you girls tomorrow," he said, aiming his words toward Eddie.

Jessica wanted to say something but was afraid Eddie would get mad. She was happy when Marilee piped in that he needed to cool his jets.

"I know you feel like you need to protect me, but seriously, no boys are ever going to come near me with you around. And Jessica really likes Paul. You chased him away for no reason."

"Paul isn't boyfriend material," Eddie stated.

"Why?" Marilee asked.

Eddie got in close so not everyone would hear. "Because he's a total burnout. Look at his eyes. Those alone should warn you that he's messed up."

"What'd you mean, drugs?" Marilee questioned.

"Yeah, and other things. He's a freshie, and I know who he is just by the neighborhood rep. Jessica, you're easy picking for someone who knows a hell of a lot more about life." Jessica was not sure to take that as a compliment or insult, but either way his words were hard to ignore. So Paul was a burnout, which—as Jessica learned in her first few days of high school—meant he liked to party. She was not so sure what "party" entailed, but was pretty confident Pin the Tail on the Donkey and drinking soda pop were not on the agenda.

Paul did not show up for Humanities, and as Jessica walked down the concrete steps, she was surprised to see him walking toward her with a strange look on his face. He was alone, however his group of friends stood in a circle not far off smoking cigarettes, talking, and laughing. She noticed that the circle of friends now included a few girls who liked to smoke too.

"Hey," he said.

"Hi," she said as she stepped over to the side so as not to get trampled by exiting students. She could smell that pungent odor again and his eyes looked tired.

"What did I miss in class?"

Jessica felt a twinge of anger. *Why should I tell you when you blew class off to "party" with your friends?* "Not much."

"Cool."

They stared at each other for a couple of seconds.

"Do you wanna hang out with us?" He motioned toward his friends. "We're goin' over to Alicia's house and then back to mine."

Jessica could not believe what she was hearing. He thinks she wants to party. The thought scared her, and for the first time, she understood what Eddie warned her about.

"I have to go. I have to watch my little brother until my mother gets home from work." She felt guilty lying but thought she had no choice in order to get out of the invite with her reputation intact.

"Sure. Whatever."

"See you tomorrow," she said and walked off before Paul could say good-bye.

That night in bed, she had two worries about the following day: seeing Paul in homeroom and her father's return home.

Chapter 6

When she'd gotten back from school the day before, she'd seen the Polish cleaning ladies' van in the driveway—Father was coming home. Before her father's return, her mother always hired a cleaning crew to ensure perfection. Even though her mother was an immaculate housekeeper, her father could always find something not quite clean enough. And as usual, Jessica's insides were a frenzy of oppression and turmoil. Life at home was more relaxed when her father was away. Her mother carried out the rules, but not as forcefully. Her mother would never make anyone stand in the corner holding books above their head as punishment for a messy bedroom, although that type of chastisement had not been doled out in a while. Now bedroom doors were removed to ensure no mistakes were made at all. Jessica started to ache about the situation that led to her door being removed.

It was over the summer. All the neighborhood kids were out playing Ghost in the Graveyard. Even the high schoolers got involved, so they could hide with their sweetheart and make out, or at least that's what Marilee thought. Jessica would peek from behind the curtain in her bedroom at all the kids. Marilee and Barbara were allowed to play, and sometimes Marilee would sneak over and wave to Jessica, who was at the closed window. One night, trying to impress a boy she liked—according to Marilee—Barbara decided it would be funny to throw rocks at Jessica's window, trying to get her to come outside. Barbara's aim was not very good, and she started hitting other parts of the house. When Jessica heard the commotion, she opened the window to see Barbara and some of the neighborhood boys whispering for her to come down because one of the boys liked her. Jessica told them to leave before her father came, but it was too late. The next thing Jessica knew, she was being dragged back into her room by the neck of her nightgown and thrown onto the bed. As soon as Barbara saw Jessica get tugged in she took off, but the boys, who did not catch on as quickly, just stood there. When her father stuck his head out the window, the boys started running in different directions.

"Step back on my property again you'll find bullet holes in your heads," he bellowed.

Her father yanked the window down, locked it, and then turned toward Jessica, who was hugging her pillow with her knees pulled up to her chest. Her mother dashed in just as her father unleashed a bunch of expletives.

"Jim, please," her mother said.

"She was about to climb down the window and meet a group of boys."

Her mother looked at Jessica. "Is this true?"

She shook her head no as she stuffed in the tears. She would not show them her tears.

"Bullshit! I will not listen to any more of it." Her father's face was contorted and small beads of sweat had built around the edges of his buzz cut. His fists looked like tightly wound pieces of barbed wire.

"Jim, will you please go downstairs? I want to make sure those boys don't try to get into the house."

Her father's chest was heaving. "You're a whore and a liar."

"Jim, please," her mother pleaded. He backed up and slowly walked out of the room with her mother following. Jessica could no longer hold in her pain. Her tears tumbled out, spilling all over the pristine Egyptian cotton comforter.

Later that night, she was awoken by the sounds of drilling. Standing between the hall and her open bedroom door with an electric drill in hand was her father. His large mass was shaded in dark as he worked with only a headlamp. He decided the only way to keep a better eye on Jessica was to take off her door. This way he or Katherine would have easier access to the goings-on in her room. Jessica pretended she was sleeping when her father announced this out loud, but it did not matter to her anyway. He had won.

Before Jessica left for school, she placed a welcome home letter for her father on the kitchen island. Leaving a note was an easier way to bridge the hello and awkwardness of him not being in her life for two months. In the note, she included her grades, the Honor Society and Key Club information, along with a few tidbits of her personal life. She was unsure if he cared about that last part, but it was a continued effort for Jessica to connect with him on an intimate level.

During homeroom, Jessica sat with the regulars, and Paul. No words were spoken about yesterday. Even Jeff did not bring it up. As abruptly as Jeff asked her out, he had stopped paying her any attention. The whole situation made Jessica feel strange, but she was glad there was no weirdness between them. She just wanted things normal again.

At lunchtime, she spotted Paul with his friends heading toward the outside door. A girl named Alicia chased after them and grabbed Paul's ass. Jessica couldn't believe what she saw. Paul turned around and put her in a playful headlock; it was the type of headlock a boy would give to a girl he liked. Jessica lost her appetite watching the scene play out.

Alicia was a sophomore according to Marilee. She liked bad boys and the rumor was she'd had sex with at least five. The girls couldn't deny why he'd be attracted to her—perfectly feathered blond hair, kick-ass body, and makeup to show off her model-like face.

Marilee pushed away her tater tots and threw her napkin in. "How can we compete with that?"

Jessica never thought about having to compete for a boy. It was new territory for her, and she couldn't picture herself fighting for her man. Paul was not even her man, well at least in real life. Her fantasies were a different story. At night, she would put pillows alongside her body and pretend they were sharing the same bed together. Part of her felt it was wrong, but the lonely part that ached for love and affection wanted more.

"I wonder if that's his girlfriend," Jessica said.

"Who knows? But hey, look around. We're in paradise."

Jessica and Marilee scanned the lunchroom looking for cute boys. All they saw were guys who had not reached their full potential or puberty. Some of them still looked like they were ten, all skinny with acne and nervous twitches. The girls looked at each other and busted out laughing.

"I guess we need a new plan," Marilee said.

During Humanities, Jessica thought she saw a hickey on the side of Paul's neck. She had learned about them in computer class when a sophomore girl was showing off her hickeys, bragging about who gave them to her. Jessica was unsure how the hickeys got there, so she asked Marilee, who then asked Julie.

"Like, a boy sucks on your neck so he can leave that mark. Gross," Marilee exclaimed.

"My parents would kill me. No, they would kill the boy," Jessica said.

"You're not kidding. Your dad would come up to school and shoot him."

Jessica thought about that. Would her father be capable of murdering a boy over a hickey? The answer she came up with did not surprise her. It was a definite yes.

The day after the "boys-under-the-window" incident, her father told Jessica they needed to have a talk. Jessica waited for him in the office, seated on the capacious leather sofa, staring at the angry-faced bear. When her father entered, he placed two Colt .45s on the table between them. Jessica was used to seeing weapons in the house. Her father was a hunter and ran a business in which he used weapons and had special containers with locks for the arsenal he would take on business trips. He also had a large collection of antique swords, knives, and other devices that inflict catastrophic harm displayed on the walls. Jessica often thought no one in his right mind would ever want to break into this residence.

"I need for you to understand that I will not have you jumping out the window to hang out with boys." He leaned forward in his chair. "You see these on the table?"

Jessica looked at them and nodded.

"You ever have any boys outside your window again, they will be filled with bullets from these two guns. I will tell my cop friends that they were trying to break in. I will be completely absolved of any wrongdoing."

Jessica held her breath for a few seconds so she could steady herself.

He stared at her with an intense yet distant look. It was as if he had roadblocks in front of his emotional highway and was not sure how to navigate around.

"You are my daughter, and I will not allow anything bad to happen to you. Do you understand?"

Jessica started to dig her nails into the palms of each hand. How was she going to control Barbara or anyone else in the neighborhood who thought it would be funny to throw rocks at her window? The pressure she felt at that moment was insurmountable. Kids could be killed, and none of it was in her control. Where was her mother in all this? Just a casual observer in a possible murder case?

"I understand but . . ."

"No, no buts. I have made it clear what the consequence will be if you disobey my rules again."

And with that, he collected his guns and walked out of the room, leaving Jessica to wrestle with this newfound madness.

At dismissal time, Jessica was surprised to find Paul walking with her to her locker.

"Are you going home to watch your little brother?" he asked.

She looked at him puzzled, until the lie from yesterday came rushing back. "Oh, no not today."

"So you wanna do something?"

"You mean right now?"

"We have been set free."

Jessica smirked at that statement. Free was definitely relative. "Um, I wish I could, but my father's coming back from a business trip so I have to go right home."

"Okay. What about tomorrow?"

Jessica started to blush. She realized that he was asking her out.

"Uh . . . I . . . I don't know."

Paul was staring at her face. He looked around as they slowly approached her locker. "I wanna go out and do something."

"Do you mean with just me?" she whispered so the other students around could not hear.

"Yeah," he said, looking straight into her eyes.

This moment was one she had fantasized about for the last two months. Funny thing is she had always daydreamed about scenarios in which they were already a couple, never about that first moment when he asked her out. Despite mounds of excitement that piled into her, reality began to bare its ugly teeth. She could never be Paul's girlfriend, her father would see to that.

Jessica stared back at his crystal clear blue eyes. There was no heaviness or glassy look to them this time.

"Paul . . . I want to go with you, but I can't." She put her head down.

He leaned closer. She could smell his clean scent.

"So you want to go out with me?"

"Yes," she said, looking back up. "But I can't." Before Paul could ask the next question, Mrs. Daley stepped out from homeroom and asked to see Jessica for a few minutes. Paul and Jessica looked at each other like two pieces of stuck candy that needed to be pulled apart.

"We'll see you tomorrow, Paul," Mrs. Daley said as she put her arm around Jessica's shoulder and led her into the classroom. Mrs. Daley's coat and large multicolored satchel that she carried all her school papers in were on top of the desk.

"Come, sit down over here," she said, pointing to a chair as she lifted herself onto the edge of the desk. Jessica could not imagine what Mrs. Daley would want to talk about. She did not think she had done anything bad.

"Listen, I know this is really none of my business, but I feel I need to make it mine. You're a good student, the best in my homeroom, but don't go repeating that." Jessica smiled.

"And I've been watching the way things are progressing around here. Some boys think they can take advantage of you because of your homeroom job, but I have been very proud of the way you've handled yourself. You've stayed true to who you are. I can tell your parents taught you well." Jessica felt a slight flash of nausea over that comment but continued to listen. "And I can see that you and Paul seem to like each other. I have been watching y'all, well I watch everyone, but you two are obvious. I want you to be careful. Things that seem new and exciting can get old and dangerous with a flick of a switch. I'm not telling you what to do. I'm just letting you in on some wisdom that you may want to use when making choices down the road."

Jessica felt privileged that Mrs. Daley would stay after school to help her. "Thank you for caring about me."

"Aw, I care about all my students," Mrs. Daley said as she stood up and started putting on her coat. "Even the knuckleheads."

Jessica realized that she was late for home and started to panic.

"Mrs. Daley, could you please write a note so my parents know I was speaking with you after school?"

Jessica noticed Mrs. Daley looked at her funny. She figured that Mrs. Daley probably heard the anxiety in her voice, but at that moment, she did not care.

"Are you in some sort of trouble?"

"I will be unless I have a note. My parents are kinda strict."

Mrs. Daley gave her a look but did not say another word and wrote the note in silence. Just as Jessica was about to run out the door, Mrs. Daley asked if she still had her personal number. Jessica said she did.

"Good. You use that if you need to, baby girl."

Jessica ran all the way home forgetting to pull the Heritage sweatpants and shirt over her clothes. When she entered her house, she realized before she took off her coat that she still had the tight clothes on. At that same moment, her father came out of his office and greeted her with a hello.

"Hi, Dad," Jessica said, and made a line to hug him, coat on.

Her father returned her hug and said he enjoyed the letter she wrote him. "Take your coat off. We'll talk in my office."

Jessica panicked—he could not see the clothes. "Uh, I have to go to the bathroom really bad. I'll be right back down, okay?"

"All right," he said.

She raced upstairs, praying her mother was not in her room. Jessica changed her clothes quickly behind a locked bathroom door and flushed the toilet so it sounded like she actually used it. When she came back downstairs, her father was sitting at his desk sifting through a stack of papers. He looked up and grabbed her letter off his desk, going through each section and asking her questions, almost like an interrogation with a hint of goodwill. Jessica learned early on that this was the best way to acclimate her father back into her life. In her youth, she tried jumping into his lap, internally begging for his protective arms to engulf her as she regurgitated memories from the past couple of months. But he never responded the way she envisioned and was left with a bigger hole in her already damaged heart. The letter came out of desperation and in the end seemed the most humane.

Once he concluded his questioning, he pulled out a thinner version of the canister of Mace she already had.

"The potency is the same, but this will be easier to conceal in school."

Mace? Aunt Lodi brought her a beautiful necklace with a cross and dream catcher charms, and here her father sits offering a gift of Mace.

Jessica's curious mind wandered for the moment wondering how her father could think this was a gift a teenage girl would want.

"Oh, thanks. Yes, a smaller version will definitely be better."

That night in bed, Jessica held up the Mace to the light streaming in from the streetlamp outside. She understood the notion of keeping yourself protected, but his ideas were too extreme. Marilee and her sisters got claddagh rings from their parents; that seemed far more normal than Mace. She decided she needed to figure out the puzzle called her father and believed that Aunt Lodi held the answers. On a few occasions when Jessica prodded about their past, Aunt Lodi's carefree expression would change. She would give a few short answers and then cut it to an end by saying, "It's not appropriate to speak someone else's story. That's for them to tell." Jessica decided she needed to at least try to collect some information about why her father was this way. It would take some ingenuity, but she felt up for the task, especially when the hopeful payoff would be figuring out how to navigate around the oppression. And lead a life with Paul.

Chapter 7

In the morning before school, her father had Jason engaged in a workout consisting of calisthenics and resistance training. Because of Jason's age, he was a perfect fit for such a workout. He seemed to enjoy the jumping jacks and pull-ups. As her father was ordering Jason to finish another set of twenty, he mentioned that Jessica might want to join in.

"You're starting to get flabby around the middle."

"What?" said her mother before Jessica had a chance to say anything.

"Jessica needs to get back on a workout regimen. Bob's kids are involved in numerous sports. Jessica should be too."

Her father had no right to comment on her size, and she did not think she was flabby at all. In fact, she thought she weighed less because of not eating the disgusting school lunch. The only things she really liked were the tater tots and fries.

"Jim, I would like to speak to you about that in private," said her mother.

Jessica caught her father's surprised expression. It also surprised Jessica how firm her mother appeared. Usually her mother was fine with being second in command, but not today.

"All right, Katherine. After they go to school, we will discuss it in my office."

Jessica could not wait to get out of there. Her worries about Paul all but faded. Now she had to contend with possible flabbiness and how to get out of joining sports.

Jessica thought about "the jocks," and she wanted no part of that group. Working that hard in sports did not spark a desire of any kind. She needed a plan and was willing to break an arm, a leg too, if necessary.

Marilee was equally appalled by what her father said. "I'm sorry, Jess, but your dad's an asshole."

Jessica knew she was right but felt too loyal to agree. "Well, maybe I do need to lose a few pounds."

"Are you crazy?" Marilee retorted. "You're perfect just the way you are. Don't let those words shake you!"

But they had. Just like *whore* and *liar.*

"Okay," Jessica said with a smile.

Paul approached the girls as they took a shortcut through the green-and-brown spotted lawn in front of Heritage.

"What's up?" he said.

"Well," said Marilee. Jessica shot her a look. "We were just talking about how parents can be a real pain in the butt."

"Okay," Paul said slowly. He started to fidget. "Can I talk to you for a minute?"

"Sure," said Marilee. Jessica and Paul looked at her. "Oh, you mean talk to her, alone. Fine, I know when I'm not wanted," she said with a grin and walked toward school.

Paul looked around before speaking. "Can you meet me in the park by the swings at lunch?"

"Uh, sure," Jessica said.

"Alone, okay?"

"Yeah, sure."

"And don't tell anyone."

Jessica's insides felt loose. Her father had pounded into her the difference between good and bad secrets and right now, Jessica was not sure what side Paul's request was on.

"Do you mean adults?" she asked.

"Yeah, and friends."

Jessica's gut flipped. Both Eddie and Mrs. Daley had warned her about Paul.

"I want to meet you, but I have to tell Marilee. She's my best friend and we don't keep secrets."

Paul hesitated. "Okay. But no one else."

All day Jessica felt antsy. She sat in homeroom pretending everything was normal, but she really wanted to whisper the secret to anyone who would listen.

In Spanish, she told Marilee about the secret and begged her not to tell Eddie.

"Like are you kidding? He would ruin any chance you and Paul have. I'll tell him you had to meet with your counselor about classes."

When the lunch bell rang, Jessica exited a door that was not being monitored and walked alone to the park. Her insides were a mix of desire and alarm, and she laughed in her head about being thankful for the thin Mace her father had just given her. It fit nicely in the front of her tight jeans.

The sun decided to take a break, and the gray, which hung heavy above, covered the entire sky as a sharp breeze blew, making the scratching of leaves sound constant. She approached the swings and sat down on one that did not squeak as much as the others. The chains smelled of rust and metal, and she lifted her head so she did not inhale the fumes. Looking to her right, she saw Paul advancing quickly.

He looked uneasy as he approached and sat on the squeaky swing next to hers.

"So you must be wondering why I asked to meet you like this."

"It crossed my mind," she said coolly. The tone of her response even surprised her.

"I overheard what Mrs. Daley said to you."

Jessica felt bad, not for herself but for Mrs. Daley, not wanting Paul to treat her badly.

"Mrs. Daley was talking in general terms, you know. Not so much about you."

"Well, I just need to clear something up," he said and made a sound in his throat. "I was asking you to go out with me. Not like be my girl-friend, but just go out. Maybe it would be cool for us to be together, but I need to go out with you first."

Jessica's heart fluttered. Her dream was coming true.

"You said you wanted to go out with me, right?"

"Yes, I really do," she said, looking at him but then not being able to stop herself from looking past his silhouette and onto the street she turned down to get to her house. "But my parents won't let me date."

"Well, maybe if I come over and meet them."

"Out of the question," she said quickly, never wanting to see Paul's handsome face with Colt .45 bullet holes. "My parents are extremely overprotective. It won't happen."

They sat with only the squeaking sound of a swing to break the silence. After a few minutes, Paul looked at her. "So we're finished even before we started?"

"I guess so."

Paul tightened his jaw and squinted his eyes. "What about sneaking out to see me? Or I could sneak into your house to see you."

Jessica saw Colt .45s. That was all she could see.

"Paul, my father's not the type of man that you can sneak around on. I'm scared to death to even try."

"But maybe you can try to see what happens."

"What will happen is that *you* will get a bullet in the back of your head. And I cannot have that on my conscience."

Paul's eyes widened. "Are you joking?"

"Sort of."

"Is your dad a cop?"

"Something like that," Jessica said, quietly trying not to let her tears bear themselves. "I'm so sorry."

The leaves that had been thrashing around took refuge around their feet, hovering until someone picked up a foot to swing gently.

"Well, if you decide to take me up on my offer, you know to sneak, I'll be ready."

"And until then still friends?" Jessica asked.

"Yeah, still friends," he said and held out his hand to shake. They shook on their friendship but instead of letting go right after the shake, he hung on for a few alluring seconds. Just enough to give Jessica a taste of what it would really feel like to have his skin next to hers.

The rest of that day, and the weeks and months to come, the pleasure center of her brain would refer to that moment as pivotal in her desire to be with Paul. Pillows were not going to be the standard fill-in anymore now that she was exposed to the real thing. The thought of his touch would make her body feel tingly. Oh, how she wanted more. Sometimes in Humanities, when they sat bunched up in their foursome plowing through their project, she would lean her shoulder to purposefully touch his. He didn't seem to mind. Sometimes he would give her a gentle nudge back, inviting her in for more.

Cassandra and Mickey, their partners in Humanities, noticed.

"Are you guys going out?" Cassandra asked.

"I've been wondering the same thing," Mickey blurted. "You act like you're glued to each other."

Jessica and Paul would just smile and deny, but inside they held the secret of the swing conversation between them like an umbilical cord. It continued to feed the relationship they wanted but could not have. And for a month or two, Paul seemed satisfied with that. But his boy hormones, which appeared more forgetful and impulsive, soon took over. Jessica would catch glimpses of him holding hands with a freshman for a month or so, then a junior for a while. Jessica and Marilee made up a game—"Paul's flavor of the month club." They would rip apart every new girlfriend.

"So who is the flavor this time? Redhead? Blonde?" Marilee asked.

"Actually, brunette. I think it's that girl who wears a jean jacket *in winter* with cigarettes sticking out of the pocket."

"I did see him walking real close to that black girl, Kenyatta."

"An equal opportunity dater," Jessica said. "Impressive."

Jessica made light of the situation because she had no other choice. But seeing Paul with a new girl every couple of months was starting to make her feel worthless—a feeling that she knew should not be lost on a boy, but she could not stop herself. Her only shelter was their friendship. They talked all the time in school, even writing notes and passing them during the day. Once in the hallway while they were walking to lunch, one of the "flavors" stopped and asked Paul where he thought he was going with Jessica.

"To lunch."

The flavor eyed Jessica up and down. "I don't think so. You need to find your own man."

Jessica stepped back stunned, and Paul lurched forward into the flavor's face.

"You don't own me. And you don't tell me who I eat lunch with. Got it?"

"Fuck you, Paul," she said and stormed away.

Jessica looked at Paul. "I don't want to cause any problems."

"You're not," he said. "No one tells me who I can hang out with."

As they got back onto the track they had just derailed, Paul said, "And truthfully, I'd rather hang with you anyway."

They locked eyes for a brief moment. His smell was making her pulse rise—brisk and clean, like a bar of soap. And his eyes appeared fresh and open. It reminded her of a pristine pond where she swam in the UP. Before she knew what was happening, Paul grabbed her hand and rubbed his thumb gracefully along hers. Her body and mind were digesting every second of his touch, so that it could be played out again and again in bed, next to her pillows.

Paul looked at her longingly. "Are you ready to sneak?"

Without another thought, her instinct to protect kicked in, and she let go of his hand.

"I'm sorry. I can't," she said in a defeated tone.

"Jessica, I know one day you're gonna come to me and say you're ready. And when you do, I will be."

Jessica found Paul's effort valiant; however, he did not know her father. Besides the whole "shooting a boy who steps foot on the property" threat, Jessica had a lot of self-control. All thanks to her self-control training. Her father would put marshmallows in front of Jessica at the age of two and make her wait before eating one for fifteen, twenty, even thirty minutes. If she tried to reach for it, he would hit her hand. No squirming either. Her father took pride in Jessica's ability to sit still with her hands folded in front of a marshmallow treat for thirty minutes at age two and a half.

But in bed that night, Jessica cried next to her pillows. Her soul was forever being scarred by watching Paul with his slew of girls. The self-control she took so much pride in was starting to wane, and in the dark of the night, her thoughts started to bend toward taking Paul up on his offer to sneak. She thought it would be easier if her father was away on a business trip, but she'd heard nothing about him traveling again. And it had been four months since his return home.

The only bright spot in her life was Aunt Lodi's visit. Aunt Lodi always came to Chicago in the spring for a week. Her mother prepared the guest bedroom as if someone was being laid to rest. Jessica loved the fact that this was one of the only times that music was played on the radio in the kitchen. Usually it blasted news coverage 24-7, but with Aunt Lodi around, sounds of peace and yesteryear prevailed.

Chapter 8

Genealogy is a word that calls forth memories and stories to be told. Some memories and stories are laden with words like adventure, courage, and hope. Others are represented by stoic faces and muted clothing, framed and hung on the walls of their ancestor's home. Jessica's home was lacking in both stories and memories from the past. The only item that was kept was a chest in the attic that her mother said was given to her by her grandmother. It contained some old clothes that did not appear that important; otherwise, they would have found life in the closets of the living. Every once in a while, Jessica would sneak in the attic or into her parent's bedroom and look around. She was not searching for anything in particular, but the thought of finding clues to their past lives was compelling enough to bypass her fears of possible video surveillance.

There were two pictures in her parent's bedroom. One was on her mother's dresser; a round, shiny silver frame showed a black-and-white photo of a man in a hat and suit holding a baby. He was not smiling even though it looked like a special day. The baby was dressed in all white, with a little bonnet. Even the blanket that wrapped the baby in warmth was white. On her father's nightstand was a simple black frame with a picture of him and Aunt Lodi on horses in the woods. They looked young, maybe in their twenties. Snowcapped trees and white hills surrounded them as a crisp baby blue sky hung low. It almost looked like they could reach up and touch it with their hands. Jessica was amazed at how beautiful the scenery was in that picture. The natural elements helped, but her father and Aunt Lodi looked so intertwined with it all, like they were one with the earth. It was the type of picture that should be showcased in the office. But as she thought about it further, its mere presence amongst the harsh visuals of war would no doubt drown out its beauty. Maybe that's why her father kept it in the bedroom, behind the closed door, because it's too easy for a beautiful memory to be engulfed by a room full of harsh ones.

Jessica sat at the desk in her bedroom contemplating how to lie to her parents. She already lied to Aunt Lodi. Well, she didn't think of it as a lie but as a way to gather information about her family history. She'd told Aunt Lodi that she had a genealogy paper to complete for Humanities. Mr. Gambino did assign a paper; however, it was on her heritage. Jessica knew she was German, Swedish, and Norwegian. Her father taught her that as he lectured, using a map, about the history of America at war. The missing pieces were the stories about her grandparents and those before them. Why is her father so different from his sister? Why does he seem to care about his children but can barely put his arms around them?

At dinner that night, Aunt Lodi brought up the paper before Jessica had a chance to formulate her lie.

"A family tree?" her father questioned. "What does that have to do with your academics?"

"Well, I'm not sure, but it's an important part of history according to Mr. Gambino."

Her father and Aunt Lodi looked at each other. She smiled at him and gently said, "You know, I'm sure this is something we can figure out."

Jessica watched their apprehensive expressions. Aunt Lodi did not seem that concerned when Jessica had told her alone, but now, in her father's presence, she seemed more rattled. This was the third day into Aunt Lodi's visit, and her mere presence made Jessica feel like she could challenge the status quo of the household. Not head-on, but in small chipping away steps.

"It would be nice to know more information about your parents," Jessica said.

"What exactly do you want to know?" asked her mother.

"Well I need to make a family tree and put the names and birth dates of your parents and their parents before them. I also need to include immigration, like when they came through Ellis Island, and any stories that are relevant in our family history."

"You sound so professional, you straight 'A' student," Aunt Lodi said with a grin. "Aren't you so proud of her?"

"Of course," her mother said. "But let's not get distracted. So you need your father and I to tell you about our ancestors?"

"Yes," Jessica said.

All three adults looked at each other. Jessica stared at Jason as he shoved more venison stew into his mouth—one of Aunt Lodi's concoctions. *What is wrong with our ancestors?* Jessica wondered.

"When is your paper due?" asked her father.

"Next Friday."

There was a long silence before her father spoke up again. "We will have a talk over the weekend, in the office."

"Sounds like a plan," Aunt Lodi said, slapping the tabletop. "Now who wants some of my famous homemade brownies?" Aunt Lodi pushed herself up from the table and made her way to the kitchen. "And don't give me that look, Katherine. My hard-core hippie days are over."

*　　　*　　　*

One of Jessica's favorite times with Aunt Lodi was in the morning. She would wake up extra early, without the help of an alarm clock, and tiptoe to the guest bedroom. Aunt Lodi would be meditating on the bed, and Jessica would quietly slip under the covers while Aunt Lodi took cleansing breaths. Then, Aunt Lodi would pull Jessica in close. They would whisper, do exercises like the bicycle, and sometimes Aunt Lodi would read her palm. The most wonderful predictions about Jessica were made on her palm. Jessica will have a very successful career helping others, maybe have two children with a man that is very loving and generous. He will be big, like her father, but in a more teddy bear kind of way. Jessica always giggled about that. Aunt Lodi had been telling her that since she was little. As she got older, it would lead into the question: is there a special someone in your life? Jessica would always laugh, and Aunt Lodi would tickle her. But that was before, when it was impossible to have a special someone. Things were different now. Paul was someone special, but Jessica was not sure she could trust Aunt Lodi with that secret. If that secret ever crept into her father's ears, who knows what would happen to Paul.

"So, do you have a special someone?"

Jessica hesitated. "Well, there are lots of cute boys at school, but no, they're not into me."

"What?" Aunt Lodi whispered. "Jessica Turner, you're probably intimidating those boys with your smarts and looks. You know, boys who like girls are usually too shy to say so. They do all sorts of dumb things to get your attention."

"Like what?"

"Oh, they take your mittens and hat, so you have to chase them down. They try to act too tough or too funny and end up looking idiotic. Is any of this ringing a bell?"

Jessica thought about it. No one had ever taken anything of hers to make an impression. Plus a lot of what Aunt Lodi was referring to sounded like something that happened in elementary school, not high school.

"No, none of that has happened, but I'll keep my eyes open for that type of behavior."

Aunt Lodi laughed and squeezed Jessica tighter. "Yes, please keep an eye out for that 'behavior,'" she said, playfully mocking her. "Then you'll know for sure that a boy likes you."

It struck Jessica in a funny way. Since Aunt Lodi was around, she wasn't having as many lonely thoughts or feelings. And while she did think about Paul a lot, she didn't crave his company as much. She wondered why, but she shrugged it off as another way that Aunt Lodi and her contagious self worked. The brightness in her could fill a void in anyone's soul.

Springtime brought about a renewed love of the outdoors, so the lunch table sat empty of the seniors since many would walk two blocks to JJ's Gyros for lunch, or go to someone's house nearby. Eddie now had a girlfriend and would sometimes go to her house with their friends. He never invited the girls along, so one day Marilee asked him why.

"Because you're my little sister."

"What does that mean?" Marilee asked.

"Well, things that seniors do aren't the same things that freshmen do."

Jessica and Marilee looked at each other. "So you're making out and drinking?"

"That's none of your business," Eddie said and walked away. The girls watched Eddie and his girlfriend lean their heads together as they made their way outside.

"I wonder what he's doing over there. You don't think he's having sex, do you?"

"I don't know. What do you think of his girlfriend?" asked Jessica.

"She's nice, you know, one of those cheerleader girls. Always like, '*hi*' and '*rahrah*.'"

Jessica smirked, but then wanted to cry. "Speaking of cheerleaders, did you notice who Paul is with?"

"No, who?"

"Donna Double D. Do you think she's pretty?"

"Like *no*. Do you see how much makeup she paints on her face? Like a flippin' clown."

Jessica smiled but felt sad around the edges. "I think they're having sex. Donna's in my computer class. I overheard her say that she and her boyfriend have sex all the time and that they went to the beach one night and did it like four times in a row."

"Is that even possible?" Marilee asked.

"I don't know."

"Jess, you know I think you and Paul would be great together, but I think you pining away for him isn't good for you. You don't have that easy feeling about you anymore."

Jessica felt tears come to the surface. "But I like him so much. Do you know how hard it is to like someone and they really like you back but you can't be together because your father might kill him? And not just the *kidding* kill him but the *for real* kill him."

Marilee put her hand on top of Jessica's. "I'm sorry. I wish you could live with me, but I can't date until my sophomore year."

"Well at least that's in a couple months. I can't date until I'm twenty-one, which is in forever."

"Having a lover's spat?" came a voice from the end of the table. It surprised Jessica to see Paul there with one of his friends. Marilee's hand was still on Jessica's as she pulled it off slowly.

"No, we were just talking about how boys can be real assholes."

"Oh," Paul said. "Well, I hope you're not talking about me."

Jessica couldn't take it. Without thinking, she jumped up and headed outside. Her strides were quick as she made her way out the stainless steel door and onto the cement courtyard. The brightness of the sun blinded her but that didn't slow her pace. As she passed the benches full of students and was making her way to the baseball field, she felt a pull on her arm; swinging around, she saw Paul holding onto her sleeve.

"Just leave me alone, Paul. I can't pine away for you anymore."

"Jessica, please stop."

Jessica tugged her shirt sleeve away from Paul's grip. "I can't keep watching you with all these girls. I just can't do it anymore."

"Let's talk over there," Paul said as he motioned toward the bleachers by the baseball diamond.

Jessica didn't move, but her tears kept falling despite her desperate wish they go back inside. She hated crying in front of anyone; it made her feel so vulnerable.

"Come on, there's hardly anyone over there," Paul said with a concerned look on his face.

She moved away from him. It was too easy to brush up against him and forget how hurt she really felt.

The baseball field had randomly placed puddles from the spring rainstorm that had come through the night before, and all the bleachers contained small groups of students who were eating lunch and talking. Jessica and Paul ended up on a small section of the bleacher at the very bottom, hoping this put them out of the range of gossip.

Paul stared at Jessica as she continued to wipe away any hurt she showed him.

"Did I do something to you?" he asked.

"No . . . well, yes." Jessica took a deep breath and touched the necklace Aunt Lodi gave her.

"I feel stupid right now. You did nothing wrong. It's me."

Paul looked at her unconvinced. "So is that why you said you can't, 'pine away,' for me anymore?"

Jessica felt embarrassed. "Look, you're free to be with anyone you want. We're not together."

"You can change that."

"What? Oh, you mean sneaking around?"

Paul looked at her intensely. "Do you know how easy it could be? On our half days you could tell your parents you have stuff at school so you have to stay the whole day. Or we could change our schedules in the computer to show that we have study hall at the end of the day even though we don't."

Jessica lifted her face to smell the spring breeze. It made her feel like she needed a fresh start. "On the computer?"

"Yeah, on a day when the lady lets you enter the attendance you can change your schedule."

"How do you know about this?" asked Jessica.

Paul's devilish smile came out again. "Let's just say I had a class or two adjusted."

"And your grades?"

"No. I'm not that stupid. Plus my grades are fine."

Jessica stared long and hard at Paul. The idea of changing her schedule sounded so appealing. And it sounded easy to do but not now. Her parents would question it immediately.

"I could never do that now. It's too late in the year. My parents would investigate that in a second."

"You could do it for sophomore year. We're gonna pick our new schedule in the next couple weeks. You could add last period study hall to both of ours in the computer, print it out, and show it to your parents."

Jessica could hardly contain the mix of feelings running around her body and brain. "What would we do? Where would we go? I can't be wandering around the neighborhood for my parents to see."

"That's easy," he said with a smile. "My house."

My house did not sound like a safe idea to Jessica. In fact, it downright scared her. Even though she felt more comfortable around Paul, she knew he had way more experience with relationships, more specifically sex. She was not ready for that adventure yet.

"Uh, who's home at your house?"

"Depends on the day. Sometimes my brothers, my mom . . . sometimes nobody."

Jessica started to pick the cuticles of her nails.

"Jessica, I'm not bringing you to my house to do anything you don't wanna do. I'm not that kinda guy."

"What kinda guy are you, Paul?"

He laughed. "I'm not sure how to answer that, but if I like somethin' I go for it. Like with you."

Jessica hid her grin, not really understanding why Paul chose her in the first place.

"Would you ever take my hat or mittens and make me chase you to get them back?"

"Well, that's something I did when I was nine, but if that makes you happy, then sure."

The bell rang as they continued to smile at each other on the bleachers.

"Can I do something?" Paul asked.

"What?"

"Kiss you?"

Ohmigod. Jessica had never been kissed before, and she did not want Paul to know how bad of a kisser she was going to be. She was hoping to get some practice by kissing her pillows.

"Don't you have a girlfriend?" she asked.

"Yeah, you."

"I know you're with Donna."

"Donna? The cheerleader?" Paul laughed out loud. "I'm not with Donna. My buddy Freak Boy is. I did have to help her out one day when this guy kept buggin' to go out with her. Freak Boy went in rehab and asked me to watch over her in school."

Jessica felt relieved and stupid because she completely misread certain events.

"So you and Donna are not going out?"

"No," said Paul shaking his head. "Not my type."

Jessica felt one step closer to kissing Paul, but it didn't feel right to do it outside where everyone could see.

"Not yet, okay?"

Paul looked disappointed. "Okay. Are you good with changing our sophomore schedules to show we have study hall last period?"

Jessica knew this step was taking her out of her father's grip and placing her into the unknown. While she worried for Paul's safety, her being in a relationship was a normal part of teenage life. And all she desperately wanted to be was normal.

"I'll do it. You'll have to tell me how when the time comes."

Paul grabbed her hand and held it tight as they made their way back to school. "This is gonna be great," he said.

Jessica returned the pressure of his grip. Holding on was all she could do.

Chapter 9

Before Aunt Lodi returned to Cedar Creek, she took Jessica shopping for some new clothes. Aunt Lodi told her parents that Jessica's clothing would certainly place her in the ostracized group in school. Her mother put up a fight, stating Jessica never said a word about being made fun of, but her father said he saw her point. Jessica's eyes widened, and her hands balled up as her nostrils flared. She wondered why it took her father this long to let her go.

As Jessica sat in the car waiting for Aunt Lodi, her father handed her a list of don'ts. Once again, makeup was on the list. *So much for "letting go,"* Jessica thought.

"Be honest. You've been sneaking out clothes," Aunt Lodi said as they drove away.

Jessica didn't want to lie. "Yes. I change at Marilee's. She and Julie do my laundry and give me clean clothes and shoes to wear."

"Honey, I understand. I would be doing the same thing. Crazy, sending you to school looking like a boy. These should be some of the best years of your life."

That statement made Jessica feel much better about her choice to change her schedule. Aunt Lodi was right. This is the time to be young and adventurous.

"Will you be here when Dad talks to me about the family tree?"

"I wish I could, but I need to get back to the reservation. I need to help plan our planting celebration." Aunt Lodi looked over at Jessica. "But that's his story to tell."

"And you have your own?"

"Of course, silly. We all have our own stories. You have a story too."

Jessica never thought of it like that. She didn't think she would have a story until she got married and had kids of her own.

"But I'm only fifteen."

"Fifteen years of a story. Some of it you don't remember, but that's where the people around you come in. They fill you in on the little details of your unconscious life. Your conscious life is easier to translate because you're a willing participant—well, for the most part." Jessica noticed Aunt Lodi's face saddened.

"I saw a picture of you and Dad on his nightstand. You were on horses in the winter. Trees and snow were all around you."

Jessica could see that Aunt Lodi was searching the archives for a spark of recognition.

"Oh, is it the one where the sky sits so low you could touch it?" Aunt Lodi asked.

"Yes. I thought the same thing."

"Oh sure," Aunt Lodi said slowly. "We loved those horses."

"Where were you?"

She hesitated for a minute. "In the UP, on a friend's farm." Silence fell until Jessica spoke up again.

"Can you tell me about it?"

Jessica saw Aunt Lodi wipe away a tear. "You know, honey, me and your dad have stories that intertwine, even braid. But I don't feel right telling you that one without him being here."

"Maybe you can tell it when we get home."

"I think your dad has his own plan, this weekend in the office. But when you do meet, honey, go slow with the questions."

Jessica mulled over that thought and then asked why.

"Because your father doesn't like to talk about the past. But I will tell you this," Aunt Lodi said, trying to compose herself. "That picture was taken when something we lost was returned to us. And for the first time in a long time, me and your dad felt complete."

Jessica let the statement roll in her head, trying to figure out how lost they could have been.

The Piper Mall was *the* place to hang out if you were a teenager. Although Jessica had only been to the mall twice, once with Marilee and once with her father, she heard many stories in school about it. One story she had overheard was about a secret stairwell that kids made out in. As she and Aunt Lodi walked through the crowded corridors, Jessica envisioned her and Paul in the secret stairwell. In her fantasy, she was a great kisser because of all her practice on the pillows. Even Paul was impressed.

All teenagers were supposed to be embarrassed to be with an adult at the mall, but Jessica did not mind. She was ecstatic about getting a wardrobe she didn't have to sneak out. Shirts that would be accepted into the Turner home were easy to find. Jeans, however, were not. Aunt Lodi had Jessica try on twenty different styles and sizes, but it all amounted to the same flaw: too tight.

"I don't think we're going to get around this," Aunt Lodi said with a disappointed tone. She stared at the three pairs in her hands. "These were the loosest although that's a stretch. I'll buy them but keep the receipt just in case."

Jessica took advantage of the shopping opportunity to get some cooler looking underwear. She felt so embarrassed when she changed in the locker room. All the girls had sexy-looking bikini briefs, one even wore a thong. But Jessica had what amounted to granny panties.

While changing in the locker room, some girls started laughing while looking Jessica's way. She ignored them like she usually did, assuming they were talking about someone else, but one of them yelled at her, "Hey, did you borrow those from your Grandma?"

Jessica had no idea what she was talking about. Borrow what? Jessica's hands started trembling. They were making fun of her.

"I guess she doesn't want to answer you," a girl with a loud squeaky voice said.

"Hey, you, did you hear me? Nice granny panties."

As her heart pounded in her chest, she jumped at the sound of a slamming locker from behind.

"Are you shitting me? You're staring at her undies, you creep?" blurted one of the Mohawk girls.

Jessica swallowed hard and looked over at her haters. She could see the strain on all their faces.

"We're just joking around with our friend, right?" said one of the girls. But Jessica did not respond. She looked at Mohawk girl with relief.

"Yeah, right," said Mohawk girl. "Quit fucking around with her or I'll beat your asses."

In a flash, the girls turned around and continued changing into their gym uniforms. Jessica wanted to quietly thank Mohawk girl, but before she could, Mohawk girl was in the gym getting ready to slam some of those girls into the wall during floor hockey. Later that week, Jessica saw Mohawk girl outside walking by herself. She decided it was a perfect opportunity to say thank you. Jessica walked to where she was and then realized she did not even know her proper name.

"Uh, excuse me."

Mohawk girl turned around wielding a cigarette in between her fingers. "Yeah."

"I just wanted to thank you for last week, you know with the girls in the locker room."

"No sweat," she said, as she coolly blew smoke out of her mouth.

Jessica was going to leave it at that, but she was so curious about two things: why she did it and were her parents okay with her hair?

"I really appreciate you standing up for me."

Mohawk girl smirked. "I didn't do it for you per se. I did it for all those who get picked on by the elite."

"Oh," Jessica mumbled, feeling not so special anymore. "Can I ask you a question?"

"Shoot," said Mohawk girl.

"Are your parents cool with your hair?"

Mohawk girl laughed out loud. "Funny," she said and walked away.

Aunt Lodi brought the clothes to her father for inspection. After a few tense moments, he agreed she could wear them, but he would have to see the jeans on before giving his total approval. Her mother stood back with a grim look on her face. Jessica was careful not to show her happiness, in case her mother felt the need to squash it.

The evening Aunt Lodi left, Jessica started to feel that deep lonely feeling again. She tried to cling to all the wonderful moments they had together but as Aunt Lodi's car pulled out of the driveway, desolation washed over her.

Jason turned to Jessica. "I'm sad."

No sooner was Aunt Lodi down the block when her mother demanded they get in the house. Everyone was to pitch in and help clean up the mess. The radio in the kitchen was tuned back to news coverage, and the whole family worked until bedtime sanitizing, mopping, and washing the entire house. Even her father, who rarely said one damaging word about his sister, agreed she was disheveled. Exhausted, Jessica dropped onto her bed. Before falling into a deep sleep, she pulled her pillows, including the ones she sneaked from Aunt Lodi's bed, tight against her skin.

Chapter 10

On Saturday morning, after Jason and her father returned from a jog, Jessica was summoned to the office. She brought a pen and notebook so she could be as accurate as possible with her note taking. Her father was at his desk when Jessica walked in. He told her to have a seat and then handed her a piece of paper.

"Here's my family tree. Your mother's is on the other side. Any questions?"

Jessica studied the paper under duress; this was not how she envisioned this moment. Stories and memories were supposed to be shared. Aunt Lodi said everyone has a story to tell and Jessica wanted to hear it. She took a deep breath then swallowed hard, summoning up as much courage as she could gather between her fears.

"Do you think you can tell me about your childhood?"

His face tightened. "That's in the past. This is now; this is where I want to be."

Jessica pursed her lips together. "It would add to the paper if I could have some more details."

"Be specific. What details do you want?"

"Just one story about you, you know, and your parents."

He walked to the French doors and stared out for a few moments. The gray spring day brought a few sprinkles of rain that hit the windows in little splats. While Jessica sat in silence, she continued to decipher the family tree. It appeared his parents died at the same time. She knew they were dead but the story attached to their death was never told.

"As you know, I grew up on a farm, in the UP," her father began, still looking out the window. "We had livestock, mostly dairy. Some bean and corn crops. Lodi and I worked hard; you had no choice on a farm. My parents were good people, strong morals and values, church-going folks. Everybody knew everybody where we grew up. It was supposed to be a safe place to live." He turned and looked at her. "But no place is safe." He folded his arms tight in front of him. "My parents were killed in a car accident, ol' Buddy Akers on that whiskey. You know where Buddy Akers is?"

Jessica reluctantly shook her head, afraid her father might reveal too much.

"Living in a nursing home in the UP, letting taxpayers foot the bill for his murdering ass." Her father hesitated for a few seconds. "But you know who is *not* in that nursing home?" She watched as her father grew agitated. His face shrouded in hate and his arm muscles flexed. "Ermaline and Walker."

Who were Ermaline and Walker? Those were not the names of his parents.

"Are those relatives?" Jessica asked out of curiosity.

Her father suddenly sat down in his office chair and put his fists against his forehead and slowly began to bang them against his head. After a minute had passed, her father spoke in a voice that cracked, "I hate everything about Ermaline and Walker. Even their names leave a foul taste in my mouth. I can still see it. I can still see too much."

Jessica's eyes were firmly planted on her father because she had never witnessed him being in pain. It was hard to tell, because his fists covered his face, but she was pretty sure a tear fell from his eye.

"Dad, are you ok?" Jessica asked. She was about to move off the couch to be closer to him, but then he slammed his fists on the desk and stood up tall. If his eyes did shed a tear, they were all dried up now.

"Look around this room. See all these weapons," he said, then walked toward a bayonet and ripped it off the wall. He held it up for Jessica to see. "They can only serve you to a point. It's up to you to keep yourself safe, no matter what."

Jessica fixed her eyes on the closed door, hoping to telepathically beckon her mother.

"Your job is to keep guard of yourself at all times. Know who is around your space; everyone can be an enemy."

Like a gift from God, the phone rang in the office. Jessica stared at her father, but he acted like he didn't even notice.

"The phone is ringing," Jessica whispered.

From the kitchen, her mother yelled for her father to answer it. Instead of picking it up, he lifted the bayonet high above his head and brought it down point first on top of the phone. It looked like he was spearing a shark. Jessica jumped at the sound as little pieces of plastic went flying all over the room. She crouched down on the side of the leather sofa, and peeked at her father, feeling shocked at his lack of control. He was staring at the bayonet while his hand trembled. Even though she felt protected by her father, she feared his rage made his vision blurry. She would have to take his advice and keep herself safe. Before she could make a move toward the door, her mother came lunging into the office with her apron on, batter all over her hands.

"Jim, have you lost your mind?"

He stared at her as if he had never seen her before.

"Jim, this is your wife, remember, your family, the people you love and are to protect."

He glared at his wife, bayonet still in hand. Jason came running into the room and stopped just past the threshold.

"Jessica, I want you and Jason to go upstairs, please," her mother said with a mixture of fear and firmness in her tone.

Jessica stared at her father, not sure if she could trust him being alone with her mother. Peeling herself off the leather sofa, she approached her mother and was about to say they should *all* leave Dad alone, but the thin line of her mother's lips and the eyes that directed Jessica toward the door kept her quiet. Jessica led Jason out of the office, and when they entered the hallway, she heard the phone ringing in the kitchen. She wondered who was on the other end because the ringing was nonstop, but her thoughts kept going back to her mother in the office, with her father, and all his weapons. But then Jessica remembered she had a weapon of her own. "Come on," she mumbled to Jason as she hurdled up the stairs to her bedroom. She grabbed the Mace from her backpack and told Jason if anything bad happened to get under the bed and stay there until someone safe came to get him. Jason's little brow frowned up.

"I'm the boy. I should help."

Jessica had no time for testosterone. "Listen, you're only six. I'm fifteen. Do as I say." He stopped protesting and slid under her bed.

Jessica crept down the stairs with the Mace in front of her and ready, if needed, to pull the trigger on the same man who gave it to her.

There were no noises coming out of the office—no gurgling on blood, no murderous cries. Jessica leaned inside the doorframe. Her father was sitting in his desk chair, head in hands, rocking ever so slowly back and forth. Her mother was on her hands and knees cleaning up the mess. And the bayonet was safely back on the wall.

Jessica and Jason stayed in her room the rest of the morning. They played games, drew pictures, and read books. For a snack, they ate smashed cereal bars that were at the bottom of her backpack. At one point Jessica dozed off. When she woke up, she found Jason sitting at the end of her bed, stiff as a statue.

"What's wrong?"

"Shhh, Dad's up here. I just saw him." Jessica leaned over and grabbed the Mace from the nightstand. As she sat back up, her father walked in with Marilee's dad.

"Bob's going to take you to his house for the night. Jessica, pack a small bag for the both of you."

Her father did not look like the raving lunatic from earlier. Jessica tried to get a good look at his eyes, but he would not meet hers.

"Where's Mom?" asked Jessica.

"Cooking dinner," he said and walked away.

It was Aunt Lodi on the other line when her father smashed the phone into pieces. She became alarmed when she called back and the phone just rang so she called the Ripps. Jessica found this out upon entering the Ripp home and being handed the phone with Aunt Lodi on the other end. Jessica repeated that she was fine and felt safe, then started to wonder if she had done something wrong because Aunt Lodi kept reiterating she did nothing wrong.

"You have every right to know the history of your family. Please don't let that outburst stop you from asking questions." *Outburst?* Jessica could not help but wonder what Aunt Lodi would have thought being in that room watching her father unravel. If she were witness to that, would she continue to push for any more stories?

Marilee, Barbara, and Julie were still at school participating in mandatory Saturday practices but Eddie was home, so he took Jason in the basement to watch TV. Mrs. Ripp was in the kitchen writing down a pizza order for dinner.

"What do you and Jason like on your pizza?"

"Just cheese, please."

Mrs. Ripp smiled and said out loud while writing, "One small cheese pizza, and two large sausage, mushroom, and pepperoni. We eat like pigs over here," Mrs. Ripp said. "I know you guys don't eat like this in your house." Jessica was amused by the Ripps. They were more primitive than her parents. It was a refreshing change.

"Look at Bob," Mrs. Ripp said as he walked through the kitchen to the dining room. "You would hardly know that man can eat two large pizzas. Now me, I stick with one."

Jessica was unsure if she was joking, so she gave a small grin, not wanting to seem ungrateful for the hospitality.

After some polite conversation with Mrs. Ripp, Jessica lied and said she had a headache and went upstairs to Marilee's room. All the Ripp girls shared the attic on the third floor. Warm knotty pine paneling ran the entire length with a window centered on the front and back walls. The pine reminded Jessica of Aunt Lodi's cabin and gave her an instantly cozy feeling.

The sun, which finally came out after all the gray and rain, was setting to the west, beaming a large ray of light at the foot of Marilee's bed. Jessica lay down on the unmade bed in a fetal position and started to cry. The loneliness was hard to shake and was reinforced by her mother not saying good-bye or checking on them all day. Shouldn't that be number one on the priority list? See how the kids handled their dad's meltdown?

"Are you all right?" Mrs. Ripp's voice interrupted Jessica's pain, and she sat up quickly, wiping her eyes.

"I'm fine. Just tired."

Mrs. Ripp looked unconvinced. "Oh sure, sometimes I feel the same way. Sometimes I just want to lie in bed all day. But then I start to get bored and wonder, what am I missing?" She slowly walked towards Marilee's bed, picking up random pieces of tossed clothing on the floor.

"Although I don't ever miss housework."

Jessica grinned.

"Life can be tiresome. We really don't understand why people act in certain ways. But know this, you are the decider on how you handle adversity, how you deal with tough situations. Don't ever let something out of your control decide your path in life."

Jessica was getting the distinct feeling this was a Ripp pep talk, and she appreciated the effort.

"Thank you. I'll remember that."

Once all the Ripp kids got home from various functions, everyone flocked to the dinner table in the kitchen. They did not serve on china or have cloth napkins; it was paper and more paper. And it was loud: "Pass the parmesan. Pass the crushed red peppers. Hey, I wanted that piece."

"Hey, I need some cheese . . . please." Jessica watched as Jason chimed in, feeling more comfortable.

Jessica and Jason smiled at each other.

Conversation flowed as all spoke about their day: things that happened, good and bad. Mr. Ripp was not a talker, however, Jessica watched him give a lot of grins and head nods. He would interject every now and then, usually to give advice, and then get back to being silent.

"Eddie, are you going out tonight?" inquired Mrs. Ripp.

"Yeah, I don't have to work tomorrow until later in the afternoon."

"Oooh, are you going out with Sonja?" Marilee asked.

"Shut up," said Barbara. "You're so immature."

"You shut up," Marilee retorted.

"Enough," Mr. Ripp snorted.

Marilee and Barbara looked at each other with contempt.

"Jessica, you can sleep in my bed tonight. I'm sleeping at Margaret's house," Julie said.

"Are you meeting us at church?" Mrs. Ripp asked.

"If I must," Julie said while getting up and throwing away her paper plate.

After Jessica and Marilee helped clean up and get Jason ready for bed, they went to the basement to listen to the radio and paint each other's nails. Jessica would have to take the polish off before she got home, but for once she didn't care.

"I love listening to the radio," Jessica said. Music was a novelty since she was not allowed to have a radio or tape player in her room.

"Oh my God, I love this song," Marilee said and turned up the volume. After a few minutes of Marilee singing the song off tune and Jessica trying to memorize the words, Marilee turned the music to a hum and asked Jessica what happened at her house earlier.

"My dad had a meltdown about the past. I was trying to get some information about his parents, but he lost it."

Jessica shared the details and said that she'll probably stop asking questions because she didn't want to cause that type of reaction again. Marilee told her she was sorry about what happened and gave her a big hug, which made Jessica's heart fill with warmth and even put a few tears in her eyes.

After they pigged out on chips, dip, and Reese's Pieces, Jessica's stomach started to hurt. These were not the kinds of foods she was accustomed to. Marilee had her lie down on the couch with a hot water bottle on her stomach as they watched MTV videos, gossiped about people at school, and said which movie stars they thought were cute. Jessica rarely watched TV and only sometimes would go to a movie. Usually Aunt Lodi gifted her with those privileges, but that was only three weeks out of the year.

Around ten o'clock, Mr. Ripp came downstairs and told the girls they needed to go to bed. He was holding a big bowl of vanilla ice cream with sliced bananas and chocolate syrup. Mrs. Ripp was making her way down the stairs with a bowl of her own.

"There they are," she said, making a beeline to the Reese's Pieces on the table. "I love these on top of my ice cream."

Jessica picked up their mess as Marilee proceeded to kiss her parents good night. The Ripps had settled into the plush orange couch for a night of TV watching.

"Good night, Jessica," Mrs. Ripp said with a heavy tongue. "Wow, this ice cream is cold."

"Good night," she said and then hesitated before following Marilee up the basement stairs. "Thank you for taking good care of me and Jason."

"Anytime. You know we love having you."

"Sleep well," Mr. Ripp said with an ice-cream grin.

Marilee briefed Jessica on the Sunday morning ritual. Breakfast was at eight o'clock sharp because they had to be at ten o'clock Mass. Mr. Ripp did the cooking on Sundays: eggs, bacon, waffles, and freshly squeezed orange juice upon request. Mrs. Ripp was not very coordinated in the kitchen according to Marilee. Jessica could not envision her father in the kitchen cooking anything since that was her mother's job. After breakfast, all the kids cleaned up while the parents got ready for church. Marilee said it would be best if they got ready before

breakfast, to avoid much arguing for bathroom time, and set her alarm
clock for seven o'clock.

"We'll be the only ones up that early, so we'll get all the hot water
in the shower."

The night and day that Jessica spent with the Ripps was the most
love she had felt since Aunt Lodi left. This realization made her feel like
a deserted island, but it also confirmed how necessary it was for her to
be with Paul. Her decision to change their schedules was now all she
could think about. It was out of her character to do so. In fact, she did
not even tell Marilee, but desperation called for a bold plan. And all she
wanted was to feel and be told she was loved.

The sun was setting when her parents drove over to pick up Jessica
and Jason. Mr. Ripp and her father spoke alone in the basement, while
her mother was being held hostage listening to Mrs. Ripp talk about
her new money-saving obsession: coupon clipping. Marilee helped
Jessica gather up her belongings in the bedroom attic.

"I'm so sad to see you go."

"Me too," Jessica said with a frown.

"Oh, you two are pathetic," Barbara said from her bed, not taking
her eyes off a book she was reading.

"Come on, I'll walk you out," Marilee said as she gave Barbara a
dirty look. As they walked down the steps, Marilee grabbed Jessica's
arm and told her that if she ever felt scared at her home again, she was
to call immediately. "My dad or Eddie will bring you and Jason back
here."

Jessica gave her a hug. "You really are the best friend I could ever have."

In the car, Jessica's parents said they were glad to see them. Jessica felt guilty because she didn't feel the same way. And she saw what she thought was the same feeling on Jason's face too.

Upon entering the home, a strong odor of bleach with a mixture of lemon met them at the door. Her mother looked at Jessica and Jason for a minute. "I hope you behaved yourselves at Bob and Sue's."

"Mom, we did great. We ate pizza and played games, and watched TV and . . ." Jason was allowed to emote for over ten seconds before he was interrupted.

"Well, that sounds like a fun time. I want you to get ready for bed and we'll be up in a minute to say good night."

When Jessica pulled her covers over before climbing into bed, her parents came into her room.

"We are sorry about the event that took place yesterday, and it will not happen again," her mother said in a low tone. "But you need to stop digging around in the past; the here and now is where everyone belongs."

Her father stood in the doorway and, for the first time that she could remember, looked apologetic. "I'm going on a business trip next week so I would like you to put this behind us."

Feeling pressured, Jessica nodded with agreement, but inside she could not keep out the inquisitive voices. Who were Ermaline and Walker? And if they were not in a nursing home, where were they? What about them made her father turn into a raging beast?

Both parents gave her a peck on the head and before exiting the room, her father turned around with an earnest look on his face. A twinge of sorrow rang in her belly, but she pushed it away. Tougher was how she needed to be in order to survive the Turner home.

Later in the night, Jessica tiptoed to her window and looked out at the sky. It was impossible to see stars because of the lights of the city, so it was hard to wish on one. She decided to wish on the moon, with its crescent shape illuminating the area that hung around it. However, after a thoughtful discussion in her head, she changed her mind about the wishing, feeling that it was not powerful enough, and said a prayer to God. She folded her hands, like she did at Mass in the morning, and once again prayed for her parents to change, for love to wash over her family, and for forgiveness for the lies she planned on telling in the future so she could be with Paul.

Chapter 11

The next week at school, Jessica ate lunch on the bleachers with Paul. Even though freshman were not allowed outside for lunch, the enforcement of the rule seemed more lax the closer the school calendar inched toward June. They were not alone; Marilee, along with Paul's burnout friend Gary, gathered on the bleachers beside them. But in Jessica's world, it was her and Paul alone. He stole her lunch one day and Jessica chased him around to get it. He hid behind a tree, and when she grabbed at it, he pulled her into him.

"I know it's not mittens, but it's the next best thing."

Jessica was all smiles as they walked hand in hand away from the tree, to the surprise of Marilee.

"So are you officially going out?" Marilee asked later in the girl's bathroom.

"Well, sort of. We have to keep it a secret because of my dad."

"Do you have a boyfriend, Jessica Turner?"

Jessica's cheeks turned pink. "Yes."

Marilee jumped up and down for a few seconds. "This is so exciting. Did you kiss?"

"Ohmigod, no. I'm afraid he'll think I'm a terrible kisser."

"Remember that party I went to in seventh grade, where I played spin the bottle and kissed a couple of boys? It really was pretty easy. You just peck out your lips, push them on his, and pull away fast."

Jessica thought about that image. What Marilee was describing didn't look the same as when she watched those MTV videos, but then again, what did she know? Marilee had kissed at least four boys.

"This sounds stupid but I've been practicing on my pillows."

"Hey, I have a poster of Scott Baio. You could practice on that. You know, get close to his lips and do what I said."

Jessica liked the idea of practicing on something that had a real face, not imaginary.

"It folds up so you could sneak it in and out easily."

"Okay," Jessica said. "Bring it tomorrow."

In Humanities, Mr. Gambino announced he would give extra credit points to anyone who attended the school musical and brought him a ticket stub. Jessica was pulling an A+ but Paul jumped at the idea for other reasons.

"Tell your parents you have to go to the play because your teacher said so. We could sneak out and go to the mall or my house. Then I'll walk you home after the play lets out."

Jessica started to panic again. She was not ready for his house—and he could never walk her home. In fact, he could never know where she lived.

"Paul, you have to promise me you will never, ever, go to my house."

Paul looked dismayed. "I'm not letting you walk home alone at night."

"That's really nice, but you can't walk me home. I mean it. If you insist, I will not be your girlfriend."

Paul continued to look at her, confused. "One day your parents are gonna find out about me. They always do."

Jessica did not want to think about that. All she wanted to think about was the now, not the past or the future.

*   *   *

The biggest fund raiser of the year at Heritage High School was the spring musical. The drama department would direct, act, and produce a weeklong Broadway musical. This year's winner was Mary Poppins. Marilee, who had convinced her parents she could balance sports and drama, had a small speaking part that consisted of less than ten words. Jessica, supportive to the end, said at least it was a start. Next year she could try for twenty.

After praying daily for a week, Jessica mustered up the courage and finally asked her parents if she could attend the play. It took a few apprehensive days but her father okayed the mission, with the caveat that he would drop her off and pick her up.

"I won't see you for a few weeks because I'm leaving on a business trip. This way we can spend a few minutes together before I go."

Jessica suppressed her elation over him leaving and she also suppressed her deceit. She had already seen the play. The drama department had a special dress rehearsal and invited classroom teachers who donated their time and talent. One of her teachers helped with costume design, so during Jessica's computer period she was able to watch Marilee on stage in all her glory.

The night of the play Jessica felt too intimidated to go to Paul's house, so he convinced her to hang out in an empty classroom rather than sit through the performance. Jessica's face was pale as Paul, who was enjoying the adventure, tried different doors to discover one that would open, finally twisting an old brass knob that said yes.

A yellow glow from the streetlights shone through the narrow grills in the windows that ran along the wall. As they crept in, Jessica hung behind Paul until he suddenly said, "Yeah, baby." Jessica poked her head from behind his back and that's when she saw an old medical table in the corner. Jessica started to get that unsafe feeling again. Here she was with a boy who knew a lot more about everything, in a semi-dark room with a thing they could potentially make out on.

"What's this room for?" Jessica whispered.

"Don't know," Paul said as he guided her toward the table.

Jessica surveyed the room and came to the conclusion that it served as a library at one time but was now storage for old and dying books. "Wow, look at all these books," she said, trying to distract him.

"Books? Are there books in this room?" he said, walking her closer to the table. She dragged her feet, not wanting to reject him full force. He placed his hands on the table and pulled himself up, then reached over to pull her next to him. Before she could say anything else, his face was inches from hers, his hands cupping the sides of her head.

"Wait," she said, pulling away.

"What? What's the matter?"

She looked away from him, trying not to show how nervous she was.

"All I'm gonna do is kiss you . . . okay . . . nothing else."

Jessica felt worn out from her internal struggle. How would she know if she's a good kisser if she never kissed a boy? She turned her face back toward his and gave an awkward smile.

He took that to mean "game on" and once again, but a little slower this time, leaned in to kiss her. Jessica pecked her lips forward like Marilee said and for a split second thought, *I'm doing it,* but then the presence of his tongue in her mouth threw her off. She tried not to gag, pretending this was a normal part of kissing. After a few seconds, Paul stopped kissing her and asked, "Have you ever been kissed before?"

Jessica wanted to die. He could tell for sure that she was a fake, a novice, someone who thought kissing pillows and posters would cut it in the real world.

"Sort of," she mumbled. "Well, I've never been kissed like that."

"I was French kissing you, you know, with my tongue in your mouth. You're supposed to stick yours in mine."

Jessica wanted to faint. *So much for being tough,* she thought.

"I don't know if I can do that," she said quietly.

"Hey, how do you know until you try . . . and try again?"

"You sound like a twisted version of the little engine that could."

"If that's what it takes to get you to kiss me."

Jessica could not help but smile at him. He looked so beautiful, patiently waiting for her to grow some balls. (She heard that expression at Eddie's lunch table.)

"I think you can, I think you can, I know you can, I know you can," he said playfully.

"Okay," Jessica said.

For the third time, Paul gently held Jessica's face in his hands and leaned in. This time he kissed just her lips, parting them with his, ever so softly. He slowly pushed his tongue in her mouth and rolled it around, until Jessica felt the rhythm and did the same thing to him. Once she got the hang of it, she thought it was semi-enjoyable. Or maybe it was because it was with Paul. She appreciated that he did not press anything else on her and figured he must know that for tonight, she could not handle one more thing on the making-out program.

The part Jessica enjoyed the most was cuddling next to Paul, just like in her bed with the pillows next to her. They talked about their friends, gossip around school, and a little bit about his family. The part with his arms wrapped around her and her head nuzzled in between his shoulder and neck, feeling the warmth of his body, smelling his freshly washed hair—she realized how easy it would be to fall in love with someone if this was how it started.

Jessica kept obsessive track of the time so she would walk out with the students exiting the play. Paul agreed to walk out after her and not acknowledge her presence.

Her father's truck was parked right out front, exactly where he dropped her off. As she opened the passenger door to get in, she felt someone staring at her. She glanced out the back of the cab window and saw Paul half a block down. The streetlight shone on him as he walked backwards with his hands deep in his jacket pockets, grinning. She tried to hide her smile, but it was impossible. It didn't matter though. Her father didn't even notice.

The last week of school before summer break was full of excitement and energy. Students pasty from the lack of sun were barely able to contain their elation over outdoor freedom—swimming in the neighborhood pool, riding bikes, and hanging out late with friends.

While Jessica appreciated the warmth of summer, and the prospect of spending two weeks with Aunt Lodi, the thought of being in the house most of the time felt like a prison sentence. She would not have five-day-a-week access to Paul, or the empty library so she and Paul could French kiss. She was beginning to really love French kissing and believed she was getting better: B+ for sure. But she could sense Paul edging for the next level. On a few occasions, he tried touching her breasts. Jessica sent his hands away, but she believed he was not the type of boy to keep waiting. The only frame of reference she had was listening in on how girls at school talked about their relationships. Jessica and Marilee would conference about it, and then ask Julie what she thought, but in the end, Jessica was left with making the hard decision alone.

"Look," Julie said one day while they walked home from school. This was the twentieth time the girls asked her the same question. "You have to decide how far you're willing to go, and whether the boy's worth it. I've had a few boyfriends, none that deserved having sex with, but that was my decision. And God's too, because for me, my beliefs play a part in making that decision." Jessica and Marilee stared at Julie like she held the answer they were finally looking for. "But you can't make that decision based on *my* beliefs. They need to be your own."

Jessica had a strong belief in God. Prayer, and not just at night, was a ritual that made her feel better and guided her when times were tough. But Paul was a sticky matter. She knew having sex was something her parents *never* wanted her to do. And it was not like at the moment she was ready for that step either. Having a boyfriend was a brand-new experience, but she began to fear it would become complicated. She was starting to feel like she loved him. And, she was pretty sure he felt the same way too.

Jessica asked Paul to eat lunch alone one day that last week of school. She wanted to find out if Paul loved her. She knew she could never come right out and ask; she would have to play it cool to get that information. (Something she had learned from overhearing a conversation in Gym.)

They sat on the same swings that had brought them together for the first time that fall day. This time, he twisted the swings so they could face each other, and Jessica placed her legs on top of Paul's so they could look at each other as they talked. Jessica loved the way the sun shone on his auburn hair, glistening off his boyish face.

"Can you believe school is over Friday?"

"School's out for *summer*," he sang. "I can't wait for school to be out *forever*."

"Seriously, what do you do in the summer?"

Paul hesitated. "Is this a trick question?"

Jessica nudged him with her legs, and he smiled.

"Well, I hang out with my guys, go swimming . . . party. I mean, it is summer."

The partying was something Jessica did not understand firsthand. Since becoming boyfriend and girlfriend, she noticed Paul's heavy, glossed-up eyes were a rarity around her. His partying was something she never asked about, more out of fear than anything else, and from not wanting to be the type of girlfriend that nitpicked her boyfriend. (She was learning so much in Gym.)

"But I want to spend time with you, you know, this summer," Paul said. "Is that a possibility?"

She looked away, toward the expansive green grass of the park, lifting her head to gaze at the colossal trunks of the trees.

"Probably not."

They looked at each other while their swings swayed ever so slightly. Jessica leaned the side of her head on the chain, and after a few minutes, Paul spoke up and told her not to worry; sophomore year was going to be great.

A month earlier Jessica had changed their schedules to reflect study hall last period and then printed them each a copy. Paul said he didn't need to show anything to his mom; she would never know the difference. When Jessica gave the schedule to her mother, it was not even challenged.

"So I guess we won't see each other the whole summer," Jessica said.

"I guess you're right since you won't let me sneak over to your house or you'll 'break up' with me," Paul said.

Jessica felt this was the right time to broach the subject of love.

"So are we together this summer?" she asked.

"Of course, you're my girlfriend. I'm your boyfriend," he said then gave her a look. "I'm not gonna cheat on you if that's what you're asking."

Jessica felt relieved by his words even though that thought had never crossed her mind. She summoned up the courage to ask about love by saying a little prayer in her head.

"Thanks. And I hope you know I would never do that to you." She hesitated. "Because I care about you a lot."

He stared at her intensely. "I know. I care about you too. Truthfully I have more trust in you than I do most of my family."

Since their relationship consisted of eating lunch on the bleachers and sneaking into the old library to kiss, she really didn't know a lot about his family situation. The only time they ever talked at length was the night of the school play, on the medical table. He briefly mentioned his family in the form of facts—oldest of four boys, mom a single parent, lived two blocks from school on the other side of the overpass.

"Why, because you have brothers?"

He shook his head. "You'll see in the fall." Jessica agreed to meet at Paul's house during study hall. Something she had finally relented to because she feared getting caught in the old library kissing Paul. That would for sure require a call home.

The faint sound of the next period bell was heard from across the park. Their eyes met, saddened by the reality of abandoning each other for three months.

"How can we meet alone again? I want to leave you with me on your lips."

Jessica felt shy but she too wanted to kiss him good-bye. "I have Key Club from three to four thirty on Friday. We're having an end of the year party. I can leave a little early, around four. Maybe we can meet in the old library again?"

They untangled their legs from each other and started walking back to school. Paul grabbed her hand and held it tight.

"I love your idea."

The Key Club met in their usual space, around the corner from the old library. The afterschool program leader wanted Jessica to be a part of the club sophomore year. He told her she was a wonderful asset, very responsible, and added a lot of maturity to the group. Jessica glowed from the compliment and said she planned on it. Even though it was getting easier to lie, she felt criminal telling the afterschool leader she had to leave early. Especially since he'd given her a compliment that she no longer felt worthy of.

Jessica and Paul met in the old library again, but she still would only let him kiss her. Afterward, Jessica laid her head on his chest, loving the feel of his breathing. Up and down, up and down. Paul grabbed Jessica's hand and put it up to his in the air. Her fingertips were half an inch below his.

"This sucks. I can't believe I won't see you until September. Are you sure there's no way we can see each other?"

Jessica paused. She thought about plans and missions, but in the end, all she could see were two Colt .45s.

"I'm sorry. It's impossible."

Jessica's head lifted up as Paul took a deep breath in and let it out slowly.

"I'll remember this and keep you close to me," he said and pulled her in tight.

Those words comforted Jessica with the knowledge that Paul loved her and three months apart would not change that . . . she hoped.

Chapter 12

That summer, there were only three things that happened that were worth noting: Jessica sneaked out and saw *Purple Rain* with Marilee, she visited Aunt Lodi's, and Paul was spotted fighting at the local pool.

It was Marilee who suggested they sneak out to see the movie *Purple Rain*, with Prince. Jessica didn't know who Prince was, so she asked a lot of questions. Marilee, like a wise healer, answered them all in a cautious tone and added all the reasons why they should go.

"Plus," Marilee said after giving a five-minute sermon, "Julie said she would help us."

"Really? Why would she do that?"

"Because she kinda feels bad for you."

Jessica was taken aback. "Why?"

Marilee stared at Jessica like she was lost. "Because of all the bullshit your parents put you through. Because you're practically a prisoner in your own home. Because you have to sneak out clothes just to look normal."

Jessica knew she was speaking the truth, but that loyalty feeling crept up again. "They have good reasons I'm sure." Marilee looked disturbed. "But I'm not sure what they are."

Marilee softened her expression. "Look, Jess, I'm not trying to bad-mouth your family. We just want you to be happy."

Jessica put her head down and nodded.

"So whatdya say?" Marilee asked with the same devilish smile that Paul gave.

Jessica reluctantly agreed to the plan. Julie would cover at home, and Eddie would drop them off, go to his girlfriend's house, and then come back to pick them up when it was over.

At dinner, Jessica couldn't believe the turn of events when Mr. Ripp said he had to run over to his sister's house because of an emergency furnace problem and Mrs. Ripp said she had a commitment that evening to take the nuns from the convent shopping. All the kids looked at each other like a gift just poured down from heaven.

Marilee did a happy dance after watching Mrs. Ripp drive away and a few seconds later grabbed Jessica's hands and twirled her around, jumping up and down, singing, "This is *so exciting!*"

Jessica took part in the festivities and put on a spirited front, but her insides were on a roller coaster ride. Eventually she rationalized that this type of behavior was something she needed to get used to, considering what she'd agreed to do in the fall with Paul.

The plan worked without a hitch. They squeezed into two middle seats in the front right section. Once they shifted themselves into comfortable positions, they looked at each other with amazement. Jessica thought the people in the theater looked older than they. Probably because it was an R-rated movie.

When the first song came on, Jessica was blown away by the choreography and sound; her senses had never been plugged in and put into overdrive. *Purple Rain* aroused feelings Jessica had never felt before. The sex scenes were so visual that flashes of hotness swarmed over her entire being. Watching Prince and Apollonia during their intimate moments felt like an invasion of privacy. But she loved the music—it made her feel alive. She especially loved "The Beautiful Ones" scene. Even before the movie let out, Jessica made up a fantasy in which another boy loved her and was trying to take her away from Paul. Paul, who could sing and dance like Prince, sang "The Beautiful Ones" to her during the school talent show, and all the girls who made fun of her because of her granny panties were envious that she had two cute boys who loved her. But in the end, she stayed true to only one . . . Paul.

One week later, the cleaning ladies arrived, and Jason said in a soft tone that Dad's coming home tomorrow.

"Next week we're going to Aunt Lodi's for two whole weeks, just you and me."

Jason brightened and then asked Jessica to play a game with him. They carved out a small space on his bed and played Candy Land around the feverish energy of the cleaning ladies.

Dinner was served in the dining room, on china as usual, and her mother announced their father would be home tomorrow and that they were all going to the UP the day after. They would be spending five days together as a family, then her parents would return home, and the kids would stay the two weeks as usual. This spending family time together in the UP was highly unusual. Her father always drove them to his sister's, stayed a couple of days, and then drove back to Chicago. That's how it had been since Jessica could remember. When she was younger, she would ask why her mother wasn't coming and the response she hastily got was, "nature is not for me."

Her father arrived home in the morning before anyone woke up. Jessica was thankful she'd written the welcome home letter with all the details of her summer and left it on his desk before she went to bed that night. Right after breakfast, during his inquiry in the office, Jessica paid close attention to her father's physical appearance. She thought that being gone for over a month might have left clues on his body as to his whereabouts. He'd been in a sunny climate due to his tanned skin. It was obvious he'd worn sunglasses. His hands looked more calloused and dry; his right hand had a long scratch mark that was in the late stage of healing. The tops of his ears had flakey skin falling off them. And he looked tired, but not dejected. He said he was glad she was enjoying her summer so far and that she looked forward to spending time as a family at Aunt Lodi's.

"It'll be good for all of us to get away from the city for a while," he said with a smile.

Burning sage hit their noses as they entered Aunt Lodi's cabin. She'd told Jessica's father that she might have to work late, but the door would be unlocked and food would be on the stove. Her mother could barely move past the front door. Aunt Lodi's cabin was much smaller than their home, with an L-shaped living room, dining room, and kitchen. A stone fireplace kept the cabin warm and even heated the loft area where Aunt Lodi's and Jessica and Jason's rooms were.

Jessica thought her room was the coziest of all. Its walls were painted in an earthy orange tone that was framed by light oak molding and was the only room in the cabin that had carpet. Framed art that Jessica and Jason made during their visits hung on the walls. Aunt Lodi had written their ages and the year on each one. Tightly grouped on another wall were paintings of sacred Michigan animals: wolves, eagles, and moose. Small dream catchers were attached to their bedposts and handmade quilts that reflected the color of the northern lights covered each bed. A built-in bookshelf contained photo albums of their visits so they could reminisce about the past.

"How long did they say they're staying?" Jessica asked as she and Jason unpacked their belongings.

"Maybe a week," Jason said.

Jessica crumpled her face and then pushed open a window, breathing in the sweet and dewy smells of the outdoors, listening to the sound of the chickadees, and watching a bluebird in flight.

Her mother was complaining about the space, the lack of a dishwasher, and the nonexistence of modernity. Jessica could hear it all from her room. Her father told her sternly that she had agreed to this and in no uncertain terms would he be leaving. If *she* wanted to go to a hotel, she would be going alone.

To the sound of growling stomachs, her mother began serving dinner on the back deck. A few mosquitoes made an appearance that were not as lethal as the nighttime ones but Jessica's mother complained that she had no choice but to eat indoors. Her father stayed outside, lighting the citronella candles around the deck, and Jessica ate with a strong scent of mosquito repellant floating around her nose.

After dinner, her father grabbed his fishing pole and bait from the refrigerator and was about to set off toward the creek when he was interrupted.

"Jason would love to go with you," her mother said.

Her father looked surprised and then turned to Jason. "Sure, go get your shoes."

Jason looked disappointed but did as he was told. Jessica was glad she was not part of that outing; she had no desire to be eaten up by mosquitoes. When Jason was younger, he had to be rushed to the hospital because he had fever, vomiting, and shortness of breath, all due to a severe allergic reaction to mosquito bites. As Jessica thought about her mother's suggestion, something occurred to her. Maybe the suggestion was made because Jason *would* be eaten by mosquitoes, get sick, and have to leave Aunt Lodi's, her father in tow. Jessica waited for her mother to get mosquito spray, but she never did. This only solidified her original thought; a heinous act was being orchestrated by her mother.

"Wait!" Jessica yelled, running after her father and brother as they were making their way toward the back door. Jessica opened the cabinet underneath the kitchen sink and pulled out the repellant, long sleeve shirt, and hat that Jason wore when they went out after dark with Aunt Lodi. Jessica thought she saw her mother flash an annoyed look. "Aunt Lodi always has Jason wear this. Otherwise he'll get sick from the mosquito bites and have to go to the hospital again."

"Good thinking," her father said and gave everything to Jason to put on.

Aunt Lodi came home an hour later, eager to grab a hold of someone for a hug. Her mother backed away and claimed she felt a cold coming on.

"For Christ's sake, Katherine, you're staying in my home for the first time in years. This is how we greet family." And before her mother could protest, she was in the loving grip of her sister-in-law.

Jessica hung out underneath Aunt Lodi's arm on the couch the rest of the night. They talked, played cards, and watched TV until her father and Jason came back from fishing. He was wearing the same headlamp he'd worn when he took off Jessica's bedroom door, and she had to hold down a flash of nausea, swallowing hard on her spit. Aunt Lodi pulled herself off the couch and gave everyone a hug, gleefully looking at the caught fish in the pail. "Dinner for tomorrow? Jason, thank you so much."

Aunt Lodi was working during the day but that didn't seem to impact her father because he was in his element: guns, woods, and fishing.

Her mother, however, walked around like a city cat that was stuck in a box, fearing the bugs and other inhabitants of the natural surroundings. Jessica noticed her parents barely said a word to each other. At the first sign of light, her father set off with his fishing pole, sometimes with Jason dragging behind, and they would not be seen until lunch. Food in mouth, they were off again to shoot at something, or chop this or that, then back for dinner at six thirty sharp. Aunt Lodi returned from work around that time, and they would sit together as a family on the deck and eat. Coming together for a meal made Jessica glow.

One evening, Jessica took notice of the sky and basked in all its glory. The sun was setting slowly over the woods in the west with hues of pink, orange, and yellow shining through the leaves on the trees. Jessica wished she could stay in the moment forever.

She glanced over at her mother, who was wearing a bandana tied around her chin, a long sleeve white shirt, fitted black trousers, and flat dress shoes. Her sunglasses stayed on even after the sun went down; wrinkles were a frightening thought. Then she looked at Aunt Lodi's outfit: a light blue-and-yellow summer tank dress that hit at the ankles, a floppy hat from the '60s, and no shoes. The large jewelry she wore was embellished with Native American symbols and stones. Despite being complete opposites, there was one thing both women agreed upon: the wine Aunt Lodi opened nightly. Jessica figured if her mother could, she would drink from the time she got up in the morning to the time she went to bed—anything to cloud her current circumstances. Jessica was hoping her father would reach for a beer, but to her disappointment, he never did.

One afternoon, Jessica sat at the edge of the creek making circular motions with her feet, looking through the clear water to the sandy bottom and studying the multi-speckled rock formations. Jason and her father were wading upstream, trying to catch a trout dinner. Jessica realized she had not thought about Paul until now. It's not that she forgot about him, but being in a place where she felt free to roam, being around nature which seemed necessary to fill her soul, and being surrounded by all her family made her feel more whole. She reasoned that this was the most fun she'd ever had with her father, and it brightened her day.

That evening, her mother announced they'd be leaving in the morning.

Her father gave a small grin. "So you won't have to cook those huge meals anymore."

"Oh please," said Aunt Lodi, "do I look like I eat birdseed?" Everyone laughed, except for Jessica's mother who smirked. "But I've got to say, I really enjoyed these last four days. And your kids look like they have a renewed sense of life with you two." Everyone looked at each other around the patio table.

"Yes, Lodi, I've had a great time," her mother said with a smile.

Jessica was not surprised to hear her parents pack up and drive away before dawn. She crept downstairs and watched the back of their truck with the taillights swishing back and forth as it rolled over the gravel and grass path to the road. A note was left on the kitchen table in her mother's handwriting thanking Aunt Lodi again for a wonderful visit and wishing them fun the next two weeks. It also included rules that should be followed, but that was a given.

The next two weeks for Jessica were joyous. They drove to a waterfall, went hiking and canoeing, and attended the state fair. At the state fair, Jessica and Jason spent the whole day riding on the Tilt-A-Whirl, the Zipper, and Ferris wheel, trying not to throw up the candied nuts, deep fried cheese curds, or funnel cake. This was the most junk food Jessica had eaten since being at Marilee's. The state fair also had live animal auctions, barns full of every farm creature imaginable, and a draft horse pull. Jessica loved horses, so they walked around the two barns attached to the arena, trying to touch them through gated wire. Most of the people in the barn were kids from 4-H, many Jessica's age, showing and selling the animals they raised.

The draft horses were Jessica's favorite because they stood tallest of all, strong and muscular, exuding a look of confidence and wisdom. An older boy was inside the stall of a draft horse named Moses, raking out the hay and manure.

"Looks like a smelly job," Aunt Lodi commented.

The boy softly laughed and said, "Yes, ma'am."

"Is this your horse?"

The boy stopped working and looked at Aunt Lodi. "Well, he's my brother's, but he's been having too much fun here with his friends." The boy looked up at the horse and gave him a rub behind his ear. "Couldn't watch him stand in the muck one more minute."

"Why, that's mighty kind of you. Look here," Aunt Lodi said to Jason and Jessica, in particular. "This boy is a hard worker and loves animals."

Jessica did not know where Aunt Lodi was going with this but did not like the turn it was taking.

"Your horse seems like a big teddy bear," Aunt Lodi said, shooting a look at Jessica. *Oh no*, Jessica thought, knowing now for sure where she was going. "These are my niece and nephew, Jessica and Jason. They're from Chicago so they don't get to see this very often. Can they pet Moses?"

Jessica almost died, but she couldn't be mad at Aunt Lodi; she didn't know about Paul.

"Sure," the boy said and raked out a small path for them as they entered the stall.

Moses towered over them, but the boy told them where to stand and how to touch him behind the ears and gently on the nose. The boy started talking about the draft horse breed, giving them a brief lecture on anything they wanted to know. Jessica felt a strong pull to jump on Moses's back and take off out of the barn and into the woods, holding on tight to his majestic black mane.

"You want to ride him, don't you?" said the boy.

Jessica tried to hide herself but there was nowhere to go. "Sort of," she mumbled.

"I don't," Jason said, looking straight up at the beast and backing away.

"Moses isn't a riding horse. We have other horses that pull people; they're more manageable."

Jessica leaned away from Moses, not sure what to make of all that information.

"He won't hurt you if you touch him. He likes that, but I wouldn't go jumping on his back."

Aunt Lodi engaged him with more questions about the horses, but it all led back to getting information about his life. Moses, and the boy, lived on a farm near the Wisconsin-Michigan border, where his family raised and trained draft horses for competition and pleasure. While he was answering all of Aunt Lodi's questions, Jessica sneaked a look at him. He was tall, probably around six foot, with a small extended belly. His brown work boots were scuffed and stained with green streaks running down the sides, and his overalls and T-shirt looked well worn. The John Deere hat he wore was pushed back as he kept wiping the sweat that was rolling into his eyes, which were brown, but definitely not the same color as his boots. They were more like a piece of caramel, she thought.

After Jason started getting fidgety and some kids, including a cute blonde, walked up to the stall, Aunt Lodi ended the conversation. Before walking away, Aunt Lodi thanked him and then abruptly apologized, realizing she hadn't asked his name.

"My name's Matt," he said. "And thanks for listening to my lesson about horses." His friends started laughing at him, and the cute blonde grabbed his hand.

"This boy loves horses," she said, smiling at him. *They're obviously going out*, thought Jessica, who was now feeling completely uncomfortable.

They stayed to watch the heavyweight draft horse pull contest, clamoring onto the metal risers to find a place where Jason could see without anyone blocking his view. The arena smelled of hay, dirt, and manure, but Jessica loved it. Teams of two horses competed against each other to see which could pull the heaviest load the farthest. The team driver, usually an older man, sat on a flat sled loaded with concrete blocks, waiting for two men to hitch the team onto the sled. The horses then charged forward together, moving slowly ahead.

"Look, there's that cute boy, Matt." Aunt Lodi gestured to the far end of the arena where Matt was hitching his father's team. His father looked to be about seventy years old. Another taller boy who looked a lot like Matt, but much blonder, was on the other side helping; Jessica assumed it was his brother. She didn't think Matt was as cute as Aunt Lodi thought. But as she continued to watch him, the way he handled the team, how strong yet gentle he appeared, she started to see something she considered appealing: kindness.

*   *   *

As their last days together neared, Jessica decided it was time to inquire about the family's past, craving the shared history and stories of her family.

Jason was sleeping, and Aunt Lodi and Jessica were in the kitchen preparing a picnic lunch for the next day's adventure.

"Can I ask you something?" Jessica asked as she poured crackers into sandwich bags.

"Of course, anything," Aunt Lodi said, reaching for a strainer in the cabinet to wash strawberries in.

"Who are Ermaline and Walker?"

Jessica jumped when Aunt Lodi dropped the metal strainer onto the floor.

"Dear Lord," she said, and then looked at Jessica. "Where did you hear those names?"

"From Dad, the day I was supposed to hear stories."

Aunt Lodi stared through Jessica for a minute, and then bent down carefully to pick up the strainer.

"What did he say about them?"

"He said they were *not* in a nursing home, unlike Buddy Akers."

Aunt Lodi pursed her lips together then pulled a chair over to where she was standing and lowered herself down. She set the strainer on the counter and then studied her wide hands before she spoke.

"Buddy Akers killed our parents in a drunk driving accident. He was a wormy man, but everyone in town thought he was harmless. I guess he would've been if it hadn't been for the drinking. I was eleven and Jim was seven when we became orphans. Those people you spoke about, they took us in because they were our closest kin even though we hardly ever saw them growing up." Aunt Lodi wiped a few tears off her cheekbone with the back of her hand. "Our lives changed with the turn of a steering wheel." Aunt Lodi stared deep into Jessica's eyes. "I know you think your dad's over the top sometimes, but he can't help it—he really can't."

Jessica sat silent, breathing in the words that were just laid out. "So Ermaline and Walker are family?"

"No," Aunt Lodi said fiercely, and then stood up. "They were associated by blood, that's it."

Jessica could feel the energy in the room twist with her effort to press for more information, but she bore on.

"Where are they now?"

"I'm sorry, honey, but I have to stop. The rest has to come from your dad."

Jessica felt like a ball that was being held underwater. No matter how hard you push it down it wants to come up; it has to go somewhere. After many minutes of stillness, Jessica thanked Aunt Lodi, then thought it best to say good night and leave her alone. Aunt Lodi hovered over the kitchen sink, tears dropping in.

The last day at Aunt Lodi's was spent celebrating Jessica and Jason's birthdays. They were both born in September, and it played out the same way every year: a movie, lots of butter on the popcorn, roller-skating or swimming, homemade pizza with their favorite toppings, and of course presents. Aunt Lodi always bought them something to bring home and something to keep at her house.

Jessica was in complete shock when she opened up an envelope: horseback riding camp for one week in July next year. Jessica jumped up and hugged Aunt Lodi. "Thank you! Thank you! Thank you so much!"

As she sat back down, she wondered if Aunt Lodi were trying to play matchmaker. "Wait a minute, is this . . . ?"

"Don't be silly. I wouldn't embarrass you like that. Plus, they don't offer lessons on Matt's farm, only hay and sled rides."

Jessica gave her a playful pinch and smiled brightly.

When Jessica returned home from Aunt Lodi's, her father said he had to see Bob and told her she could come along too.

When Jessica arrived at Marilee's, she was whisked up to her bedroom where, upon entering, the door was locked behind them. Before Jessica could recover from the speed of the moment, Marilee said she needed to tell her something important, and that she should sit down. Jessica slowly lowered herself onto Julie's messy bed.

"So I went to the pool today and guess who I saw?"

Jessica was still in shock at how dramatic Marilee was acting. "Who?"

"Your boyfriend . . . and he was in rare form."

Jessica's heart sank. "What do you mean?"

"So, me, Barbara, and a couple of Barbara's friends were sitting on our towels and talking. All of a sudden we hear a bunch of commotion right outside the fence of the pool." Marilee sat down next to Jessica. "I look over and see Paul and two boys, who I later learned were his brothers, fighting a man. The man was getting stomped and then the man pulled out a knife."

Jessica put her hands over her mouth and whispered, "Oh my God."

"The lifeguard, the really cute one, jumped the fence and started talking the man down. He kept saying it was not worth going to jail over these kids, stuff like that. Two more lifeguards got out there and were able to break it up."

"What happened to Paul?" Jessica asked, with her hands still covering half her face.

"Well, he kept trying to go after the guy, but one of the big lifeguards held him against the fence. His brothers backed off and stood by Paul until he calmed down, then they followed Paul into the park before the police arrived."

"The police came?" Jessica put her hands down.

"Yeah, but the man refused to press charges. I heard from someone at the pool that Paul and his brothers jumped him because he beat up their mother."

Jessica sat in silence, letting the information play out like a violent scene from the movie *Purple Rain.*

Marilee's bedroom was consumed by the direct heat of the evening sun. It was about ten degrees hotter in her room than the rest of the house, and sweat was starting to run down Jessica's back and collect under her bra. She wiped sweat away from her hairline and looked back at Marilee.

"Did Paul see you?"

"Not sure. There was a huge crowd all crammed on the fence. Everyone was trying to see what was going on. I did get a good look at his brothers. They hardly look alike at all. One had blond hair and the other black. Weird."

Jessica sat on the bench under her window staring at the full moon. She gave up trying to sleep when she saw it was 2:30 a.m.; her last look at the clock said 2:05 a.m. The house was quiet, and that's how she moved around, not wanting to wake her father. Paul was on her mind. What kind of life was he living, that as a kid he would seek revenge on an adult in such fashion? Paul said his mom was a single parent but never mentioned his father. Even though Marilee's description of the fight was disturbing, Paul never showed any violence toward Jessica. She was reminiscing about all their time together and never once did she feel as if he would physically harm her. She fell back on the knowledge that when they returned to school she would find out more about his life. Paul had said something, almost warning her, that his life was different and to be ready. Jessica frowned, thinking that her life was the one he really should beware of.

Chapter 13

Jessica quickly turned off her buzzing alarm and sat straight up in bed. The day she had been fervently waiting for since the last day of school had finally arrived. She felt more relaxed about her first day of sophomore year compared to freshman year, but she was also apprehensive because she had not seen Paul in three months.

Besides Marilee reporting Paul's actions outside the pool, he was spotted at a party that Eddie and Julie attended, drinking and smoking pot with his burnout friends. According to Marilee, Julie said that Alicia was hanging on him and trying to get him to go with her somewhere alone. Julie noticed that Paul treated Alicia like a friend and showed no interest in being with her or any other girls at the party. While the news was supposed to relieve Jessica, she could not help but feel tense about the drinking and smoking pot, which in her opinion were disgusting habits, although she didn't think she had a right to say anything about it.

Jessica put on a purple dago tee and striped shirt that was designed to hang off the shoulders, but in her case, she wore it as conservatively as possible. As she pulled on a pair of jeans that were not as skintight as the rest of the teenage population's, she pushed the Mace down into her front pocket in case her father inspected for it.

Before going down to breakfast, she made sure to double-check her fake schedule. It reflected that she had study hall from 3:15 p.m.–4:15 p.m. daily. She caught her reflection in the full-length mirror and tried not to call herself a liar. She reasoned that having a boyfriend was a normal part of being in high school, and if her parents were going to deny her that right, then she would do whatever it took to make it happen.

Her family was in the kitchen eating pancakes, eggs, and toast when Jessica entered. Her father stared at Jessica and asked if she was wearing makeup.

"No," Jessica said, trying not to sound annoyed. She could see him glaring at her wardrobe.

"I think those jeans are too tight."

She looked at him coolly. "They're the same ones I wore freshman year. Aunt Lodi bought them in the spring."

Upon hearing his sister's name, he relaxed slightly. "You look too mature."

Her mother interjected that Jessica was sixteen now and developing into a young woman.

Her father gave a disgruntled look at them both. "You should look like a respectable young woman, not a . . ." He stopped himself, but she knew the word he was thinking.

Jessica turned her head and tried to eat her breakfast, but her father's absent words replaced her appetite. Her mother said that she would like to see her father in the office for a moment.

"No, Katherine, I'm not going to see you in the office," he said, then walked out of the kitchen.

As soon as he was out of sight, her mother turned toward Jessica. "Your father made a poor choice of words."

Jason looked at Jessica and told her he thought she looked pretty. Jessica's eyes got watery as she breathed in the only ray of sunshine she'd felt all morning.

*   *   *

After she'd shown her father the Mace and the fake schedule, and he'd told her she had seven to ten minutes to get home from study hall, Jessica said good-bye and good riddance to her parents and made her way to the corner to meet Marilee. The girls hugged and exchanged excited talk as they cruised over to Heritage. They both agreed how strange it would be to not have Eddie or Julie in school with them, although Marilee acknowledged boys would be hanging around her more, so that was a plus. Jessica never told Marilee about changing her schedule and going to Paul's house. She reasoned there was no need for all the attention Marilee would offer up.

After big greetings and a brief catching up with friends who they hadn't seen all summer, the girls proceeded to the entrance. Jessica kept a watchful eye out for Paul, her skin begging for his touch again. As they turned the corner, Jessica caught a glimpse of some boys crowded around the edge of the building, almost out of sight, next to a Northern Catalpa shaded tree.

"Is that who I think it is?" asked Marilee. "What is he doing?"

Jessica's pace slowed as she took in the scene. She saw Gary, a kid with black hair, Freak Boy, and two Mexican boys with Paul. Paul was wearing a jean jacket despite it being seventy degrees and was pulling something from his pocket. It looked like a dark substance in a large baggie.

Marilee slowed to a stop. "Is he doing what I think he's doing?"

They watched the two Mexican boys giving Paul money in exchange for the baggie.

"Ohmigod, is he selling drugs?" Marilee whispered as she grabbed

Jessica's arm. At the same moment, she saw Paul spot her. He mouthed something, two of the boys looked her way, then they turned away quickly, trying to act like nothing was going on—real casual. But Jessica knew what she saw: he was selling drugs.

"Come on, let's go," Marilee said, dragging Jessica toward the entrance.

The girls did not say another word to each other. Jessica's heart was frozen. She knew Paul was a drug user, but she never thought he sold it too. That information was more than she was prepared to handle and she started to panic at the thought of seeing him right now, in homeroom.

"You know, I couldn't wait for this day to begin, and now I wish it never had."

Marilee looked at her cautiously. "What are you gonna do?"

"I don't know," Jessica said as she dodged people in the hallway, trying to get to class.

Marilee gave her a hug before she left and said she would meet her after homeroom, so they could walk to gym together.

Mrs. Daley greeted the students with the same enthusiasm and openness as that first day of freshman year and proceeded to give Jessica a big hug, saying how glad she was to see her again. Jessica beamed with pride at the greeting and returned the embrace enthusiastically. Jessica was all smiles as she sat down next to a few students she'd become friends with last year.

"Where's your man?" asked a girl in her group.

Jessica's face dropped at the reminder of her current situation, and before she could get out the words, "I don't know," Paul stepped into the classroom and walked toward Jessica. He was sporting a huge smile, but Jessica could see the angst underneath. He knew that she knew.

"Mr. Peterson, thank you so much for getting to homeroom without a minute to spare."

"I missed you so much, Mrs. Daley, and couldn't wait to see you," Paul said as he took his eyes from Jessica to address her.

"From the looks of things, we have the same homeroom as last year, with only two transfers out and one transfer in." Mrs. Daley continued on with introductions and the generic speech she gave on the first day of school. Paul took a seat two rows away from Jessica and tried to get her attention, but she refused to pay him any. She was unsure how to respond to him because she loved him and felt worried about the choices he was making, but she also knew, deep in her heart, she could not go out with someone who sold drugs. Jessica was aware it was a double standard; she accepted his smoking pot, but selling it just seemed so delinquent.

Paul was trying to be slick, asking people to move their seats so he could sit next to Jessica, but no one budged, mostly due to Mrs. Daley's stern gaze.

"Paul, is there something you need?" Mrs. Daley finally asked.

"No, just can't wait to see my schedule. I think last period is gonna be the best."

Jessica felt his stare, but she continued to ignore him. Mrs. Daley gave him a curious look and began where she left off with her lecture.

Eventually updated schedules were passed out, and friends conferred with each other on who had what with whom. This time Paul got directly up and stepped in between Jessica and the classmate next to her, putting his schedule on her desk.

"Last period study hall, remember?"

Jessica looked up at him. His tanned skin looked too dark, and his feathered hair needed a desperate trim.

Her eyes narrowed. "I remember."

"Can I see your schedule?"

She begrudgingly passed it over to him and he sat down on the edge of her desktop.

"So we have Chemistry and Art together. No lunch, bummer. And definitely study hall." Paul passed her schedule back over and touched her hand. Jessica pulled back without thought.

Paul looked at her longingly. "We need to talk," he whispered.

"I guess during study hall," Jessica replied and turned away to talk to another classmate.

Outside of chemistry class, Paul was waiting for Jessica. She stopped when she reached him and looked at him up close. His face carried a callous look, and his eyes appeared sad. He had grown taller; his chest and arms had filled out, but his body looked tight and constricted. Paul held out a note and asked her to read it in private. That's when she noticed his knuckles had cuts that were trying to heal. She slowly took the note from his hand and walked into Chemistry alone. Paul followed behind but did not sit near her, although the teacher's new seating chart soon had them sitting together once again.

At lunch, Jessica and Marilee sat outside on the benches to eat their beloved tater tots with ketchup while discussing the contents of Paul's note.

"Read it to me again," Marilee said, leaning closer to Jessica so no one would overhear.

Jessica took a sip of her Coke and then whispered, "I see you're pissed at me. I think I know why. Can we talk during study hall in the old library?"

"What's he talking about, the old library?" Marilee asked.

Jessica unveiled the truth about the room they had been kissing in.

Just saying it made Jessica feel self-conscious, like she was doing something wrong.

"Jessica Turner, what other secrets are you keeping?"

Jessica looked apologetic at Marilee, not wanting to expose all her badness. "Nothing."

Marilee did not look convinced. "What doesn't come out in the wash comes out in the rinse. Remember that."

Paul was sitting in art class when Jessica arrived. As she walked past him, she slipped a note on his desk and sat down a few seats behind him. Jessica watched Paul open it, read the contents, then stuff it in the front of his jeans pocket. Gary, one of Paul's burnout friends, was also in art class, but Paul wasn't sitting by him, which made Jessica wonder why. He was one of the boys with Paul this morning before school. Gary gave Jessica a nod to acknowledge he saw her. She gave a small smile because she did not want to be rude even though she didn't care for him.

After the bell rang, Jessica was collecting her things to leave when Gary approached her.

"Hi, Gary."

"So where you going?"

Jessica looked surprised. "Uh, home."

"Home, huh?" Gary gave her a hard look. "Don't mess with Paul's head. He likes you. Isn't that enough?"

Jessica didn't know what to say and started to fidget with the papers she was holding. Gary stared at her and then walked away.

Jessica was on high alert as she walked down the hallway, unsure what message Gary was trying to send. In no way did she intend to give the impression she was messing with Paul's head. She agreed to meet with Paul so she could hear him out, praying that he had a perfectly good explanation for what she saw. But Jessica was also firm, even if it shattered her heart; if Paul were selling drugs, she would break up with him—she could not be associated with someone who was involved in such illegal activity; it was not safe.

The old library had been reorganized over the summer and was not the same cluttered mess from before. The shades were rolled and tied at the top, so the blazing sun came through without hesitation. For the first time, Jessica noticed how much the wood floor creaked.

The medical table was in the same location although a few labeled boxes had been placed on top. Jessica started removing them and putting them on the floor when she heard the door open. She looked up, and Paul walked toward her and gave a weak smile. She returned it with one of her own.

"Hey," he said softly.

"Hi."

Paul removed the rest of the boxes so he and Jessica could sit on the nurse's table but at a safe distance apart.

Jessica felt very uncomfortable. She wasn't good at standing up to others—all she wanted was to slink away and hide deep inside herself.

A few more moments of silence passed before Paul spoke up.

"So you're pissed at me because . . . ?"

Jessica answered slowly, "I saw you this morning, with your friends."

Paul did not budge. "Yeah, so?"

"You had on a jean jacket, and it's seventy degrees."

"And you're pissed because of that?"

Jessica started to feel he was toying with her emotions. "I saw you take out a baggie and those Mexican boys paid you for it."

"Yeah, so, they're tamales. My mom makes and sells tamales."

Jessica stared at him. "Tamales?"

"Yeah, you know, cornmeal with pork inside wrapped in a corn husk."

Jessica had never tasted tamales and had no idea how one even looked. "Your mom makes and sells tamales?"

"My mom's are rad."

Jessica narrowed her eyes because while she desperately wanted to believe Paul, her gut did not feel calm.

"I saw you take out something very dark from your jacket."

"My mom burned the husk cause she didn't put enough water in the pan in the oven, but those guys don't care because like I said, my mom's are the best."

Paul's description made sense, and he sounded very convincing. Jessica's eyes started to loosen.

"What did you think I was doing this morning?" Paul questioned.

Jessica looked down at her dangling feet, trying to decide if she should tell the truth.

"I thought you were selling drugs."

"So that's why you treated me like a piece of shit?"

Jessica looked tenderly into his eyes. "I'm sorry. I . . . I'm kinda new at this, you know, having a boyfriend."

"I hate when people give me the cold shoulder. If you're pissed at me, just tell me."

"Okay," Jessica said then reached over and touched his bruised-up hand, intertwining her fingers with his. They turned their bodies toward each other, and he gently put his other hand on the side of her face. Her hand reached around his waist and pulled him into her body. The movie *Purple Rain* gave a visual to things Jessica had no previous knowledge of. Paul kissed her gently at first, and with the image of Prince and Apollonia in her mind, Jessica became highly excited. She leaned in and kissed Paul with more passion than she ever had before.

Paul didn't protest. His hands made their way under her two shirts and onto her arched back as he kissed her neck and ears. It scared Jessica how much she wanted to be with Paul, but she knew she was not ready for that yet. After many minutes of making out, Jessica finally pulled away when she felt Paul edging for more.

"Okay. Okay," he said and stopped. They cozied up on the table, catching up on the events of the summer.

Jessica was stunned by Paul's brutal honesty about his life. He explained the bruises on his knuckles and the other scars were all due to fights he got into over the summer. He'd even defended his mother by beating up her abusive boyfriend. He told her about a couple of parties he went to, and that he thought the reason she was mad at him was because Alicia was all over him at a party that Eddie was at. Paul was sure that Eddie told her he was cheating. He explained that he partied, drank, and smoked a lot of pot, but did not cheat on her.

"Do you like Alicia?" Jessica asked.

"As a friend. We went to elementary school together, and she likes to party. That's it."

The door to the room suddenly opened up. Jessica froze at the sound, deathly scared of being found and a call home being made. They listened intently to the creaking of wood as the person shuffled through boxes at the front of the room before finally leaving.

"Are you all right?" Paul whispered.

Jessica did not realize she was clinging to Paul and shaking. She shook her head no.

Paul gathered her in closer. "No one knows we're here. I promise you're safe."

Chapter 14

The big day had arrived. Jessica was going to Paul's house. She tried not to dwell too much on what she was doing because she trusted Paul, but there were certain fears she couldn't dispel—like fearing that Paul's home was not a safe place because his mother was beaten by her boyfriend there.

They sat together in homeroom, and Paul warned her that his home was probably not as clean as hers.

Jessica smiled. "I'm sure it will be fine."

After Art, they went to their lockers and then got Danny, Paul's younger brother, who was now a freshman, and walked home together. This was the first time Jessica had met Danny, and she was surprised at his appearance. His black hair was messy and long, and he stood almost as tall as Paul. His build was stocky, and he looked like he was pumping iron already. He seemed nice enough, but Jessica felt he lacked the carefree gentleness that she felt in Paul. Danny seemed rough.

Jessica felt nervous walking in the opposite direction of her home. She had never walked this neighborhood, only ran through it with her dad at her side. And she had never crossed over the overpass on foot. Jessica had made sure to find out what time Jason got picked up from homeschool, so there would be no chance of being spotted by her mother, who was a creature of habit and would rarely deviate from her daily routine. Jessica soothed her thoughts knowing that there would be no errand running after Jason was picked up—home immediately.

Crossing the overpass, Jessica was instantly struck by gusts of hot wind and the loud noise of traffic on the expressway below. Jessica fought to regain control of her hair as it whipped around.

They approached a group of small one-story brick bungalow homes with tiny yards in the front to match that faced the expressway. There were five homes in the row—four had trimmed lawns and an appearance of being kept up. Danny ran ahead of them, flicked the butt of his cigarette into the brown grass of the fifth house, and walked up the crumbling concrete steps. Paul squeezed her hand and grinned.

When Danny opened the torn screen door to push the front door open, music that could just be heard from the sidewalk came pouring out. Jessica's heart pumped faster as she approached the steps. There were missing awnings and a window that had plastic covering it on the inside. Paul stepped in after Danny, pushing a small pile of clothes out of the way. The smell was what hit her first—stale and musty with cigarette smoke and a hint of sweat. It was also very hot; no windows or doors were open to allow the warm breeze from the outside to blow through. The living room walls were barren and dirty. An army-green-colored couch was pushed against one wall, a TV and stereo with huge speakers against the other. There was a small curio cabinet in the corner that held two glass sculptures and disorganized papers. Paul turned the stereo down; it was playing something hard and sad.

"Paul, is you home?" yelled a brassy voice from the kitchen.

Paul was leading Jessica toward the voice when two boys came running up from the basement; both had blond hair. Paul gave them playful punches and continued to lead Jessica into the kitchen.

"Who are you?" the taller blond boy asked.

"That's Jessica," Paul said before she had a chance to respond.

"Is she your girlfriend?" the smaller boy asked. The taller boy punched his arm, and he started to blush.

"These are my brothers Marcus and Brian," Paul said, trying to get past them.

"Nice to meet you," Jessica said as she followed Paul, who grabbed her hand to lead her into the kitchen.

A woman in a white dingy robe was curled up on a kitchen chair, talking on the phone. She had a cigarette in one hand and the phone tucked in between her head and shoulder. Jessica stared at the woman, trying to see any resemblance of Paul. Her thick curly black hair was messy and poked out every which way. She looked like she had just woken up and had a half-eaten bowl of soggy cereal parked in front of her.

"Ma, get off the phone," Paul demanded. Jessica looked at him, shocked he would order his mother to do anything.

Paul's mother gave him a dirty look and pushed her cigarette-holding hand in the air as a sign to shut up. Paul turned toward Danny, who had emerged from a back room and was searching the kitchen for food.

"Is she on the phone with that fucker?" Paul asked.

Danny looked at his mother and just shrugged his shoulders. "Let's not get into that again."

Jessica could feel Paul's anger. "Maybe we should go."

She looked at the faces that were staring at her; they looked amazed that she would want to come *here* for a visit.

"Jess, come here," Paul yelled from the back room. Jessica stepped down into a small enclosed porch that had room for a twin bed and a TV on a crate. The black-and-white TV was playing a cartoon with the sound turned all the way down and Paul was sitting on the edge of the bed, looking out the window at the barren backyard.

"I don't think I should've brought you here."

Jessica pushed a ball of blankets to the side and sat down next to him reaching her arm around his shoulders. "It's all right." She leaned in and kissed him on the cheek.

Paul's smile was crooked as he continued to stare out the window. It took Jessica well over twenty minutes, but she finally got him to start talking, even laughing, when they caught Brian spying on them. Jessica finally told Paul she'd have to leave in another ten minutes. Paul grabbed her, wrapping his arms and legs around her whole body and pulling her onto the bed.

"Nooo," Jessica shrieked, trying to maneuver out of the wrestling hold as Paul's mother walked in.

"Paul, stop," his mother said, surprising them both. Paul let Jessica go, and she straightened out her clothes and stood up to say hello.

"You need to stop getting' in my business," his mother said, not acknowledging Jessica.

"You wanna go there right now?" Paul asked.

"I don't give a rat's ass who hears me. And you should be the one to talk, beatin' up an old man in front of the whole damn neighborhood." Jessica slinked over as far as she could so that she was out of the way of their words.

Paul jumped up. "Nobody's gonna beat on you and get away with it."

"Jesus Christ, it was one black eye. One. First and only time he done that."

"And last," Paul stated.

For the first time, Paul's mother looked Jessica's way, casually lifting her hand to push down her hair and close up the robe that was slipping open at the top.

"I'm guessing you're Jessica. Call me Dee Dee or Dee. Whatever. It doesn't matter," she said, holding her robe together.

"Hi. Thank you for letting me come over."

Dee Dee snorted. "Honey, I'm thinking you won't be coming back." Paul shot her a mean look.

"Jessica's my girlfriend, and she'll be back every day after school."

"Well, it's nice to see you got someone more decent than those hoes you keep bringing over."

Jessica almost fell over in embarrassment. Just as Paul's mouth opened, Danny stepped in and said those "hoes" were his friends, not Paul's. And he would appreciate it if she would refrain from talking about his girls like that.

Dee Dee grumbled, walked down the hall to her bedroom, and slammed the door. Danny grinned at them both. "Someone didn't take her happy pill today."

Marcus put on a band called Metallica, which Jessica had never heard of, and cranked it all the way up as she got ready to leave. Paul walked Jessica onto the front porch and grabbed her hand.

"I promise it won't be like this every day. Ma is only home Mondays and Tuesdays."

"Who takes care of your little brothers?" Jessica asked.

"Grandpa Joe and sometimes my Aunt Darleen, when she and Ma aren't fighting."

While Jessica hated the thought of returning home, she hated leaving Paul at his home even more.

"Are you going to be all right?"

Paul gave her a puzzled look. "Trust me; this isn't even a bad day for her."

Jessica could not imagine what a bad day looked or sounded like.

The screams from the stereo were making her feel sick; *Metallica is not feel-good music,* she thought.

At dinner that night, Jessica appreciated the quiet sounds of her home and gave thanks for cleanliness, no smoking, and her dad not beating on her mother. She'd never appreciated these things before, but being at Paul's home was an eye-opening experience.

While Jessica lay in bed that night, she felt grateful that Paul's mother would not be around tomorrow. She was debating telling Paul that they needed to have a different plan because of how uncomfortable she'd felt today.

Jessica slid out of bed and sat on the bench under her window, taking notice of the brilliance of the moon, completely round and bright. She prayed to God while looking at the night sky, believing that her prayer would be heard the closer she was to nature's beauty. Jessica's prayer for Paul and his family was to find harmony, serenity, and the Polish cleaning ladies.

Chapter 15

The fall and winter went relatively smoothly. Jessica and Paul continued to meet at his newly cleaned home, not by the Polish cleaning ladies, but by Paul and his brothers. Jessica mentioned to Paul after her first visit that her hair smelled like smoke and it was too risky to continue to meet at his home, so Paul decided to do something about it, making a cleaning schedule that mimicked a military regimen. Most days Dee Dee was sleeping in her bedroom or running errands, so Jessica was rarely exposed to her direct cigarette smoke.

But today, Dee Dee was curled up on the worn-out tan couch in the basement watching *Jeopardy*, sipping on something she called a hot toddy. She was fighting her yearly bronchitis infection.

Jessica noticed that sometimes Dee Dee would call Paul, "Pa." When she inquired about why, Paul just shrugged his shoulders. Finally, after six months, Jessica mustered up the courage to ask her.

"Damn, that boy's thinkin' he's everybody's daddy," Dee Dee puffed out after a coughing attack.

"But that boy ain't nothin' compared to my daddy. Paul calls him Grandpa Joe—now he's a real ass." She coughed hard into her blanket then took a swig of her drink. "Me and him get along, then we don't. He thinks he can be the boss of me. I hate people who tell me what to do."

Paul was in the kitchen making ramen noodles for dinner while his brothers were yelling and wrestling upstairs. Dee Dee banished the boys from their room in the basement so she could get better in peace. Paul thought it would be less chaotic downstairs, so Jessica sat on the least stained orange chair keeping his mother company.

"What's your daddy like?" Dee Dee coughed.

Jessica had never been asked that directly. "Well, he's muscular and athletic."

Dee Dee drank some more before asking, "But what's he like?"

Jessica wanted to give an answer that was loyal, even though her insides were not completely agreeing. "He is confident, intelligent, and very responsible."

There was a minute of silence before Dee Dee said, "So that's why you came lookin' for Paul."

Jessica gave her a quizzical look.

"Cuz your daddy sounds like an ass, just like mine." Dee Dee finished her drink and asked Jessica to go upstairs and have Paul make her another. Jessica really wanted to find out what she meant by "came lookin' for Paul" and could not wait to get back downstairs to ask. But Paul had other ideas.

He grabbed Jessica and started to kiss her in the kitchen, in front of Danny. Jessica pulled away, embarrassed that he would do that in front of someone. Danny was eating a donut sandwich—a donut on top of donut with Cool Whip in the middle—and looking at a comic book, not paying them any attention.

"Stop," she whispered, shooting a look Danny's way.

Paul look dejected. "Here," he said and handed her the drink. Jessica felt bad but was still uncomfortable with public displays of affection.

Jessica gave Dee Dee the mug full of what smelled like alcohol and sat back down. Dee Dee was yelling out the correct answers to *all* the *Jeopardy* questions. At the commercial break, Jessica wanted to ask Dee

Dee what she meant but too much time had passed, and she became shy.

"That's a pretty necklace."

Jessica's hand reached up and grabbed the two small hearts attached to a silver chain that hung around her neck. It had replaced the necklace Aunt Lodi had given her. "Thanks. It's my Christmas present from Paul."

"Did he just give that to you? I ain't ever seen that on you."

"Well yes, two months late. It took him a while to save up his money."

Jessica watched Dee Dee smile for the first time since she had been with her in the basement.

"Paul's a good boy. No wait," she said, holding out her wiry arm, "man. He helped pay our bills so many times. None of my boy's daddies stuck around, but Paul, he comes through even when I think we're not gonna make it."

An overwhelming feeling of love for Paul engulfed Jessica because Dee Dee's words strengthened the feelings of desire she had for him. Maybe she was not being as open as she could be and now thought she may have come across as a prude earlier in the kitchen.

"Do you need anything else?" Jessica asked.

Dee Dee coughed hard into her blanket and shook her head. Jessica told her she had to get ready to leave, hoped she felt better, and would see her next week.

Dee Dee gave a good-bye wave as Jessica climbed upstairs, even though she had fifteen more minutes before she really had to leave. Marcus and Brian were drinking Kool-Aid and eating noodles and donuts in the kitchen while Danny was nowhere in sight. Paul was lying on his bed in the back porch watching *Jeopardy* too. He looked like a little boy, curled up fetal style under his blankets, pillow folded in half to support the side of his head. The temperature in the back porch was much colder than the rest of the house.

"Paul," Jessica said, standing by the doorway.

He looked up. "Hey, how's Ma?"

"She seems a little better. Funny you guys are watching the same show."

Paul gave a small grin. "She gives me a run for my money but sometimes I can beat her."

Jessica smiled and sat down on the edge of his bed. Paul rolled over on his back, folding his arms under his pillow, and looked at Jessica. She put her hand on his leg. "I'm sorry about earlier."

Paul looked at her funny. "Earlier?"

"Remember, when you tried to kiss me in front of Danny?"

"No biggie, I forget you don't like kissing in front of people."

Jessica suddenly felt like she was some sort of control freak, having all these rules Paul needed to remember just to be with her. Why did she have to be so complicated? Jessica looked at this boy she loved and coveted, then lifted her leg over his body so she could straddle him, leaning down to kiss him hard. It took Paul by surprise and he barely got his arms out from under the pillow to take a hold of her waist. Jessica started pushing the blanket from his body so she could lie on top of him. She laid her body on his as she found a way under his shirt to caress his chest. Then she moved her hand down, past his stomach, toward the top of his jeans and rubbed back and forth until she un-buttoned the top button and slowly unzipped the zipper. Paul bucked forward, thrusting his erection against her hand. Jessica had done this before but had stopped when she saw how hard his penis had become, not wanting to be a tease.

But at that moment, she wanted to show Paul that she really did love him and was not the control freak she made herself out to be.

Jessica pulled the blanket over their bodies in case his brothers came in and started to stroke him from the outside of his jeans. Paul was highly aroused and kissed Jessica passionately. Cautiously, she slid her hand beneath his underwear, but the tightness of his jeans made it hard to go any farther. Paul started pushing his jeans down, so Jessica helped. Once his jeans were knee level, she placed her hand on top of his underwear and rubbed. This was the first time she had been this close to him. While she'd initially felt this was something she had to do to please him, she could not deny the excitement overcoming her body. Paul was obviously feeling a lot of pleasure, which made Jessica even more excited. He reached and pushed a side of his underwear down. Jessica played follow-the-leader and did the same on the other side. Even though her hand was not yet on his penis, she could feel it throbbing. Knowing it was too late to turn back, she laid her hand on the warm hard body part and stroked it softly, not sure what else to do. Paul put his hand on hers, helped her hold it tight and made a quick up-and-down motion. He did not let go until she had a steady rhythm. Jessica had no idea what would happen next, but she was sure it was going to be good because Paul was making small grunts and telling her to slow down or speed up.

When it was all over, Jessica felt grossed out. She had no idea that a big mess would occur. Maybe if she'd known she could have prepared with paper towels and a wet wipe. Paul was the happiest she had ever seen him.

"You are awesome," he said, sitting up and kissing her again and again. Jessica held her hand high, frozen in place as she tried not to touch anything with it.

"Hold on," he said, as he reached over the side of the bed, pulling out a Kleenex box. He gave her a bunch and helped her wipe off the stuff, then cleaned off his stomach and balled up one of the blankets and threw it on the floor.

"I'm shocked you did that," he said as he adjusted his clothes.

Jessica was about to say that she did it because she loved him but suddenly realized that twenty minutes had passed. She was going to be five minutes late getting home. Jessica jumped out of bed and ran to the front room, throwing on her winter coat, mittens, and scarf. Paul followed behind with his jeans unbuttoned, helping adjust her backpack.

"Are you late?"

"I have to go," Jessica said and ran out the front door, catching a glimpse of Danny in a car parked across the street. She thought she saw Alicia in that car too.

On her way home, she kept opening and closing her glued hand, nervous her father would spot the evidence right away. Jessica thought touching a boy's penis would get her fifteen to life and Paul would get death if her father had anything to do with sentencing. Jessica ran half the way home and was only three minutes late but her father was on the front porch as she approached.

"Where were you?"

"Sorry I'm late. I forgot my mittens in my locker and had to run back to get them."

Her father gave her a stern look. "Let me see your Mace."

Jessica took off the mitten of her clean hand, unzipped her coat, and dug it out of the front of her jeans.

"No," he barked. "You'll be in someone's car before your fingers even touch the canister. The Mace stays in your hand as you walk home, got it?" Before Jessica could answer, her father walked back into the house. Jessica realized she'd forgotten to take off the necklace. Panicking, she quickly unfastened the clasp and plopped it in the front pocket with her Mace, then walked into the warm aroma of pot roast and homemade biscuits.

On the way to school the next day, it crossed Jessica's mind to tell Marilee everything, but she was scared Marilee would judge her. Even though they were best friends, Jessica had shameful thoughts about how she'd behaved. *What would Marilee think or say about her touching Paul's penis and making that white stuff come out?* Jessica didn't feel her self-esteem could weather an attack from the only friend she had. Instead, the girls talked about all the boys Marilee thought were cute, French kissing versus regular kissing, and gossip at school—normal high school stuff.

After their last encounter, Paul was putting more pressure on Jessica to move the relationship to full throttle. He continued to be respectful of the word *stop,* but he'd changed from being patient and gentle, to acting, simply put, on fire. There was romantic music playing when Jessica entered his home and sometimes even candles burning, which concerned her as his brothers could bump into one and start a fire. She didn't touch his penis again, to his obvious disappointment, but stuck with the old game plan, kissing and rubbing fully clothed bodies next to each other. Jessica could feel Paul getting bored and impatient and was unsure how long she could continue the old way of making out. And now that Danny's girlfriend Alicia was coming around, flirting with Paul right in front of her, Jessica felt there was a greater need to put their relationship on higher ground.

Springtime entered gently with warmer days becoming more frequent. The burly limbs of trees were covered with small budding leaves, and daffodils and tulips did not stay hidden any longer. Jessica loved the smell of spring and all its newness. It made her feel empowered and reminded her of last spring, when she'd made a decision to take more control over her life, accepting Paul's plan to be together.

Heritage was once again preparing for the spring musical. Marilee won the role of a supporting female actor in the play *Grease,* so Jessica got permission to sleep over at the Ripps' to help Marilee practice her lines. When the girls were alone in bed with the lights turned out, Marilee asked how far she and Paul had gone.

Jessica was glad she was in the dark. "Well, we kiss and, you know, touch each other."

"Have you gone all the way?"

"No," Jessica said quietly.

"Do you love him?"

"Yes."

"Does he love you?"

"I think. He's never said," Jessica admitted.

"Have you told him?"

"No, but I think he can tell."

"You may wanna say it. This way it'll be a for sure," Marilee said.

Jessica thought hard over Marilee's words that night. She had never said "I love you" to anyone but family, and truthfully could not remember the last time those words left either of her parents' lips in her direction. Aunt Lodi was the only person that those words easily flowed toward and away from. It took Jessica a long time to fall asleep, but before dozing off, she decided to tell Paul her true feelings come Monday.

*   *   *

After school on Monday, Jessica and Paul made their way to his house. She took in deep breaths to let her spirit know that it need not be scared, that telling someone you love them was a normal part of life. They held hands, and Paul told her he had a surprise for her. A rainstorm had followed the morning mist and washed away all the dirt and grime that lingered on the sidewalk and streets. The sun pushed out of the clouds and was beaming soft rays, filling the air with liquid warmth.

As they entered, Paul told her to wait one second. Jessica sat on the front room couch that was now covered with a clean sheet and waited as Paul put a record on the player. Paul's home was constantly flooded with music from different decades, and Jessica had become accustomed to it. She enjoyed the way certain music influenced her feelings and emotions and would study album covers, making a game of matching the face with the voice.

Paul walked into the kitchen as the music started playing. The instant Jessica heard the voice she knew it was Johnny Cash, one of Dee Dee's favorites. She listened intently to the words, as Johnny sang deeply about his heart, and how because a girl loved him, he walked the line. For a minute, she felt very close to Johnny Cash, like he was speaking to her, but quickly shifted her emotions back to Paul, knowing this was his way of telling her he loved her. When the song ended and the needle on the turntable picked itself up and returned to its original position, Paul reentered the room with a bouquet of flowers. He gave her a bashful smile, which surprised Jessica, seeing how confident he usually was.

"I thought that since we got together around this time last spring we could make this our anniversary date."

Jessica was speechless. Besides Aunt Lodi, no one had ever made her feel as special as Paul was right now. Jessica's eyes welled up with tears.

"Oh man, I didn't do this so you'd cry," Paul said as he sat down next to her, putting his arm around her waist.

Jessica wiped away the tears she couldn't control while she covered her face.

"I . . . I . . . this is the nicest thing anyone has ever done for me." Jessica paused, seeing Paul fill with pride.

"You should see what I cooked for you in the kitchen."

While she hadn't envisioned telling him she loved him in this way, the moment felt too right.

"Paul . . . I . . . I . . . I love you."

Paul leaned forward and looked at her deeply then reached his hands up to cup her face. "I love you back."

Beams of light aimed themselves through the windows with no awnings and onto the couch Jessica and Paul were sitting on, offering instant brightness.

Paul leaned in and kissed her so intensely that it made Jessica feel as if he was peering into her soul.

His thumbs caressed her cupped face as she lifted her arms and wrapped them around his upper back. He tore his mouth from hers and started kissing her neck, breathing heavy he pressed his lips against her ear.

"I want you so bad."

He didn't need to say it; Jessica felt it loud and clear. But she was scared that her inexperience with sex could make Paul not love her anymore. She was afraid she wouldn't measure up to Paul's standard. As quickly as her passion for him overflowed, fear now overpowered.

"Paul . . . Paul . . ." she said, pushing him away.

"Jessica, please," he said, his face hot.

"What do you want from me?" she hissed.

"What do you expect from me?" he hissed back. "You take me from zero to ten and leave me there. I'm not made of stone. My body, my heart, it doesn't work that way. No man does."

In that instant, Jessica realized how much she had led him on when she touched him that day and that there was no going back, not if she wanted his love.

"I'm sorry. I thought I was doing the right thing when I, well, you know, touched you. But I can see all it did was make you want me more."

"And that's a good thing," he retorted. "Don't you want your boyfriend to want you?"

"Paul, this is all so new. You know I never had a boyfriend before you. I thought I was doing the right thing before, but now I feel like I teased you and you won't forgive me."

Paul smirked. "Jess, you haven't done anything that I need to forgive. If anything I'm thankful, I mean come on, you made me feel awesome!" He scooted closer, smoothing his arms around her waist. "And it's because I love you that I want to be with you, all the way."

Jessica stared at his beautiful pleading face while anxious thoughts spread through her mind. Now that she'd told Paul she loved him, she felt a huge relief. But she had to know everything before saying yes to what he was asking.

"Have you ever loved another girl?"

"No," he said in an instant. "Not even close."

"Why me?" Jessica felt as brave as Marilee and, in fact, was channeling her to get through these questions that needed to be answered.

Paul leaned back so he could look at her from a distance. "Well, you're gorgeous. I love the way your hair looks, so long"—he reached out and wrapped a piece around his finger that lay on her chest—"and wavy. I love the fact that you didn't let any of those bozos in homeroom push you off your square, you know, you never let them compromise

your job. And you didn't give Gina the answers in Biology. You're shy—
I like that. But you're smart. I like smart. And you're loyal. You proved
that when I asked you not to tell people certain things and you never
did. I trust you . . . more than I trust a lot of people in my life."

Jessica quickly realized that Paul really did love her.

"Why do you love me?" he asked in a low tone.

Jessica grinned and her cheeks heated up; even with the honesty
and openness, she still felt uncomfortable with it all. "Well, I also think
you're gorgeous. Your eyes grab me." Paul sat back and put his hands
behind his head and his feet up on the crate, which served as a table,
looking smug.

"Ohmigod," Jessica said nervously.

"Please go on," Paul said, grinning.

"Well, I know you're also smart, which I also like. You're loyal, like
over the summer when you had a chance to be with Alicia and didn't."
Jessica waited a few seconds, formulating her words so they came out
the way she meant. "And you make me feel loved, like I'm the only one
for you. You give me more love than anyone else in my life."

Paul sat up slowly, bringing back the intense look he left earlier.
Jessica felt like crying again but did not want to look weak. Her tears
were more of joy and relief that she really could be open and honest
about her feelings, but acknowledging that Paul gave her more love
than anyone else, besides Aunt Lodi, made Jessica feel lonely.

"Why do you look so sad?"

Jessica smiled to cover the pain. "I'm not. In fact, I'm the happiest
I've been in a long time."

Paul grabbed her hand and held it tight. "Jessica Turner, know this;
I will never do anything to hurt you, ever. When you're ready to be with
me all the way, I will be *very* ready to oblige."

Jessica smiled weakly at his statement. It reminded her of freshman year when he told her that when she was ready to sneak, he would be ready too. And she was reminded of the fact that she *did* go to him. But she needed to know one more thing before going home and ending the conversation that made her feel excited and worn out at the same time.

"One more question."

"Yep."

"Have you ever, you know, gone all the way with anyone?"

Paul shifted on the couch but kept holding her hand and didn't break eye contact. "Yes."

"But you said you never loved anyone else."

"Jessica, I'm a guy."

Jessica yanked her hand from his grip. Paul looked at her like she just didn't get it.

"Are you serious? You're pissed because I've had sex before?"

"No, I'm mad because you don't have to love someone to take their hormones on a ride."

"What? What does that mean?"

"So you love me, *great*, but you still would've had sex with me any-way. You would've gone all the way with me without even loving me."

"Jessica, you're talking crazy. Yeah, I had sex with girls I didn't love. But know this. You are the *only* girl I have ever loved, the *only* girl I want to be with completely."

It was hard for Jessica to have a comeback to that because it sound-ed very real.

"Go ask my friends, or Danny. They'll tell you the same thing. In fact, they say shit to me about it all the time."

"Like what?" Jessica felt intrigued.

"Excuse my French, but they call me pussy whipped."

"Disgusting," Jessica said.

"They've never seen me this hung up on someone, to the point I don't party like I used to."

Jessica liked what she was hearing. "Did you stop all the partying because of me?"

Paul smirked. "Did you listen to the song I played for you?"

Jessica met his eyes with love again. "Yes, I heard what you were telling me."

"I'm not perfect . . . I still party, but not like before. Smoking weed makes me laugh and gives me the munchies, but it doesn't fill me up the way your smile does when you're looking at me. Or when you hold my hand when we walk to my house. Or when you get on top of me and kiss me so hard that you make me think you're gonna rip off my clothes . . . and then don't . . . but even then, I'm so glad you're mine."

Jessica reached over and touched the hand she brashly pushed away earlier. "I think I understand. And when I'm ready to be with you, all the way, I will let you know."

Jessica had ten minutes before she had to leave the confines of love to return to her loveless home life. Paul invited her to indulge in the meal he prepared for her last night and was heating in the microwave: scrambled eggs with cheese and sausage. He put the bouquet of flowers in a vase, knowing she could not bring it home, but told her she could look at it and remember this moment every time she came here.

"I wish I could do something for you," she said, diving into the eggs with her fork. "I feel like you're always doing things for me."

"Well, I wouldn't say that," Paul said with a look of pleasure.

Jessica caught wind of his thoughts and rolled her eyes while she blushed. "I mean something else. You put a lot of time and thought to this, and other things, like the necklace. I want to give you something too."

"Surprise me," Paul said.

Jessica looked up at him from her almost empty plate. "Okay," she said, thinking hard about the only thing she really thought he would want: her.

Chapter 16

Aunt Lodi arrived on one of the hottest days recorded in spring. It was eighty-five degrees, and Jessica's mother was not prepared for how stuffy and hot the house would feel.

"Jim, I think we may need to turn on the air conditioning. You know how Lodi can sweat."

Jessica watched her father ignore her mother's request and continue to clean his guns. Jessica and Jason were in the office with their father spending "quality time" together. He had returned from a business trip and was more animated than usual.

"Look at this." He held up a Mini UZI submachine gun. "This is a magnificent piece of machinery." Jessica and Jason gave the mechanical answer their father wanted to hear, "awesome."

The rumble of Aunt Lodi's car could be heard as she pulled into the driveway.

"She's here," Jessica said as she and Jason jumped up to run outside.

"Hey, my lovelies, I have presents," Aunt Lodi sang as she was closing her driver's side door. Jessica ran up beside her and was pulled into a big hug. Aunt Lodi put Jessica at arm's length and took a good long look at her. "Jessica, you look stunning. Like a young woman."

Jessica flushed, not used to hearing compliments about herself, especially in front of her father, who did not appear fazed by the comment.

*   *   *

During Aunt Lodi's visit, Jessica was surprised at how much time she wanted to spend with Paul. Even though Aunt Lodi was at her house, waiting to take her on a shopping spree again, she couldn't get enough of him.

From the day they confessed their love for each other, Jessica felt a shift in their relationship. So much of their love before was patient and gentle, him teaching her things she knew nothing about. But now she felt on fire, too. Passion was the only word that came to mind.

Their kissing and grabbing at each other's bodies became more intense, to the point that Paul started pulling away and asking if she was all right. Was this her way of telling him she was ready to go all the way?

Jessica was building herself up to that point. She appreciated that Paul always left the decision up to her; when she was ready, he would be too. Paul never made it seem like he would break up with her if she didn't do what he asked. Jessica overheard horror stories in school about boys who would say. "I love you" to their girlfriends so they would have sex, only to dump them soon after. Sometimes the girls were even called sluts. While Jessica could see most of Paul's friends, and even his brother Danny doing this, she could not envision that from Paul. He was not made that way, which is one of the traits that drew her to him in the first place.

Jessica and Paul's bodies were tangled together in the basement as they lay on the couch that was covered by a Bozo the Clown sheet. Danny was at Alicia's house, *probably having sex*, Jessica thought, and everyone else was at Grandpa Joe's or running errands.

Paul was stroking her face, tracing her lips with his finger. "I love your lips," he said as he kissed them ever so slightly.

Jessica smiled as she placed her fingers on his face, stroking around his eyes. "And I love these." She pulled Paul's face closer to her lips and kissed each eye gently.

Paul started nibbling on her neck. "God, I love making out with you," he mumbled.

Jessica suddenly drew back. Paul had never mentioned God's name in all the time she had known him. In fact, they never discussed religion whatsoever; she was afraid he would be turned off by that conversation. But it was different now. She could ask him anything.

"Do you believe in God?" Jessica asked as his lips continued to make their way up to her ear.

"Um," he said, pulling himself away to look at her. "I do, but I don't go to church or anything."

"Well, you don't have to go to church to believe in God."

"I used to go, when I was younger. Aunt Darlene took all of us to her Catholic church, except for Ma. She stopped believing after Marcus's dad left. Asshole left all of us. We thought he was gonna be the one, the one who was gonna stay."

"Why did he leave?"

"I'm not sure. But there was a lot of fighting and drinking. Ma was never very good at holding her tongue, as you know."

"How old were you?"

"I think about nine." Paul looked far off as if trying to remember. "He was supposed to be one of the coaches on my little league team. But he left me high and dry." Paul looked back at Jessica. "Got kicked off that team for fighting." Paul half smiled. "Brian's dad tried, but we didn't give him much of a chance—we had already been through three others. Plus he got put in jail. He told Ma he plans on coming back to help her. I think he gets out in '87 or '88."

Jessica saw in Paul a little boy, a boy who also craved love from a dad, but like her, was left standing at the checkout line without a cashier.

"But I'll tell you one thing," he said, breaking Jessica's train of thought. "I will *never* leave my kids. I don't care if I gotta beg on the corner to support them. I will never abandon them. I will not make the mistake my asshole dad and all the other assholes made after him."

Jessica placed her hands softly around the sides of his face. "Thank you for telling me that story. And, for the record, you'll make a great dad someday."

Paul gave her a halfhearted laugh. "Am I freaking you out, with all this shit?"

"God, no. If anything, it makes me want to be with you even more. I don't know, it's weird, but your honesty makes me want you. I mean, the kind of want that has no clothes to confine it."

Paul looked at her stunned. "Is that your fancy way of saying you want to have sex with me?"

A spark traveled from Jessica's head to her toes. "I'm getting there."

Paul smiled and hugged her. "Just tell me when," he whispered in her hair, "and I will be ready."

A smile spread over Jessica's face as she looked out the car window at the setting sun against the businesses that ran along the street to the mall. The conversation with Paul was running fresh in her heart and mind. How much she wanted him made her insides burn, something she never experienced in her life.

"Whatcha thinking about?" Aunt Lodi asked, biting into her thoughts.

Jessica hesitated. "I was thinking about all the great stuff we're going to buy tonight. And how grateful I am to have you."

"Thank you, honey. That's sweet to hear." Aunt Lodi paused and her tone changed. "But really, Jessica, what were you thinking?"

Jessica turned and looked at her. Aunt Lodi had a small smile as she took a quick glance her way. "I can feel something different in you. Your energy has changed . . . for the better, I think."

Jessica tried to suppress the shock her face was clearly projecting. But then she quickly questioned herself; why did she have to hide this from Aunt Lodi?

Colt .45s, that's why.

"Well," Jessica said, carefully picking her words, "there's a boy at school who likes me."

"Wonderful! Tell me more."

"He doesn't know I know, at least not yet. Dad would never approve."

They sat in silence for a minute.

"You're right about your dad. But dating is what you do in high school. Seeing what's out there, who's compatible for you. Maybe I should talk to him."

"No!" Jessica said. This was exactly what she was afraid of—too much exposure. It would be harder to stay under the radar if her father had an inkling that someone liked her. "Please don't ever mention this conversation to him. I already know the rules: no dating until I'm twenty-one."

"For Christ's sake, you're sixteen now. This is supposed to be the time."

Jessica looked at her with pleading eyes. "Dad doesn't see it that way. But I'm fine with it. I don't really like him that much anyway. It was just nice knowing someone likes me."

After a few moments, Aunt Lodi spoke. "I won't do anything you don't want me to. I would feel terrible looking at your frightened face all the time."

"Thank you," Jessica said, trying to breathe in a regular fashion again.

"Just tell me one thing," Aunt Lodi said. "If you could date this boy now, if your dad was fine with it, would you?"

Jessica thought hard about this question, once again measuring her words. "Maybe, yes."

Jessica watched the corner of Aunt Lodi's mouth turn up. "I'm glad to hear you haven't lost the spirit of finding love." They sat in an uncomfortable silence before Aunt Lodi spoke again. "I feel deep within that you will have a great love someday. Maybe even two."

Aunt Lodi's visit was too short once again, but Jessica reveled in the fact that this time, compared to all the other times Aunt Lodi left, she did not have the heavy sinking feeling that consumed her entire being. Paul was the reason, the only reason.

As the days passed, Jessica embraced her alter ego who was cheering her to move forward with Paul. But certain thoughts continued to immobilize her. Number one, she knew nothing about sex. At Mary Carter's school, unlike public or private institutions, sex education was not part of the curriculum. And at Heritage when sex education was being taught in health, Jessica had come down with the flu and missed the entire section. She thought about doing some research in the school library, but was afraid someone she knew would walk up for casual conversation, only to discover her deviant ways. She also thought of having Marilee call Julie at college for information and advice, but Jessica could not bring herself to expose her deep, dark secret to Marilee. Ohmigod, Jessica thought, *I'm keeping a secret.* All her life, keeping secrets was pounded into her head as being a big no-no. *Was this secret in the same category?* she wondered. As quickly as the erratic thoughts twisted her thinking, a warm calm washed them away; how could being in love ever be lumped in with something not safe?

Jessica made her decision. The night she was to attend the school play would be the night she would give all of herself to Paul, *a surprise,* she thought. *Didn't he say he wanted to be surprised?* Jessica finally asked Danny if any night of the week they would all be out of the house. Danny didn't seem to care why and told her Friday. In her estimation, she would get dropped off at the play ten minutes before it started. She would have plenty of time to walk to Paul's house, and then (her cheeks started to burn) have sex, which could last for maybe an hour? With at least forty-five minutes to spare, she could make it back to school and walk out with everyone from the auditorium. Paul would be completely surprised. Jessica could barely hold in her titillation as she grabbed her pillows and squeezed them tight in her bed.

Paul almost threw off her plan. He got excited hearing that she was going to the play on Friday and looked at her with a devious grin. "Are we sneaking into the old library?"

"Is that what you want to do?"

"Hell yeah, living life on the edge again. It's starting to get boring at my house."

Images of the old library conjured up feelings of arousal but also panic and fear, remembering when they were almost discovered.

Jessica calmed herself as she said, "sure," knowing instead that she would meet him in the hallway of the auditorium, take his hand into hers, and lead him back home, where he would get the surprise of his life.

Chapter 17

Jessica's father said he would drive her to and from the play, same as last year. Jessica kept her poker face, not wanting to show any small deviation in her demeanor. Her father was a Special Forces man. Surely he may be able to sniff some of this out. But as Jessica studied him, he appeared to be completely free of suspicion. While this was something she prayed for and wanted, there was a small piece of her that felt shameful; he trusted her so much he never thought she might be sneaking around with a boy, much less having sex. Jessica closed her eyes to get the word *sex* out of her head in front of her father, at least she felt she owed him that.

Drop-off went without a hitch. Once her father finished watching her walk safely inside, Jessica could not help but peek out of the building to make sure he drove away. A soft fluttering from inside her belly made her feel weak, like she wanted to fall down and cry, but she willed herself back, away from the doorway, away from the secret faults that were racing inside her head. *This was right. This was normal. This is what teenagers in love are supposed to do.* She played that song so loudly in her head that she did not even hear Paul call her name. Only a loving touch on her arm pulled her out of the trance.

"Man, you look like you're on another planet."

Jessica's eyes widened and then softened. "Paul, I have a surprise for you."

His face lit up. "Did you get that Iron Maiden tape I wanted?"

Jessica stared into him. "No, something better."

"Judas Priest?"

Jessica took his hand and led him towards the door, looking around the perimeter, making doubly sure there were no traces of her father.

Paul squeezed her hand tight and pulled it back a little. "What's going on?"

Jessica turned toward him as they walked along the side of the building. "It's your surprise."

Paul looked dumbfounded. Jessica turned away and continued to lead him toward his house, not saying a word. She tried not to make eye contact, afraid she would give away the gift. While holding his hand, her eyes were darting around, making sure if she spotted her father they would have a chance to run and hide.

The wind blew softly as they walked on the sidewalk and increased its pressure when they crossed the overpass. Jessica loved the look of the sky, dark blue with gray-and-white clouds that hung above like a canopy. It looked inviting and ominous at the same time.

As they landed in front of Paul's home, she turned around and looked at his face. It displayed a mix of shock and excitement, something that made her heart sing.

"This is my gift to you," she said carefully. "Me. All of me."

Jessica tried to read Paul but he looked completely stunned. He was still for a few seconds and then snapped out of it.

"You're ready? Now?"

Jessica tried to meet his eyes but hers took shelter. "Yes."

"Holy shit," Paul whispered. "I really thought this wasn't gonna happen for a while."

Jessica started getting nervous. She was feeling like he did not share the same passion for her as she held for him, and could tell Paul saw that on her face. He grabbed both her hands. "I want this, *real* bad, but I was not . . . prepared."

Jessica had no idea what he was talking about. Prepared? What? Music? Candles?

She leaned in and kissed his lips, slightly placing her tongue on them. He could not resist. He grabbed her up, and she lifted her legs so they were wrapped around his torso. He held onto her as they continued to kiss and made their way to the crumbling porch, tripping up the cracked stair.

"Whoa," Jessica said, as she put her arms out to brace the fall.

"Sorry," he muttered as he clattered around, trying to get his footing and keep hold of her. He pulled his keys out and tried to open the screen door with her in his grasp but it was not working. She finally had to slide off him so that he could successfully get them inside.

Funny, she thought, because in real life this moment was harder to pull off; *Purple Rain* made it look so easy.

They stood inside the living room, front door closed and locked. Both had uneasy grins but loud heartbeats.

"Paul, I . . . I . . . I'm really nervous."

He reached out and grabbed her by the waist. "It's okay." Jessica saw a cocky look come to his face. "You're with a professional."

Jessica laughed and pushed him away and then ran to the basement. She had a burst of adrenaline that could not be explained. All she knew was that she wanted to run, run away maybe, but she became more alive feeling Paul chase behind her. Jessica stopped short of the couch that would be the place they would probably have sex. Feeling Paul's breath on her neck made the adrenaline surge even more. Paul, without words, grabbed her from behind and pulled her into him. His kisses on the back of her neck were making her pulse quicken to the point she started to breathe so heavy she felt like she was panting. She pulled away to catch her breath.

"You sure you're ready?" he asked, misreading her cues.

"Yes," she said slowly. "You're making me hyperventilate."

Paul gave her a gentle look and told her he needed to get some blankets and would be right back.

Jessica didn't know what to do with herself, so she sat on the edge of the couch but jumped up because she could not sit still. She felt jittery and to her surprise, aggressive. Her fingers were laced together in front of her as she paced back and forth, trying to control her racing hormones.

Paul returned with blankets and sheets in hand and looked at her carefully.

"I'm gonna lay these on the floor like a bed, okay, 'cause we can't mess up Ma's couch. But please know that I don't care where we lie. I just want to be with you."

Jessica smiled at his reassurance.

"Um, I'm going to need some direction," she blurted.

Paul was making the bed on the floor and reached up, pulling her next to him.

"If you want me to stop I will."

"Is . . . is this going to hurt?"

Paul hesitated a moment. "Well, it's not gonna hurt me, but I really don't know about you. You're gonna bleed," he stated matter-of-factly.

Jessica's mouth fell open. "But Ma has those things you girls wear when you're on your monthly. They're in the bathroom. I'll get them for you, okay?"

Jessica felt a sudden rush of cold feet. *Maybe this wasn't such a good idea.*

"Jess, you'll be fine. I promise."

Paul bent toward her and kissed her cheek, then the other one, then her nose, then her forehead. He continued to kiss all the parts above the breasts until Jessica finally relaxed. She felt herself slipping into his hands, and eventually out of her clothing. Modesty overtook her, but having blankets on top of her body made her feel more at ease, along with very dim lighting. Jessica was thankful that Paul knew exactly how to make her feel more comfortable. He did not rush anything and took each event slowly. As new moments of exploring their bodies passed, Jessica was in awe at how beautiful Paul's body looked. His stomach was rippled but not in a gross bulky way; it was slim and trim. The warmth of his skin felt silky as it rubbed on hers—he did not have as much body hair as she thought. She loved how his hands caressed every part of her, touching places he had never been before, looking to read her face so he could react quickly if he had gone too far. Jessica smiled, knowing that Paul did not understand that there would be no stopping him this time. She came prepared to give all of herself to the boy she loved. There would be no turning back.

Chapter 18

On the makeshift bed, Jessica took mental inventory of her body as Paul lay on his side looking at her. The basement was silent with only a ticking clock to keep her thoughts in line and a faint light in the corner brought a hazy appearance. The trapped warmth in the room made her feel like a baby in the womb.

"Are you all right?" Paul asked in a whisper.

Jessica took in a breath and answered slowly. "I think so."

"Are you . . . are you in pain?"

Jessica turned her head to face his. "It hurt a little."

Paul's face turned to worry before Jessica's eyes.

"Paul, it's okay." She smiled. "It was worth it."

Paul relaxed and intertwined their fingers. "Did you like it? I mean, would you do it again?"

Jessica turned her body to face him. "Yes," she said, feeling a little self-conscious. They leaned their faces into each other's and kissed, very softly.

After getting dressed (Jessica under the sheets because of a moment of awkward shyness) and cleaning up the evidence, Paul put on music and made scrambled eggs in the kitchen. Sitting on the hardwood chair made Jessica ache but she did not want Paul to see her grimace. Glancing at the clock she was surprised that sex did not take anywhere near an hour. The entire act itself only took minutes, which did not bother her in the least. What Jessica really enjoyed was the before and after—the caressing, the touching, the loving looks, and Paul making sure she felt safe. She liked that part a lot.

"What are you smiling about?" Paul asked from the stove.

Jessica did not realize her thoughts were showing on her face. A flush of pink colored her cheeks, and then Paul smiled.

"Oh," he said with a grin. "I really am a professional, huh?"

Jessica hid her face in her hands as Paul walked over with a plate for them to share. She peeked in between her fingers.

"You're beautiful, so, so beautiful."

Jessica noticed Paul sounded a lot like the music playing; a scratchy voice from the stereo speakers was singing about how someone was so beautiful to him. Her entire being filled to the brim with emotion. Paul had become an essential part to her feeling good about herself, which scared her, knowing he had that much influence in her life now.

After they ate, Jessica burrowed herself into Paul on the couch in the living room, listening to songs, until it was time for her to leave. *Purple Rain* came to Jessica's mind and she wondered if Paul had the album.

"Prince?" he said, offended. "I don't think he'd make it next to Anthrax."

"Oh, I think he can hold his own," Jessica said.

"You really like his music?"

"Yes," she said with conviction. "I really love that song 'The Beautiful Ones.' It makes my insides throb." Jessica started to feel silly but after everything they just shared she believed her deep thoughts would be safe from reprisal. "I sometimes daydream that you're singing that to me because you want me to choose you over him."

"Who's him?" Paul asked.

"Not a real life him, an imaginary him."

"Oh," Paul said. "This is a girl thing?"

"I guess. You don't think like that, huh?"

"No," he laughed. "But hey, dream whatever you want. Just make sure you choose me."

As their time together was coming to a close, Jessica pulled his arms around her tighter.

"I don't want to leave you."

Paul accommodated, hugging harder, kissing her hair. "Man, I know." He hesitated for a minute. "Are you sure your parents can't know about me?"

Jessica looked at him head-on. "Remember I told you, I can't date until I'm twenty-one."

"Yeah, I forgot." After a few moments, Paul said, "What kind of control freaks do you live with?"

Jessica felt her heart tumble like a weed in the desert. "They're overprotective."

"Yeah, like in a crazy way."

Jessica did not like the way Paul was talking about her parents, even though she agreed with him. "They think they're right."

After a long pause, Paul said, "You know, this sneaking around is keeping things exciting. I think I can handle that for the next, what, five years?"

Jessica felt shocked. Paul was talking long term, rather than just living in the moment.

"Oh, so you think I'm going to be hanging around you in five years, huh?"

"Yes," he said without hesitation.

Jessica closed the gap between their faces and showed him how much she was all right with being together for now, for the next five years, maybe even forever.

*   *   *

Jessica spent fifteen minutes in Paul's bathroom, afraid her father may sense something different in her look and smell when he picked her up. Paul reassured her that nothing on the outside of her had changed, but she continued to stare into the mirror, rearranging her hair and rubbing down her exposed skin with vinegar and water. As they walked back to Heritage, a brisk wind sent shivers down her body and her stomach balled up.

Jessica's grip was tight on Paul's hand. "Jess, it's okay. Your dad won't suspect a thing."

Jessica gave him a slight smile but could not keep the fear at bay.

While waiting for the play to let out, Jessica grabbed a program so her fingers would have something to fiddle with and her nervousness could take a break. Paul walked out first, turning around under the streetlight, smiling at her despite her father's presence. Jessica hid her happiness and, just like the year before, her father didn't even notice.

Warmer days were easing into each other now that summer was peeking around the corner, but Jessica didn't feel like herself. She opened the window in her bedroom. Usually breathing in outside air would refresh her, make her feel energized, but all she felt this morning was the desire to crawl back into her cocoon of warm blankets.

"Jessica, you don't look well," her mother stated at the breakfast table.

"I think I have a cold."

Her mother got the thermometer to take her temperature. "A little elevated but nothing to be concerned over."

Jessica's father walked in from the outside with Jason in tow, looking hot and sweaty.

"What should we not be concerned over?" he asked in perfect step with his breathing.

"Jessica looks sick, don't you think?"

Her father took a deep look at Jessica, and she felt this was the first time in a long time he paid any attention to her.

"She looks a little peaked. A morning workout regimen would be the best thing for her."

Jessica almost threw up at that thought. God, now she felt so nauseous.

"I think I have to . . ." Jessica jumped up and ran to the bathroom. There, she dry heaved because she hadn't had a chance to eat her breakfast. She could hear her mother saying it was the flu she got around this time every year. No school, bed rest, and the garbage can next to the bed.

Jessica felt nauseous all day but did not throw up again. She was able to hold down saltines, 7UP, and clear broth. Despite the fact that she was resting comfortably, she was consumed by the idea that Paul would be wondering where she was and might try to find out where she lived.

In the evening, Jessica asked permission to call Marilee to get the assignments for the day, but she really wanted to know if Marilee talked to Paul. Jessica tried her best to get as far away from her parents as possible, timing the phone call with her mother cleaning up dinner and her father cleaning his guns with Jason.

Jessica was able to get out a few words before she was interrupted by Marilee.

"Paul cut class just to find me. He wanted to know where you were."

"What did you tell him?" she whispered.

"I figured you were sick so that's what I said. But he kinda didn't look convinced. He wanted to know where you lived, but I didn't tell him . . . Jess, are you still there?"

"Yes. I'm just nervous."

"He'll never find out anything from me. I don't want to see him dead either."

The next morning, Jessica forced herself to go to school. *You will be all right. You will be all right,* she repeated in order to will herself into not throwing up as she looked at the scrambled eggs sitting in front of her.

"Can I have a pancake instead?" she asked. That sounded more appetizing than the plate of slimy yellowness staring at her.

"Are you sure you're ready for school?"

"I'm fine. You know how it is when you get the flu and your usual food doesn't look that appetizing. That's all it is."

Jessica met Marilee at their corner spot, and they walked to Heritage slowly because Jessica felt very low on energy. Approaching the school, Jessica spotted Paul sitting on the concrete stairs, looking around the grounds. His friends and brother, along with Alicia, were also there, talking and smoking cigarettes.

"Someone is searching for you," Marilee said. "How romantic."

Jessica smiled and watched to see if he'd notice her since she was not one to bring attention to herself, unlike Marilee, who was now yelling in Paul's direction. Paul turned his head toward them and then jumped off the stairs.

They smiled at each other as he drew closer, and Marilee cleared her throat as a reminder she was still there.

"Hey, Marilee," Paul said.

"See, she's fine. She had the flu yesterday."

"I see," Paul said, turning back toward Jessica. He reached out for her hand, and she met him halfway.

"I'm fine. All in one piece."

"So you had the flu?"

"Yep."

"Come on love birds, or we're gonna be late," Marilee said.

In homeroom, Paul again asked what had really happened to her yesterday. Jessica told him again that she was sick with the flu and couldn't understand why Paul looked so concerned.

"I was worried that maybe your parents found out about us and did something to you."

Jessica gave him a careful look. "You're the one who should be worried if we're discovered. My father would probably kill you."

Paul laughed out loud, which got Mrs. Daley's attention, but his quick apology sent her away.

"Kill me?" he whispered.

Jessica realized she said too much and needed to backtrack fast. "Well, not 'kill' you but want to hurt you bad. I told you—overprotective."

Paul seemed to accept that answer but let her know that if there was a problem at home, he wanted to know about it. Jessica appreciated Paul's attempt to be protective, but it would never work against her father. He was just too dangerous.

Throughout the rest of the school day Jessica crawled from class to class, even her beloved tater tots looked unappealing.

After school, Paul gave her a piggyback ride to his house as she was still feeling ill. Jessica burst with laughter when he galloped across the overpass like she was on the back of a racehorse.

Upon arriving at his home they both fell onto the couch in the living room. Paul was panting and sweating and Jessica poked fun at his obvious need to get into shape. After drinking some water and resting, they folded into each other, kissing at length. Jessica stopped protesting Paul kissing her, due to her just having the flu, after he kissed her what seemed like twenty times.

Eventually they took a breather and talked about their relationship. What was going to happen in the summer which was approaching quickly?

"It'll be difficult but if there's any way, I'll try to see you," Jessica said.

"I'm gonna need that. I don't think I can handle going from five days a week to cold turkey."

"I know. I'm really going to miss you. I kind of need to see you, to feel you every day just to be normal."

Paul smiled. "Yeah, I know what you mean."

"If we can't see each other, what will you do?"

Paul hesitated for a moment. "I'm in a bad place with my friends. They're pissed that I'm with you every day after school."

"But you can go out with them after I leave."

"True, but I usually don't. Not because of you, because I don't feel like doing the same stupid shit. I want something better, you know. I want outta here." He started looking around his house. "This place is a shit hole, I mean, sure, we cleaned it up, but it's not where I want to be the rest of my life." Paul took a moment. "I want to be better than any of the men I have known."

Jessica's heart skipped a beat because she felt he wanted to be a better man for her.

"I think you already are."

"Thanks," he said, looking away. "But you're a little biased."

Eventually he returned her gaze with a grin. "I have time to work on that. I mean, you're gonna be with me till at least twenty-one. I can't wait to meet your parents. I'll be thinkin' the whole time we really pulled one over on them."

Before leaving his home, Jessica grabbed Paul extra hard and looked tenderly into his eyes.

"I love you, Paul. I will love you always."

Paul smiled. "You are my true love, Jessica Turner—now and forever."

Despite her exhaustion, Jessica walked home on her tiptoes. Paul's words ran through her head over and over, *now and forever, now and forever, now and forever.* They were meant to be together. It was absolute.

Entering her house, Jessica was met at the door by her mother.

"Hi, Mom," she said, then looked up at her face. It was twisted with anger.

"I need to speak with you immediately. In your room."

Jessica started to swoon; she felt like daggers were being jammed into her.

"What's wrong?" Jessica asked.

"And be quiet. Jason is sick and sleeping in his room."

Oh no, Jessica thought. *If Jason's home now, Mom drove past Heritage.*

"Did he get sick at Ms. Carter's?" Jessica needed to know.

Her mother stared her down. "Yes. I picked him up early. The same time as dismissal. Oh, but I forgot. You go to study hall."

Jessica's head swished as she grabbed onto the railing that would support her walking up the stairs to her bedroom. She took deep breaths to extinguish the fire running through her body and her vision blurred as she hung onto the railing and pulled herself toward her room. She dropped onto her bed, backpack slumped to the side. The blood that was racing inside of her was now rushing to her face and chest, and she could feel hives blooming on her skin.

Her mother pushed in behind her. "Damn it, I forgot you have no door." She stood above Jessica's slumped body. "Your brother is sleeping. For his sake, keep your voice low."

Jessica nodded feebly.

"I saw you, so do not deny it. You were on the back of a boy, and he carried you to his home. You were in there for well over fifteen minutes. It looks like a homeless person lives there. Jessica, what have you been doing?"

A whirlwind of lies blew through Jessica's mind, but it was difficult to catch one. Plus her energy level was being tested and was failing miserably. She felt herself crumble, unable to keep up the façade, but not ready for the whole truth to be uncovered.

"That boy is a friend, and sometimes I go to his house to study."

"He is not a friend. He is a boyfriend. Do not take me for a fool."

Jessica watched her mother study her face. "And I don't think you have the flu. I think you're pregnant."

That word—pregnant—shocked Jessica as much as hearing her mother say it out loud. Jessica's body started to shake; she could barely lift her hands.

"No," she said, surprised by how weak her voice sounded.

"You've had sex, haven't you?"

Jessica's head fell onto her pillow.

Her mother made a muffled sound and after a minute said, "There is a pregnancy test in the bathroom waiting for you."

Jessica's frail and trembling body followed her mother to the bathroom. She was then instructed to urinate on the stick and to open the door when she was done. They sat as far apart from each other as possible, Jessica hunched on the toilet seat, her mother perched on the bathtub's edge, waiting for the results.

After fifteen minutes, her mother picked up the stick showing a vibrant pink line and placed her hand over her mouth. Jessica followed suit, not yet fully understanding why.

Her mother finally broke the silence. "Jessica, what did you do? What did you do?"

A blur of tears clouded Jessica's vision. There was no way out of the nightmare; she and Paul would be punished.

Her mother's hard shell started to break away. Jessica had never seen her mother crack, let alone watch her emotions spill onto her face and clothing. It was obvious her mother was not accustomed to this either as she struggled to grab tissues and place them on the appropriate watering holes.

"Hello?" her father's voice rang out from downstairs, making Jessica and her mother jump.

Her mother blew her nose, looked in the bathroom mirror to wipe away the tears, and straightened her clothing out.

Despite anger still oozing from her pores, her voice was level again.

"Go to your room and stay there until I come to get you," she said and hesitated before opening the bathroom door. "And do not go anywhere with your father, understand?"

Jessica nodded, feeling grateful at her mother's attempts to save her life.

Jessica's body was shaking so hard she barely made it back to her bedroom. She huddled on the floor next to the bench feeling self-conscious as she lightly touched her abdomen. *Pregnant? How stupid could I be?* Thinking she and Paul being together would never be discovered, and having sex that now produced a baby growing inside of her. Jessica was not ready to be a mother. And Paul? He wanted to be a better man but would he be able to handle the pressure of being a father at sixteen? Would she have to move into Paul's house? Jessica did not see herself surviving in his home, but there was no question, he could not live here. That is, if her father allowed Paul to continue living at all.

The daylight from outside started to dim as wind began picking up speed, preparing for a storm. Jessica pulled herself up and sat on the bench, praying to God to make things better, praying for a miracle. Her hair flapped as the breeze whistled through her window screen. The smell of a storm brewing made her feel desperate and the desire to have Paul's arms around her became so strong she thought about climbing down from her window and running to his home.

As her quivering fingers touched the metal tabs holding the screen in place, her mother whisked through the doorframe. Jessica studied her face, looking for a clue to her fate; there was nothing but a blank stare. Her mother placed a suitcase on Jessica's bed and made her way to the closet and dresser, filling the suitcase with clothing items that did not match.

"What's happening?" Jessica asked quietly.

Her mother did not respond.

Jessica sat in silence for a minute before she heard loud pounding and crashing sounds coming from downstairs. Jessica's insides panicked. What if her father was preparing to torture Paul in the basement?

"Mom, what's happening?" she asked in a firmer voice.

Her mother did not stop her task. "You are leaving here . . . for a long time. And your father is trying to control his . . . disappointment in you."

Jessica's eyes widened, and a flash of lightning streaked across the sky just as thunder rolled over the house. The rain began tumbling on top of the roof, making angry drumming sounds.

"Where . . . where am I going?" Jessica asked with what little breath she could muster.

Her mother was silent for a minute. "You will know soon enough."

"But . . ." Jessica was afraid to say Paul's name out loud, but this was his child too. "What about the father of this baby?"

Her mother stopped her work and looked at Jessica. "It's out of my hands, and now in your father's."

"He will kill him," she whimpered.

Her mother's flat face boiled over. "You should have thought of that before you made the choice to have sex." She returned to her methodical packing of Jessica's things.

Frozen in pain and grief, Jessica slid off the bench and curled on the floor. The window remained open as rain threw itself on top of her. Jessica folded her arms around her stomach and rocked to soothe the pain. How could she ever survive without Paul? How could she live with his death on her head?

As she rocked faster, flashes of running out of her home at full speed to Paul's came into focus. But the more she studied it as a viable option, the more it seemed insane. She could never outrun her father. Mrs. Daley's voice came to her saying, "call me in a home emergency." But Jessica could not bring herself to find and search the backpack that held her savior's phone number.

Her mother finally noticed the open window with rain pouring all over Jessica. She walked over and shut it, placing her hand underneath Jessica's armpit and lifting her off the ground.

"Go in the bathroom and put this on. We're leaving when you're done."

A dazed Jessica walked to the bathroom with sweatpants and T-shirt in hand. Her mother followed behind to monitor her every move.

Wearing the clothes her mother gave her, Jessica was led downstairs and pushed against the wall at the foot of the stairs, so her mother could grab her keys and purse.

"Katherine," her father said from the darkness of the kitchen. Jessica turned her head to look at her father through a spiderweb of hair, but could only make out an overpowering dark silhouette.

"Address."

Jessica's eyes focused on her mother, who clumsily searched her purse, eventually digging out a piece of crumpled paper.

"6142 W. Rolling."

That was Paul's address.

Jessica's body started shaking even more, and she was screaming inside her head, *No!* But the word with sound would not come out. Her heartbeat was so strong that she could hear it in her ears and it muffled all noises around her. Jessica was maneuvered through the front door and pushed into the backseat of the car, with suitcase in trunk, and driven away in the darkness. As they crossed over the overpass, Jessica dragged her head up and looked at Paul's home. A small patch of soft light flowed out of the living room window and onto the overgrown bushes below. Jessica turned her whole body around to watch the light out the back window despite the pellets of rain making it hard to see clearly. The light eventually faded. She felt numb as her mother proceeded to drive north on the expressway, not caring what happened to herself anymore.

Jessica woke up from the worst nightmare she had ever had. Or at least thought she had. Her mind was trying to trick her, but the harsh reality of sleeping in the backseat of a moving car in the dark of night was no illusion. She pushed herself up from the leather seat that her face had rested on and looked out the window, remembering exactly where she had been, now knowing exactly where she was going.

As her mother made a left turn onto a grassy driveway, bright lights could be seen ahead. There, standing wrapped in a blanket on the front porch was Aunt Lodi.

All the pain, all the fear, and all the hurt came rushing back into Jessica's consciousness upon seeing Aunt Lodi's face. Before her mother could shift into park, Jessica flew out of the backseat and into Aunt Lodi's open arms.

"He killed him. He killed him," Jessica shrieked. "Paul's dead. My love is dead!"

Chapter 19

Prince songs flooded through the speakers of Jessica's truck as she sped down a deserted two-lane highway. The early morning air sent shivers down her arms so she turned on the heat, hoping that it would also warm her broken heart. Before leaving home, Jessica found the *Purple Rain* CD she purchased at a flea market years ago but never had the courage to listen to—until now.

Jessica had agreed to help her friend and coworker, Jean, move her son back home after his first year at college. Jean's husband, Ray, had an accident at the paper mill and had limited mobility in his arm. The women would make the three-hour drive to Minnesota, pack up the truck, and then return to the UP.

The sun began to peek along the horizon of Lake Michigan which the two-lane highway hugged before it veered away from the water and took a path that had farms and eventually homes that generously dotted the main road into town. It was fifteen miles to Jean's home and plenty of time for unbridled memories. Some songs Jessica skipped; others she played over and over, not sure what to do with the rawness in her chest, hoping that the songs would heal parts of her that after seventeen years continued to ache.

Five minutes before arriving at Jean's, Jessica slipped the CD from the player and into the glove box so she could regain her composure.

Jean worried about her enough; Jessica did not want the careful stare or rub on the back.

Jean was in the garage searching through a workbench as Jessica pulled up, rolling down her window and breathing in the smells of oil and dust. "Hey," she said, trying to sound chipper.

"Well, hello." Jean stepped around the workbench toward Jessica's truck. "I have coffee for us and sandwiches."

"Awesome. Are they from Harold's?"

"Of course," Jean said as she placed her hand on the opening of the truck window. "I can't thank you enough for this. I could never do this alone."

"Please, Jean. You've been there plenty of times for me, so this feels a little like payback."

"Call it what you will. Tonight, dinner is on me. Of course, I hope we'll be up for dinner. Jake's dorm room is on the third floor—thank goodness you have youth on your side."

After locating bungee cords and rope, they cruised onto the highway at five o'clock. Jessica was thankful Jean's communication skills were up to par early in the morning. This way she would not have to fake happiness.

After one quick bathroom stop, they arrived at Jake's door a few hours later.

Jean stood in the middle of his dorm room, which was only half-packed. "For goodness' sake, Jacob."

"I know, I know," Jake said as he shoved clothes, shoes, and miscellaneous items into a large black garbage bag.

"Looks like you had some fun last night, Jake," Jessica said, looking at crushed beer cans in the corner.

"For goodness' sake," Jean said again.

Jessica grinned and started picking up the party remnants while Jean wandered around the room shaking her head and pointing to items Jacob forgot to pack.

Jessica's truck was fully loaded and Harold's sandwiches eaten when they got back on the road. Jake followed in his old beater.

"Thanks again for helping," Jean said. "And I'm taking you out to dinner so don't protest like I know you're going to try to do. Ray would be furious with me if we didn't treat you to a meal after all this work."

Jessica was in no mood to socialize. All she wanted was to listen to the CD burning a hole in her glove box.

"And I would love for Matt to join us. Let's give him a call?" Jean added.

Jessica hesitated. "Uh, well, he may be busy. He's leaving on Monday to take Irene to visit her family in Ireland and . . ."

Before Jessica finished her sentence, Jean was on her cell phone.

"That will be terrific. Ray will be happy he'll have someone to talk to. So we will see you at six. Bye."

Jessica pursed her lips together.

"Oh no. Did I step in when I should have kept out?" Jean asked.

"No, it's all right," Jessica said. She could feel Jean's eyes on the side of her face. "Jean," she said slowly, "please don't worry about me. We're fine."

"You deserve more than 'fine.' I hope you know that. Matt's a good man, and he loves you so much."

"I know," Jessica said softly.

Silence was not in Jean's repertoire.

"Talk to me."

Jessica could not help but smile. "You don't give up, do you?" she said, staying focused on the asphalt road that was now burning her eyes from the sun's reflection.

"Whoa, the sun is blazing," Jean said, and then fumbled in Jessica's glove box while asking if there was an extra set of sunglasses. She picked up the CD.

"*Purple Rain?*" Jean said as if it were a foreign phrase.

Jessica looked over and tried not to act upset. "Oh, yeah, I used to listen to that in high school. You know, Prince."

Jean shook her head. "I thought Lodi homeschooled you?"

"In Chicago, you know, before I was . . ."

"Ah yes, banished."

Jessica took her eyes off the road for a moment and looked wearily at Jean, who was studying the picture and song titles on the back.

"Do you have a favorite?"

She thought about lying, but why? Jean knew everything.

"'The Beautiful Ones,'" Jessica said carefully.

"Can I put it on? If it makes you uncomfortable, I'll turn it off."

It took Jessica a minute to answer. "I think it will be all right."

Last night, Jessica had watched the movie *Purple Rain* for the first time in seventeen years. "The Beautiful Ones" was something private she shared with Paul. And he was dead. While the memories held up well after all these years, so did the shame.

"Well, that was interesting," Jean said after it was over. Jessica turned down the next song, thinking it might offend Jean.

"In a good or bad way?"

"I've never heard that kind of singing before—especially at the end."

"The end is what I like best," Jessica said, feeling more at ease. "When I was sixteen, I used to daydream that two boys liked me. I could only be true to one, so I had to pick. One of the boys decided he would sing that song to me to push the odds in his favor. And it worked, of course."

"I could see why you'd daydream that. I'm sure it made you feel loved."

Jessica turned her head, afraid Jean might see her tears.

"What are Jake's plans this summer?" Jessica decided the best line of defense was a conversation changer. That always worked with Jean.

Jean rambled as Jessica nodded and interjected at the right moments, but all her head was involved in was a tug-of-war over something she could not change—the past.

When Jessica had first arrived at Aunt Lodi's, she begged for her to call her father and plead for Paul's life. Aunt Lodi did not have a phone in her home and made all calls from work or the neighbor's home a few minute's walk away. When she returned from the neighbor's, she said that their home phone rang for five minutes but no one answered. Aunt Lodi reassured Jessica that while her father may have some "control" issues, she could not envision him killing Paul because of her pregnancy.

"You think you know him but you don't. He will kill Paul," Jessica blubbered. Jessica had not stopped crying and was rarely without Kleenex or toilet paper balled in the fists of her hands.

Aunt Lodi held Jessica in her arms and talked softly, "Honey, it's not healthy for the baby to be so upset. I promise I will call your dad again tomorrow. I'm sure everything's fine and Paul's safe at his home too."

After Jessica had been there a few days, Aunt Lodi came home from work, and her face was pale and her lips without a smile. Jessica noticed immediately and asked if she had spoken to her father. Aunt

Lodi lowered herself onto the couch with her coat still on and a large bag that displayed Native American beadwork slid off her shoulder. She looked up at Jessica with wide eyes.

"Your father said Paul was dead."

Jessica shook her head back and forth with so much force that her hair flung into her eyes. This time, her voice was loud and clear. "No, no, NO!"

Jessica ran upstairs and buried herself underneath the covers of her bed. She scrunched into a fetal position and wrapped her arms around her pillows and pulled them tight against her skin. While sobbing, she spoke out loud to Paul.

"I'm so sorry this happened to you. I'm so sorry." She repeated those words over and over, and did not stop even when Aunt Lodi crawled next to her and gathered her into her arms, shushing her into eventual sleep.

For a week, Jessica rarely left her bed. She cried and prayed. She prayed for Paul, for her unborn child, and for forgiveness because she knew the risks of getting into a relationship but she rationalized them away. And now Paul was dead . . . because of her.

Aunt Lodi stayed home from work and tried to get Jessica to eat, but it was to no avail. Finally she used guilt around the baby's health as a way to coax Jessica out of a steady stream of tears to only a trickle and eventually, none. But Jessica remained in a state of slow motion. She did not say Paul's name out loud again, and never mentioned her father's.

One day, despite a headache that would not go away, Jessica was working on trigonometry that Aunt Lodi had purchased from a homeschooling program, when she found a newspaper clipping from Chicago. It was stuck to her workbook with something that looked like coffee. While she could not read all the print because the stain blotted out some of the words, she started to recognize names. Those names made her hands shake and her heart pound fiercely. It was a short notice about a missing boy named Paul Peterson. His mother, Dee Dee, had asked for anyone with information about his whereabouts to contact her or the police.

Jessica threw up in the kitchen sink. As she gripped the kitchen counter with her swollen hands, her throat constricted because she actually started to think she should call the police on her father. But then she remembered his words: *"You ever have any boys outside your window again, they will be filled with bullets from these two guns. I will tell my cop friends that they were trying to break in. I will be completely absolved of any wrongdoing."*

Her father had many police friends, not only from serving time together in Vietnam, but also his private security company trained many of the special units on the police force. Jessica was convinced her father would lie and that her mother would protect him with an alibi. Without Paul's body, or physical evidence, she believed her father's words played true; he would be completely absolved of any wrongdoing.

When Aunt Lodi returned home from work that evening, Jessica told her that she had found the newspaper clipping about Paul. Aunt Lodi grabbed Jessica's hands into hers and told her that she was going to contact someone in Chicago about the situation, and that Jessica will have to tell her version of events, and possibly testify against her father.

"It's no use to fight against him. He will never be convicted. He has too many police friends," Jessica whispered because she struggled to find her breath. Suddenly, she toppled to the floor. Aunt Lodi tried to wake her and when that did not work, ran to the neighbor's home and phoned for an ambulance. Jessica had developed preeclampsia, and when she returned home from her three-day hospital stay, she had to go on bed rest while being treated with medication. Her condition was closely monitored by a doctor, but Aunt Lodi believed that her high blood pressure was linked to the stress in her life. And so, to protect Jessica and her baby from further harm, Aunt Lodi stopped talking about Paul and prosecuting her father.

After many months on bed rest due to her high-risk pregnancy, Jessica finally gave birth to a healthy baby girl. Shortly after giving birth, Jessica learned that her father was in the hospital. She was so stressed at the news of her father's arrival that the nurse had given her extra medicine to reduce her high blood pressure. Aunt Lodi brought him to the nursery where he held his granddaughter, then left at Aunt Lodi's request, protecting Jessica's fragile being. A few weeks after the birth, her father showed up, unannounced, on Aunt Lodi's doorstep. Jessica ran upstairs with her daughter in tow while Aunt Lodi stepped onto the front porch, not allowing him in. Jessica stood at the window, clinging to her baby as if that would offer protection, and listened to Aunt Lodi's raised voice.

"I told you to not come here. You're harming Jessica's well-being."

"She's my daughter, and now I have a granddaughter. I'm not staying away."

"You killed her boyfriend, your granddaughter's father. That's sick, Jim, just plain sick."

"My job is to protect Jessica, and my granddaughter. Do you know he was a drug dealer?"

"You are not God, Jim. You don't have the right to choose who lives and who dies!"

"When it comes to my family, I do," Jim said. "And you should know that well, Lodi."

*　　　*　　　*

Despite Aunt Lodi's plea, Jessica's father showed up every couple of weeks. At first, he stayed on the front porch because he was denied admission into the home, sitting on a lawn chair for hours despite the weather. Jessica was not sure why, but seeing her father remain steadfast on the porch in the brutal winter and the gloom of spring was something she wanted to last. After many months of sneaking peeks at her father from a distance, Jessica gave Aunt Lodi permission to show him pictures of his granddaughter, Paulina. On Paulina's first birthday, he was granted entrance into Aunt Lodi's home. Jessica had not considered how her body would feel being so close to his presence. Jessica could not bring her eyes to meet his so she left the living room and hid upstairs, tucking herself into her bed and shaking underneath the covers.

Her father continued to visit monthly unless he was on a business trip, developing a relationship with Paulina, and trying to salvage one with Jessica. Eventually, her father's presence brought a little light to her darkened heart, but she placed an invisible boundary around herself, not allowing her father into her physical space, never wanting him to think that he could get closer. She rarely said one word to him, but his continual attempts to be a good grandfather eased some of her pain. Paulina ran to him for a big hello hug or a loud kiss on the cheek, and he would lift her up high. He always had a treat in the front pocket of his T-shirt, and she would reach in and pull out a lollipop, or a sticker, or a quarter.

At first Jessica, Paulina, and her father would go fishing at the creek on Aunt Lodi's property. Paulina was three and an easy buffer against any personal moment her father may have wanted to share with Jessica. Paulina continued to be a constant companion between the three of them, so alone time with her father could remain in short supply. Once

Jessica moved in with Matt, Paulina was eleven and became more in-dependent, spending time with friends and sports. So when Jessica's father would visit the farm, she thought riding the horses would be the best way to brave the time. Their moments together were quiet, sometimes uncomfortable, making talk around nature and the weather. Jessica decided that his effort with Paulina, which was more loving than she had ever remembered him being toward her, was his way of trying to smooth things out.

Her mother would visit once a month for a few days and it turned the cabin heavy.

"Lodi, do you think that's a wise suggestion?" she would ask in a light but hierarchical way.

Aunt Lodi would never address her slights outright, but instead made jokes, trying to make her laugh. But Jessica saw the twitch in the corner of Aunt Lodi's eye, and knew that if she spoke her mind, it would probably be something like, "keep your nose out of things you cast away."

Jake's friends were waiting on the front porch to help unload all his belongings and Jessica felt exhausted after the long day of driving and moving, plus only getting a few hours of sleep. At least that would be the natural assumption. Deep down she knew the true reason she felt so burned out—memories. She plopped down on the well-worn recliner and closed her eyes. Jean was right; she and Matt needed a night out with friends. Matt was a private person and did not like crowds or a lot of noise, which was fine with Jessica; she usually felt the same. But in the last year, a constant gnawing kept her from feeling comfort in their routine life and kept her from making a commitment, despite love from a very safe man. Jessica was unsure if she was bored. Sometimes she felt like the relationship needed something more, something exciting.

In the beginning Jessica took refuge in Matt's calm and predictable presence to help heal pieces of her life. Matt's heart also needed mending after the loss of his wife (and high school sweetheart) to cancer. Jessica believed they came together because of grief, but fell in love because of safety. They shared his farmhouse for the last seven years as an unmarried couple, but Matt was talking more about marriage and children. Jessica was thirty-four, and while still young enough to have children, the thought made her feel faint.

Jessica was fading into sleep as she ran through an incident that had happened last week. Matt was having a beer with his brothers in the barn. Jessica felt tired and turned in early; Matt soon followed. He tried to make love to her, but Jessica thwarted him. He lay next to her, looking up at the ceiling with his leg hanging over the side.

"Jessica, what's wrong?" he asked quietly.

She lay with her back toward him, holding in her tears. "Nothing," she said, trying to convince herself too. Jessica could tell he was a little buzzed because he hardly ever drank or initiated meaningful conversations.

"Sometimes," he said, after a few minutes, "it feels like you're miles away from me."

"Because I went to bed early?"

He turned his head toward her back. "Can you please look at me?"

Jessica let out a sigh and slowly turned her body toward the ceiling, eventually looking at him.

"What's wrong? And please don't say 'nothing' because I can see it on your face."

Jessica smirked; he was accurate about that despite being in the dark. But how could she enlighten him when she felt so clouded? The one thing she was aware of was the ache she carried for the last seventeen years was not diminishing and, in fact, was getting stronger. Before she could respond, Matt spoke.

"I know you feel like you don't deserve a happy life."

Jessica's eyes became watery. Matt was too easy to cry in front of despite her gut instinct to never show tears to anyone.

"You *have* forgiveness. You have prayed more than anyone I know. Don't you think it's time to move *us* forward?" Jessica heard him gulp and then reach for her hand under the blanket. "I love you. I want to spend the rest of my life with you as my wife. And I want children with you too."

Jessica returned his squeeze; she decided to do the opposite of what her mind was telling her, which was to pull away and get the hell out of there. She had learned from prior experiences that the mind is not always right.

"Matt," she said quietly, "I know you love me." Jessica paused for a moment. "Sometimes I feel alone even though you're around. I have an ache that persists no matter how happy I tell myself I should be."

"Not should, *can* be. You did nothing wrong to make God punish you to a life of waking misery."

Jessica appreciated the words, but her insides did not feel the same way. "I need more time."

Matt's voice eventually broke the silence. "More time to think about marrying me or more time to decide that you deserve forgiveness?"

Jessica thought for a minute and answered as truthfully as she could. "Both."

She could feel Matt's hurt but could not lie to him.

He lifted her hand to his lips and kissed it gently. "You know where I stand. I just wish you'd stop making me compete with the past." And with that, he turned over and eventually fell into a heavy sleep. Jessica wound her head with his words, unable to sleep the rest of the night.

Chapter 20

Snapping her out of her thoughts was a warm caress on her face. Matt was grinning at her like he just won a prize.

"Oh, hey," Jessica said, feeling dazed from recounting memories. She pushed the recliner up, and Matt planted a kiss on her lips and then gave her a hug when she stood.

"Sounds like you worked hard today," he said in her hair.

Jessica fell into his hold; it felt really calming.

"Yes, I think I may have lost a few pounds in the process," she mused, pulling away from his embrace.

Jessica took a good look at what he was wearing. Matt would often show up to social outings wearing clothes he wore in the fields, so she was pleasantly shocked upon seeing the dark wash jeans and button-down plaid shirt she bought him from the Eddie Bauer catalog. Jessica saw Matt catch a glimpse of her inspecting his clothes.

"See, I remembered that this goes with this," he said, pointing from the shirt to the jeans.

Jessica pecked him on the lips. "You look great."

Ray's shoulder and arm were in a sling, but his legs needed a stretch despite Jean's numerous requests that they drive to dinner. The four of them walked ten minutes to Murphy's Pub, located in the historic business district of town. The district ran four blocks and included a couple of restaurants, a dive bar, used bookstore, boating supplies, and of course a gun and ammo supply store. As they walked, Matt and Jessica held hands, and she listened to the men discuss small town business and farming. She felt both bored and soothed by the banter, like coming home to a place you never thought you would miss. Matt sped up his step to open the door to Murphy's for everyone.

They made their way to the couches gathered around the thick stone fireplace so they could wait in comfort for a table. Before sitting down, Jessica and Matt peeked in the dark green and wood room that held pool tables, shooting games, and an array of dartboards. Jessica and Matt used to go to Murphy's once a week when they first started dating to hang out with Matt's brothers and friends who loved to talk trash, drink, and play pool. Jessica liked the fact that, while Matt had a good time, he did not need to participate in all their rowdiness. That was not in his nature. Jessica could see in his face, after two beers, that all he wanted was to go back home and ride the horses with Jessica at his side.

After an assortment of Irish fare including shepherd's pie, bangers and mash, plus a couple of pints of Guinness and cider, everyone was laughing and being silly, even Jessica.

"Ohmigod, they have karaoke tonight," she exclaimed.

Jean almost spit out her beer. "Well, I'll be. I think you're drunk."

"No, I'm not," Jessica said, sitting up straight in her chair. "I am perfectly sane . . . in the membrane."

Matt started laughing at her. "This is going to be fun. Do you plan on singing in front of everyone?"

"No, darling, you are," she said playfully.

"Matt, did you ever hear the song that Jessica used to daydream about in which a boy who loves her would sing to her?"

Jessica's mouth dropped open. "Jean, that was between me, you, and Prince."

Matt looked surprised. "What's this about?"

Jessica took another gulp of the cider Ray bought her; it was her fourth one.

"Well," she said, trying to focus her eyes. "Way back, when I was a big city girl, me and my best friend Marilee snuck out to see *Purple Rain,* you know the movie with Prince?" Matt and Ray looked lost.

"Come on, you know Prince . . . purple rain, purple rain . . ." she sang off pitch.

"I remember it a bit," Matt laughed.

"Well, anywho, there was this song that he sang to his love, Apollonia."

"Apple what?" Ray interjected.

"Don't interrupt the story, Ray," Jessica said.

"Sorry," he muttered, turning to Matt as they both started laughing.

"Oh, now where was I? Oh, okay, so . . ."

The stream of consciousness was being filtered, at first, by her strong self-discipline. However, like anything controlled from within, it collapsed with the overflow of cider.

"Paul was supposed to sing that song to me."

"Who's Paul?" Ray asked, and then was hit in his healthy arm by Jean.

"We were supposed to be together 'now and forever,' 'now and for-ever,'" she said.

Matt leaned over and tried to pull Jessica away from the table and escort her out the door. Past experiences taught them both that alcohol and Paul did not mix well together.

"No, Matt. I don't deserve all this. He's dead because of me."

"What the hell's going on?" Ray asked, with his stare barreling down on them both.

"You should take her home *now*," Jean said.

"I don't wanna go home," Jessica cried.

Matt stood up and pulled Jessica into his body so he could handle any resistance. Her head fell low as she quietly cried, tears dropping onto the scuffed wood floor.

On the drive home, Matt pulled his truck over three times, so Jessica could throw up on the gravel that ran along the two-lane highway. He held her hair as she choked out past pain and her present embarrassment.

Matt carried her into their home, undressed her, and placed her on her stomach in bed. He got the garbage can from the bathroom and placed that on the floor, right under her face, then curled up beside her limp body to keep a watchful eye on her all night long.

The first thing Jessica noticed when she woke up was that her body was very angry with her. Never mind that it demanded that she sit on the toilet (on and off for hours) but it was begging for all extraneous stimuli to go away.

Matt walked in the curtain drawn bedroom. "Good morning. Would you . . . uh . . . do you need anything?"

Jessica carefully turned her head to look at Matt, not wanting to make too many unnecessary movements. "Oh God," she said in a husky whisper. "What did I do to myself last night?" She started to feel teary eyed and placed her arm over her eyes.

"Oh, uh, you had a great time. You were the life of the party."

"Then why do I feel like . . . poop?" she asked slowly.

Matt continued to be positive, but Jessica was not buying what he was selling.

"Just tell me, did I do anything I should . . . regret?"

Jessica lifted her arm to look at Matt's face. It looked like a debate was occurring between his head and his heart, but after a few moments, he smiled.

"Jessica, you were funny, you were cute, and you were among friends. There's nothing that you did among people who love you that could be called regrettable."

When those words sank in, Jessica felt a huge boulder lift from her insides. It slowly rolled out of the bed, down the hall, and out the front door of their home.

For the rest of the day, while Jessica ran between the bedroom and the bathroom, Matt was her constant companion. He fielded calls from Jean, who was worried about her and concerned about getting Jessica's truck back home, and from Aunt Lodi, who heard from Jean about the "fun" they had at Murphy's. Jessica appreciated Matt's opening the window in the dark bedroom to breathe some wellness into her spirit and bringing her saltines, Gatorade, and homemade chicken broth for dinner.

In the evening, Jessica felt strong enough to get out of bed and asked Matt to sit outside and watch the sunset.

Jessica tunneled into Matt's chest, pressing her ear firmly on his heartbeat. A blanket curled around them as they sat on the Adirondack love seat that did not swing. She didn't think she was well enough to test anything that moved.

It had been a typical late spring day and the temperature was slowing, making its descent in step with the sun. Jessica felt grateful that she could now tolerate and, in fact, indulge in the sounds from outside. Masses of chirping birds flew from one tree to the next, bursting with energy even this late into the day. The whinny of horses were heard from the barn and the purring of two outdoor cats who wound themselves around Jessica's feet, excited to receive human touch. The sounds, plus Matt's strong arms around her, made her feel whole again. Jessica pushed herself up to look at Matt's face in the glimmering sunset.

"Thank you for taking such good care of me. I would not have survived this day without you."

He smiled big and leaned in to kiss her gently on the forehead.

"Matt," Jessica said carefully, "I hope you know how much I love you."

He smiled even bigger and wound his arms around her tighter, pulling her closer into his body.

"Thanks. That's good to hear."

Chapter 21

When Jessica woke up the next morning, she washed her sheets and aired out her bedroom, then got a burst of energy and decided a home-cooked meal was in order. She did not want Paulina coming home to a messy house or mother.

"Mom, I'm back," yelled a voice from the doorway.

"Hello," Jessica responded, with her head in the oven, checking on her baked chicken with fingerling potatoes and roasted carrots.

"It smells great in here," Paulina said, walking straight into her mother's arms.

Jessica held her close to her heart, eventually freeing one arm to smooth down Paulina's auburn hair. "How was camp?"

Paulina's school year ended in May, and for the last two years, she had attended a weeklong Christian leadership camp a few hours from home. It was a requirement in order to work as a paid summer camp counselor.

"Oh, you know," she said, after being released from her mother's embrace and opening the fridge, "full of fun." There was a hint of sarcasm.

"Well at least you have a paid job this summer."

"I know," Paulina said quickly. "Just think, after next summer I'll be going away to college."

Jessica felt a strong ache.

This past school year, Jessica, Paulina, and Matt made the journey to five different college campuses. Paulina was eager to be flying away, and Jessica felt unnerved by the thought. She had never gone away to college; leaving Paulina with Aunt Lodi was something she could not stomach and at that time had no desire to leave Aunt Lodi's side despite earning an academic scholarship to a four-year college. Instead, Jessica went to a local college and completed her pharmacy degree in record time, taking more than the usual amount of semester hours and summer classes. Aunt Lodi helped raise Paulina and in the same breath, Jessica.

"Remember what we said . . . ?"

"Mom, I know. I'm saving my money for college, okay?" Paulina said gruffly.

Jessica did not want their first moments together to feel like this, but it seemed almost impossible anymore that their conversations followed a smooth path.

"Where's Matt?" Paulina asked, walking over to the open back door and pushing her head on the screen.

"In the pasture. What time is it?" Jessica asked, checking on the food in the oven again.

"Uh, almost five o'clock."

"Would you go out there and tell him dinner will be ready in thirty minutes? He thought six o'clock, but this chicken is almost done."

Without words, Paulina walked out the screen door, and Jessica listened to the loud creak then thump the door made as it swung back in position.

After dinner, Matt helped clean up the dishes while Paulina scrubbed the pan that was coated with baked-on juices. Jessica slipped outside to visit the horses in the barn. She had been busy trying to forget yesterday's nightmare and craved to have her routine back. Jessica would spend time daily with all their horses, even the ones that did not mind being without her company. She had a couple of favorites, but no one could ever tell. Moses was one of them; he was just so majestic and Jessica felt that they had a special bond. They worked together for years in order for her to ride him without getting jerked about, and Jessica took pride in the fact that her patience and determination helped Moses trust her so she could ride him softly, gracefully. There was Aubrey, the Belgian, who loved his nose to be rubbed, and Mitchell, the rescue quarter horse that found refuge with horses ten times bigger than him.

Jessica would give them treats, brush them down, and of course ride them; Matt did all the hard work. Not that Jessica evaded the responsibility of caring for them. She could be called on at a moment's notice to help, but she worked a full-time job and the horses were Matt's livelihood.

Jessica was talking to them in her horse voice when Matt walked into the barn.

"Oh no, you're not making them into babies again."

"I think you're crazy when you accuse my voice of making them regress," she said with a grin.

Matt grunted a laugh.

"How does Paulina seem? Do you think she's happy to be home?"

"She seems fine," he said, while picking up buckets and moving them to the other side of the barn. "Happy. She's on the phone with Jake right now."

Jessica pursed her lips. Jake, Jean's son, and Paulina seemed to be getting closer. It bothered Jessica because for the first time Paulina had what seemed to be a relationship with a boy. She never asked Paulina to affirm her suspicions because she was too scared. Jessica was terrified of Paulina making the same mistakes she made, so with Aunt Lodi's help, they had had numerous talks about boys and sex. To Jessica's relief, Paulina never cringed away from the information and, in fact, appeared to welcome it.

"Jake's a good kid," Matt said quickly.

Jessica stayed silent.

"Don't you trust him?"

"I don't trust anyone when it comes to affairs of the heart. The heart has a funny way of taking over even the most rational part of me . . . I mean, of anyone's self." Jessica could feel Matt's stare turn into her.

"I think her heart and her head can work together for her betterment if she lets them."

Jessica did not feel like they were talking about Paulina anymore.

"I guess," she said solemnly and walked out of the barn.

As Jessica crawled into her crisp, clean sheets that night, she ruminated about the conversations she and Aunt Lodi had about Matt. Jessica knew Aunt Lodi loved her as if she were her own child, and Aunt Lodi also came to love Matt. Matt had been the boy that years after their first meeting at the state fair, and after his wife's illness and death, had interested Jessica enough to accept an invitation on a date. Matt's world—the horses, the farm, his close-knit family—helped Jessica's walls slowly fold away, allowing vulnerability to seep in so that she could enter a relationship again. But this came at a price. Jessica and Aunt Lodi disagreed on how she was treating Matt. Jessica thought it fine that they remained together without the commitment of marriage, but Aunt Lodi disagreed, believing that Jessica was holding him at arm's length and not fully giving herself a chance at happiness because of the past.

There were moments that Jessica agreed with her observations, but the hacking sounds in her head, and her heart, were hard to silence. Jessica's choices led to Paul's death, something that was impossible to erase.

On Sunday, Matt's entire family met at church, a ritual practiced every week. There were his brothers Kevin, Michael, and Seth, their wives, and lots of children, along with his mother, Irene, the matriarch of the family after the passing of her husband, Herbert, two years earlier. Jessica found solace in the throes of very loving chaos. After church, the entire clan, with an occasional guest appearance by Aunt Lodi, made their way to Irene's farm where a breakfast feast was prepared and inhaled. All members of the family had roles to fulfill. Jessica made the biscuits and gravy, Matt made the pancakes, and Paulina along with the rest of her cousins were the cleanup crew. A job they all complained about feverishly every Sunday.

"Look at that mess! You guys are doing that on purpose!" complained Maeve.

"Yeah, you're letting all that grease splatter just so we have extra scrubbing!" said Trevor.

Depending on the weather, there would be a football or softball game in the front yard of the farmhouse. Jessica would sit on the front porch with those who were not inclined to exert themselves in sports and cheered for whichever team needed it the most. It was in those moments that she lost the pain, forgot the shame, and embraced the love of a family that folded her and Paulina in acceptance and peace.

*   *   *

Jessica, Paulina, and Matt were the last family to leave Irene's Sunday night because Matt was explaining the travel itinerary to his mother and writing down all the details so she would not forget. As they sat at the faded oak kitchen table with papers spread around, Irene turned to Jessica. "Before I would marry Herbert, he had to make me a promise, a promise that no matter what, he would save enough money for me to visit my family in Ireland every three years. I figured between having children and getting folks to watch them, three years would be the best for everyone. And unless Mother Nature interfered with the crops and horses, Herbert made sure he kept his promise." Irene's eyes teared up, and Jessica placed her hand on top of her wrinkled and freckled one, and gave her a small smile.

"Love," Irene said after setting her eyes back on Jessica, "is giving everything you have and then some."

Matt agreed to take his mother on the trip this year, which he had also done three years prior when Herbert fell ill and could not accompany her. Matt's brothers and nephews worked the farm while he was gone. Jessica loved the way Matt's family looked out for each other, and she envisioned Marilee's family working the same way, wondering what they were like all these years later. When Jessica was sent to Aunt Lodi's, she was so traumatized with grief, and then her high-risk pregnancy, that her efforts to make contact with Marilee felt like climbing a large mountain. After Paulina was born, she wrote a few letters but never had the energy to send them, afraid that Marilee's father would confiscate them and give them to her father. Jessica believed that Marilee's father would follow the brotherhood code of silence and would not allow Marilee to have any contact with her. Who would want their daughter fraternizing with a teenage mother? As the years past, Marilee would pop into Jessica's mind, and heart. She thought about trying to find her but had no strength to face her tragic past in Chicago.

It was in those quiet moments at Irene's that Jessica longed for Marilee and her family—the family that also took her in way back when, giving her acceptance and peace, too.

Chapter 22

Jessica woke up to a terrible headache. She was not prone to such ailments and worried that she may have caught a cold from one of Matt's nephews who was coughing all over everyone yesterday. Dragging herself to the bathroom, she took some vitamin C tablets and while staring in the mirror was surprised at how tired she looked; small bags hung around her barely wrinkled eyes, while shades of darkness blotted underneath. *What the heck,* she thought. *I hate getting old.* It was much harder to hide the imperfections from the outside as people aged, Jessica thought, and then laughed to herself about the things her mother would put on her face and wear just to keep her youth intact. Vanity had its place in Jessica's life, but she was much more carefree about her looks and how she cared for her body. She decided a long time ago that striking a balance between Aunt Lodi and her mother would be the healthiest way to mature and grow. Her mother cared too much, Aunt Lodi not so much; the middle felt just right.

Jessica had two hours before she needed to be at work, and Paulina had already left for her camp counselor job and would not be home until late evening. Matt was outside with Seth, discussing details about the farm that only he would know about. Jessica pulled a robe around her body, slipped on the nearest pair of shoes by the back door, and walked outside with orange juice in hand. The light morning air felt soothing on her face as she inhaled deeply, telling the powwow going on in her head to give it a rest. She put her hand up over her eyes to block the sun flickering from the east and greeted the men.

The three sat on the cushy patio furniture, drinking coffee and eating the fresh baked muffins Seth brought from home. Jessica quietly listened while Matt and Seth discussed caring for the farm. Jessica was used to Matt's family being over and having any one of them around did not make her feel like she needed to entertain. They came and went into each other's homes as if they lived there, something that took Jessica a long time to get used to. She could not help but laugh, especially when Kevin, Matt's younger brother, would come strolling out of their bathroom, wrapped only in a towel, plop himself down at the kitchen table with a grin from ear to ear and ask, with fork and knife in hand, "What's for breakfast?"

While in the shower, Jessica remembered the Prince CD in her glove box and felt glad that she would finally be alone, for the next ten days, to listen to it properly. Standing, with her hands pressed against the tile, hot water streaking down her body, she decided to move toward closure and purposefully tilted her face toward the showerhead so the stream of water would tumble onto her face. Her thoughts became more solid on a decision; while Matt was away, she would break free of the grip that the past had on her. She *wanted* to move forward with Matt because he was the best man for her and loved her despite her treacherous past. Truthfully, Jessica worried how long Matt would continue to wait for her to take the huge leap of faith needed to give herself fully to him. Jessica decided she would even listen to Johnny Cash, who she would turn off every time "I Walk the Line" came on, or Joe Cocker, so that she could rid herself of all scary thoughts about loving someone and death. Love and death were a detrimental mix, like four pints of cider and no tolerance. If that didn't work, she was thinking of having a ceremony and burning all things that were holding her back, something Aunt Lodi suggested a long time ago. Or maybe write Paul a letter and burn that. All she knew was that she needed to do something; she owed Matt that.

Matt entered the kitchen just as Jessica was making the final preparations to go to work.

"You guys get everything worked out?" Jessica asked with a smile.

"Yep, everything will be fine. You're okay with this, Seth and his boys helping out?"

"Of course." Jessica stepped toward him and slipped her arms around his neck. "Thanks for making sure everything runs smoothly."

Matt looked shocked and pleased at the same time and wrapped his arms around her waist.

"I like this. I need to go away more often."

Jessica made sure that before she went to work her kiss lingered on his lips.

As they pulled away, Matt asked her if she was all right. His concern made Jessica feel sad; here she was trying to get rid of the past and push forward with him, and he couldn't see it because of her ambivalence toward him. She made a mental note that when he got back from Ireland she needed to continue showing him just how much she loved him.

"I'm fine, but I'll miss you a lot. I love you very much."

Matt's face was brimming with happiness, and Jessica noticed it took him a long time to stop looking at her but eventually he did. He handed her a piece of paper that had the entire travel itinerary listed so she would know which home to contact them on what days. The last time Matt went to Ireland they only spoke once because it was too difficult to coordinate around time changes and schedules.

Matt closed Jessica's truck door as she turned the ignition, sparking to life with a deep hum of her well-oiled machine. He leaned into the cab for a last good-bye kiss, showing her how much he would miss her. Jessica drove off feeling light-headed, looking at him and waving from the rearview mirror.

All day at work, Jessica's head would throb then retreat, despite taking Advil, and she had a rawness in her belly that made her believe she was reacting to her decision to move forward. She likened it to the movie *Aliens*, when the beast (her past) ripped itself out of its human shell, leaving the body it occupied lifeless; although in her fantasy, she would become a superhuman species, more awake than she had been in seventeen years, with acute senses and vision so that those around her would always feel her loving energy.

Jean worried about Matt's absence and invited Jessica on numerous outings, enough to keep her fully occupied for the next ten days, or at least that's how Jessica interpreted it. While thanking her profusely and agreeing to one girls' dinner out—let's leave the drinking behind, thank you—she needed the full ten days so that she could complete the task she committed to in the shower, something she did not want coming to light until she was ready.

Jessica took a ride on Moses when she returned from work, making an extra effort to stay quiet and centered despite the light drumming that hid behind her thoughts. The air felt stagnant, which surprised Jessica because usually in the evening the woods were full of developing smells, changing from day to night. Little bugs that were a nuisance earlier in the day came out to fully irritate. The scurrying of small animals would dissipate and the songs of the birds, which were loud and constant, became less frequent. But this evening everything seemed to be standing still, almost pressing into themselves, surrounding Jessica silently. Even Moses, who relished these moments with an untouchable spirit, seemed cautious and wide-eyed.

After Jessica put Moses back in the stall and talked to Seth's boys, Trevor and Prescott, she took a hot shower and curled up on the couch for a night of TV watching.

The boys left well after sundown when a pair of headlights blazed into the living room. Jessica thought it was Paulina, who called earlier to say she would be home late, hanging in town with Jake and friends. But a knock on the door scattered that idea.

Aunt Lodi was shaking, tears streaking down her rumpled face.

"Jessica," she whimpered. "Oh, Jessica." The tears fell faster. "Your father . . . he's . . . he's dead."

Jessica stood in the shadow of the doorframe, her heart skipping beats, trying to get her mind to wrap around what Aunt Lodi just said.

"Dead?" she finally whispered.

Before more words could fall out, Aunt Lodi stepped forward, engulfing Jessica in her pain.

Everyone decided to drive separately to Chicago, unsure of how long each would have to stay and balance commitments back home. Jessica was thankful. She had not set foot in Chicago since she left in the back of her mother's car seventeen years ago. Jessica caught Aunt Lodi's apprehensive stare as they figured out logistics. Oh, the memories were there, stronger than ever, and Jessica knew Aunt Lodi could see that. Aunt Lodi gave her some herbal pills and a daily meditation book and begged Jessica to follow her on the drive, but Jessica said she needed to be in her own thoughts, not worrying about where someone was on the road. Jessica did not want a witness to her falling apart at this bad time, even though most of her emotions were tied to the past.

In front of everyone, Jessica was taking the loss pretty evenly. However, Aunt Lodi and Paulina were a mess.

"Mom, why aren't you crying?" Paulina commented while blowing her nose, which had turned red from using so many tissues.

Aunt Lodi spoke up before Jessica could respond. "Everyone deals with death differently; there is no right way."

Jessica had spoken to her mother the night before, with Aunt Lodi crumpled on the couch, and she called her again before leaving the farm, explaining that each of them would be arriving separately but within the same time frame—early afternoon. Her mother sounded distant and shocked, but said that all the burial plans would be made by her and she would appreciate Jessica's and Lodi's opinions to be kept to themselves. Jessica figured she must have spoken to Aunt Lodi earlier who'd expressed apprehension about the plans. Her mother didn't need to worry about Jessica's interference; what happened to her father's body did not matter. It was his soul she was concerned about.

The highway stretched on without much traffic, which allowed low rumbling whispers and strikingly loud thoughts to converge and jeer in Jessica's head. She left a message for Matt at one of the relatives' homes and worried about him, knowing how much he would worry about her. Restless feelings turned over like waves in the ocean as a strong current churned in Jessica's belly at the thought of seeing the Ripps. What would she tell Marilee? It would be easy for anyone to figure out why she left Chicago once they met Paulina, but Marilee would be the only one to think anything significant about her name.

When Jessica laid eyes on Paulina after her birth, all she could see was Paul—his hair, his eyes, and the angular nose. Jessica told Aunt Lodi the name she originally picked would not hold up. It needed to be Paulina. Aunt Lodi met her with a concerned expression and eventually told her to do what she thought best, but to think about the now *and* the later in life when making such a definitive decision. Jessica's youth would only allow for the now, so she gave her a namesake that would unknowingly keep Paul's memory front and center forever.

The traffic became thicker as Jessica got closer to Chicago. Even early afternoon did not keep the lanes from becoming busy and slow. Jessica struggled against the rude and aggressive drivers and was indebted to the small-town traffic she had become accustomed to along with the clean air; she kept rolling her windows up and down as emissions from trucks sputtered pollution everywhere.

The smell was making her feel nauseous and dizzy.

Jessica swallowed hard as she flipped the turn signal to exit off the ramp of the expressway, heading toward her childhood home. She tried to keep her head from looking toward the left; his home was to the left. Glancing quickly, not fixating on the fifth house, she shifted back and made the right hand turn toward her mother's home. Passing Heritage, she was overcome with emotion, shocked that she was choked up without being able to control it.

Jessica pulled into the driveway with her heart sagging, tears being wiped away by trembling fingers so they would not be seen by anyone. Before she could fully gain her composure, Jason was at the door of her truck, opening it up and grabbing her in a death hold. They had remained close through all their years of being separated, thanks to month-long visits in the summer and one week in the winter. As Jason became older, he visited during college breaks and then over work vacations.

Jason let her go and looked at her face. "Are you all right?"

Jessica met his watery green eyes and nodded, not wanting more concern to come her way.

Paulina's truck was already in the driveway, and Aunt Lodi had left a message on Jessica's cell that she would be arriving within the hour.

Jason grabbed Jessica's small duffel bag, wrapping his arm around her as they walked up the steps of the porch. Jessica was working hard at getting her body to stay calm. *Don't fall down now,* she quietly thought, but her body was struggling because of too many years of driving memories and feelings into the sandy bottom of her gut. Maybe if she had a gut made of cement, then things would not get shaken up as much. Her thoughts quickly turned when she saw her mother's figure approaching from the kitchen. The smells that met her at the door made her salivate, not realizing how hungry she had become on the almost six-hour drive.

"Jessica," her mother said. "Are you hungry?"

The question seemed inappropriate at the moment, and Jessica stepped back a little.

"Uh." Jessica felt like she was sixteen again, having no control in her life. "Sure."

The four ate beef bourguignon, garlic mashed potatoes, carrots au gratin, and for dessert, red velvet cake. They made small talk, avoiding the subject they were all forced into togetherness over. Aunt Lodi arrived an hour late, crabbing about city traffic, which was out of her character. Jessica assumed she was tired after the long drive plus the grief she was feeling. Aunt Lodi thanked Katherine for the food and with a few bites in her belly became more herself.

"Katherine," she said, after sipping the wine that was graciously poured for her as soon as she walked through the door, "I know you said over the phone you'd like your wishes to be honored about Jim's wake and funeral. Can you tell me more about what you're thinking?"

"Planning, actually, Lodi," her mother said quickly. "I know you think you knew Jim's wishes as far as what he wanted when he died, but he changed his mind on a few things, and I am going to honor them."

"What things are those?" Aunt Lodi asked, with heaviness in her tone.

"He told me I could have a wake and funeral and he asked to be cremated. The urn will be with me until I die, then Jessica and Jason . . . and of course you if you're still alive. You can take turns with it at the residence of your choosing."

Paulina made a small noise and asked to be excused. Jessica wanted to do the same, slink away and let these two have words over what they thought best. While Jessica could see her father softening about the wake, maybe about the funeral as long as God was not involved, in no way could she see him agreeing to be confined to an urn. She envisioned his ashes being thrown into the creek on Aunt Lodi's property, or in the woods.

"Katherine," Aunt Lodi said, opening her balled-up hands and placing them on top of the dining room table. "You really expect me to believe that Jim asked to be in an urn? *An urn?* Are you crazy? There is no way in hell Jim would want that."

Her mother started out slowly. "Lodi, you do not know the goings-on between a husband and a wife."

"That may be true, but I know my brother, from my core, Katherine, from my core, and I know there is no way his spirit would wish to be on someone's mantel."

"His family's mantel," she interjected. "His family's, where he belongs." Her voice cracked and tears fell down her face.

"Ladies," Jason said, from his quiet place next to Jessica. "I think we need some time to mull over what was said. We need to really think about what is best for everyone, but know that not everyone will get what they want."

Jessica looked at Jason, the way he eased himself into the conversation and his choice of words. She was in awe of her little brother, and after a few thoughtful minutes wished she could be more like him.

It only took a split second, but in her head, Jessica challenged herself, pushing to have a voice in a home that had made her so submissive.

"I agree," Jessica said forcefully. "Mom, I think we should take an hour or so and come back together, to figure that last part out, you know, the urn part."

Her mother blotted her eyes with the corner of her cloth napkin and nodded.

Jessica decided she would sleep in the guest room, Paulina in Jessica's old room—door back on, and Aunt Lodi in the basement bedroom. Jessica barely turned her head as she walked past her old bedroom to the guest room. The crushing feeling she had as she walked past was too much to bear. As she unpacked her duffel bag, she took notice of her body; the tightness in her shoulders, even her neck, was not letting her turn her head all the way to either side. And if her tension and soreness were not enough, her feelings were in an arm-wrestling match with her body. Jessica lowered herself on a chair and opened the window it was next to, breathing in the city smells she did not miss; no comfort was in the pollution that hung heavy and covered the grass and trees. Even the blooming tulips and daffodils seemed to be steeped in smog.

Jessica rubbed her temples slowly and methodically, closing her eyes and asking God to help her with the sorrow that was stuck in her throat and belly, to help her get through the next couple of days, and to please take away her pain.

*   *   *

"Mom . . . *Mom.*"

Jessica startled awake from the chair she had fallen asleep in as Paulina was holding her cell phone out to her. "It's Seth."

Jessica told Trevor when he arrived in the morning what happened to her father and knew it would not be long before hearing from Matt's family. She assumed most of them would do their best to make the drive to Chicago to be a part of the wake or funeral, Jean too.

After talking awhile to Seth, Jessica hung up and turned her attention to Paulina, who was sitting on the king-size guest bed, her back against the Queen Anne headboard.

"So most of the family will be coming for the wake, which I thought would be in the next two days. Seth will be at the funeral, since Matt's in Ireland. Jean's also coming to the funeral."

"Whenever that is," Paulina said sarcastically.

Jessica gave her a look.

"All that garbage down there, what to do with his ashes, the urn. Why not let Grandma decide? I mean, that is his wife. Shouldn't she know what's best?"

Jessica sighed. "Well, Grandma's intentions may appear good, but Aunt Lodi had a point. He would never ask to be in an urn. In fact, if memory serves me correctly, he announced one night that he wanted to be cremated, no church service, and his ashes to be spread on Aunt Lodi's property."

"I think Grandma should decide. She was, I mean is, well whatever she is now, she's the wife and should decide."

Jessica gave her a cautious look. "It's good to have an opinion, but let Grandma and Aunt Lodi figure out the rest, okay?"

Paulina gave her a devilish look, the kind her father used to give to Jessica, and said, "Okay."

Paul was a topic that was not often spoken about. At three, Paulina would ask if she had a daddy, which would send Jessica into the bathroom and Aunt Lodi to pick up the pieces. The only thing Paulina knew about her father was that he was Jessica's high school sweetheart, who was met by a terrible accident and died. It took Jessica a long time to say the last part. Actually, Aunt Lodi had been the one to say it, and eventually Jessica confirmed it. As Paulina got older, she would ask for pictures of Paul, or other family members, but Jessica would sidestep the requests, even saying most of his family was dead too. Eventually Matt and his family gave Paulina the father she craved and the extended family she longed for, and gradually the questions faded into silence.

The group, including Paulina, convened within the hour sitting around the dining room table, looking at each other in silence. As Lodi opened her mouth to speak, her mother's words rushed in first.

"I thought about what you said, and I will agree to have his ashes spread on your property, if you would agree that I keep a small piece of his ashes in an urn."

Jessica's mind became distracted, wondering which part of him she would want. His heart?

Aunt Lodi, whose expressive face was being weighed down by baggy eyes, acquiesced, as long as Jessica and Jason were in agreement also. Upon hearing their names, they gave each other a quick look and then nodded in unison.

Her mother pushed over a piece of paper that listed the plans for the wake and funeral. The wake would be held tomorrow, and the funeral the following day but not in a church; it would be held outside in a forest preserve that he liked to hike in when the city shredded his nerves. Aunt Lodi thanked Katherine for planning something that Jim would have smiled upon, and with those words, tears started dropping from her eyes. Her mother tried to smile, but it looked crooked as she got up quickly from the table and said she was retiring to her bedroom and would see everyone tomorrow morning.

The rest of the evening was spent making phone calls to inform out-of-towners about the burial information. Jean could only attend the wake because Ray was having surgery on the day of the funeral. She apologized to Jessica ten times, even saying maybe they should reschedule the surgery so she could be with her all week. After a lot of placating, Jean finally agreed that Ray's surgery was important and just being at the wake was the right dose of medicine Jessica needed. Matt's family would also be at the wake, and Seth would arrive the following day to accompany Jessica to the funeral. Jessica called Matt again from her mother's phone but got no answer. Seth also phoned, leaving messages at Aunt Mary's and Cousin Liam's, and tried to reassure Jessica that Matt would know soon enough.

Chapter 23

Jessica spent the night lying on top of the guest bed in a fetal position wrapped in an old blanket from her youth. She stared outside at the lamppost that was shining streaks of light onto the chair under the window, not realizing how hard it would be to sleep in a home she had been cast away from seventeen years earlier. Her father's death hung around her heart, tugging it down. Tears finally dropped onto the pillow, remembering the last time she saw her father.

He and Paulina were returning from a horseback ride when Jessica arrived home from work. He did not put his horse in the stall but instead asked if she would like to take a ride. It was cold, with only thirty more minutes of daylight and the snow was at least three feet high, but the paths had been worn down and the ride, through snowcapped trees, was breathtaking. Jessica reluctantly agreed. They rode for a few miles, her father talking about the weather, nature, sometimes mentioning things he used to do as a youngster on the farm where he grew up. Jessica had been learning more about his history with all his years of visiting and noticed he became more open in the exposed air of the woods. He had grown up with and owned horses . . . until something happened. Her father would always stop short, breathing heavy, a coarse look on his face. While Jessica still shied away from direct and exploratory questions, she embraced his words, storing them in her mind to ask Aunt Lodi about at a later time.

After a few hours of replaying past scenes with her father on the farm and fishing in the creek, she grabbed the handle and unlocked past memories of Paul. Jessica intertwined her hands together and clutched them close to her heart, trying to keep it from breaking apart. The last time she saw him—alive—he told her they would be together 'now and forever,' that he would be with her until she turned twenty-one, and could finally be introduced to her parents as her boyfriend. The image hurt so bad; loss was hard no matter what way it was delivered.

Around three-thirty in the morning, Jessica decided to drink some NyQuil, believing there was no way her mind or body would allow her to have a restful couple of hours of sleep.

When the alarm on Jessica's cell phone rang, she could barely twist around to shut it off because her arms felt like sandbags. Gently, she placed her hands on her face, feeling around to see if she was in one piece. Opening her eyes to the brightness of the guest room made her feel upside down. Her mind and body were screaming for nighttime; daylight felt too hot on her raw emotions. Pulling herself up from the bed and resting on her elbows, she looked out the window. She felt annoyed with herself because she kept looking outside, expecting the beauty and peacefulness she would receive at her home in the UP. This window delivered only loneliness.

Paulina's eyes were red rimmed as she slinked into Jessica's room and crawled into her bed, clutching onto Kleenex and Chap Stick.

"Strange but putting this on my lips helps me stop crying," she said.

Jessica smiled and pulled her in closer. "Whatever works, sweetheart."

Paulina spoke up after a few minutes. "I miss Matt. I wish he were here. He needs to be with us."

Jessica caressed her hair. "I know. I miss him too."

"This hurts so much. I feel if he were here it would feel better."
Jessica held in her tears. "Well, I'm sure wherever he is, he's praying
for us. I hope that gives you some comfort."

"It does," Paulina said quickly. "Yes, it does."

The large house allowed for a lot of privacy, something Jessica was
thankful for at the moment. When everyone met in the kitchen to eat
before leaving, it was the first time anyone had set eyes on each other,
all dressed in black, except for Aunt Lodi. She did not conform to the
old law of black at wakes and funerals; instead, she wore turquoise and
beads. Her mother's eyes looked dull, but Jessica could see the disap-
proval behind them.

Aunt Lodi broke the silence. "I just want to say that I love you all
and no matter what, we will *always* be together, as a family."

Jessica thought the words were being directed toward her mother,
but she could not be sure.

Her mother smiled weakly. "Yes. Family. Always."

The stillness and stagnant air of the funeral home made Jessica
uncomfortable. She had limited experience with death: Matt's father,
Herbert, and Paul. When she was younger, she attended wakes of former servicemen of her father's, but she did not know them personally.
They were just wax figures of hard-faced men.

Aunt Lodi and her mother brought framed pictures and placed
them on a polished cherry wood table where the casket would normally
sit. Some were random shots of them as a family before she was sent
away and one of the only pictures they took together as a family, when

Paulina graduated eighth grade. Jessica was surprised at one picture she had never seen. It was of her father, Aunt Lodi, and what looked like their parents. The picture was black-and-white, with a crease down the middle, but the faces were clear. Her father looked to be about six, Aunt Lodi ten, and they were sitting on fence posts, and behind them was a vast open range of crops, all neatly lined in rows. His mother stood next to him laughing but not looking at the camera, with her hand on top of his. His father stood next to Lodi looking content. Jessica picked up the picture to look deep at her father's face; he looked free.

Jessica and her family stood next to the pictures while people Jessica did not know came and went. For a while, a long stream of bodies were waiting in line to pay their condolences as others milled around, sitting quietly on the chairs or looking at a few straggled pictures in the back. Most of the mourners were men, all of whom shared the same look of war shaded over their faces. Jessica recognized some of the men from past visits to her home and could pick out who was doing better than others, basing this observation on their teeth. She had learned from working in the pharmacy and small-town life that teeth were an indicator of how well one was getting along in life.

Jessica's feet were not used to heels, and her legs were starting to show signs of fatigue even though she had three more hours to go. Paulina had gone upstairs to eat, and Jessica decided to take a rest on the blue couch in front, not to stray too far from her family.

"Jessica?" a voice beckoned from the side.

Jessica turned her head, looking at a woman with short black hair and beautiful cornflower eyes. Her heart leaped forward as she slowly stood up, shaking from the shock.

"Marilee . . . oh, God . . ." she said, as Marilee reached out and grabbed her. They cried in each other's arms like babies, Marilee pushing her out to look at her, then pulling her back in.

"I can't believe it's you, after all these years, it's you," Marilee cried. The two made their way to the back of the room holding hands and sat down on a love seat set off from the rest. Marilee said how sorry she was for her loss first, then dove into fifty million questions. Before Jessica could field them all, Paulina came back from eating upstairs. Jessica introduced her with pride and watched Marilee's eyes as she figured out the math. Marilee squeezed Jessica's hand tight and with a small smile acknowledged what did not need to be said.

After Paulina left Jessica's side, Marilee asked if Paul knew.

"No," Jessica said. "He never got a chance to know."

Marilee looked at her cautiously, but before she could utter another word, the other Ripps arrived. Jessica was embraced by her past: Eddie, now married with four kids of his own, was a policeman and lived in the same neighborhood they grew up in. In fact, his twins were currently freshman at Heritage. Julie was a nurse at a local hospital, married to a firefighter, with three children, also living a few blocks from her parents' home. Barbara married a lawyer; they lived downtown and had two children. According to Marilee, Tommie lived in Georgia, moving up the ranks of the Marines with his wife and four children, and Kathy was the woman's volleyball coach at Ohio State. She had two children and was the only one divorced, something Marilee did not want to expand on. Marilee was a drama teacher and was married to a Humanities teacher; they both taught at Heritage and had three children: Sophia, Curtis, and Michael.

Marilee's mom, Sue, grabbed Jessica up in a Ripp hug. "I hope you will never leave us—Marilee—again."

Sue and Bob were doing great—lost 150 pounds between them both, walked every day to keep in shape, and ate a low-carb, sometimes gluten-free diet. Jessica smiled when Marilee rolled her eyes after her mother said that. Looking at the Ripps gathered in a loving circle around her brought joyfulness beyond words; Marilee's family made her feel complete, just like Matt's.

Jessica spent the next three hours introducing and talking with the two family systems that helped shape the woman she became. Jean arrived just in time to join the reunion, hitting it off with Marilee the minute each opened their mouths.

At the end of the night, Aunt Lodi stood up and thanked everyone for coming to celebrate the life of James Lars Turner. She shared the history of a small-town farm boy who loved nature and jumping from the top of the barn loft to the bottom haystack. A boy who ran for hours in the woods, pretending he was Tom Sawyer or a Comanche warrior. A boy who picked wildflowers for his mother and made sure his father had enough snuff to make it through a day. And someone who loved his country so much that he enlisted in the Army right out of high school. Who became a member of an elite force, a Green Beret, and served his country in Vietnam for three tours. Meeting his best friend, Bob, and moving to Chicago where he would meet his eventual wife, Katherine.

"Jim was a man who made sure those around him were protected." Aunt Lodi's tender voice cracked. "My brother was someone I came to rely on too. Even though I was oldest, and I bossed him around sometimes." Jessica heard people chuckle. "Jim kept me safe, and for that, I owe much of myself to him and his family."

Jessica's mother stood up next to Aunt Lodi, Kleenex in hand, and gave her ten-second version of thanking people for coming. The funeral director announced that the service would be held tomorrow at Priest Woods, by the pavilion closest to the river at ten thirty with lunch at Jim's favorite restaurant, The Freilassen.

Exhaustion overtook Jessica as she said her last good-bye to Matt's family. Jean gave her new friends good-bye hugs and approached Jessica with arms open, whispering in her ear that she would pray for her and her family and to call her *anytime.* Marilee stood in the shadows, and Jessica was surprised she did not leave with her husband. Eddie also hung back, saying he would drive her when she was ready to leave. Jessica saw Marilee's face a lot that night, looking as if she needed more time to reconnect, but with so many people to interact with, it was difficult to escape. Marilee approached her again and was about to say something, but Paulina stepped next to Jessica.

"Mom, I need to go back to Grandma's. I think I'm gonna pass out."

Jessica looked at Marilee and mouthed sorry, then wrapped her arms around Paulina and walked out to Aunt Lodi's car. Jessica did not have the energy for anything other than taking care of her child.

Chapter 24

The drive to the forest preserve consisted of an endless river of memories, and Jessica felt she was entangled in a sticky web of her past. Piper Mall, the movie theater she and Marilee sneaked to, and restaurants she remembered from her youth passed by the window of Aunt Lodi's car as Jessica stared out. She recalled an outing with her father to get hiking boots for her. They went to five stores before he finally realized those types of shoes needed to be purchased at a specialty store, like the place he shopped for all his hunting needs. And she remembered her father's impatience and her silence that grew with every store they entered.

Jessica gazed over at Aunt Lodi who was very quiet, as was Paulina. *Everyone's lost in their own grief,* she thought, studying Paulina through the side mirror. Paulina loved her grandfather. As Paulina got older, Aunt Lodi coached him to navigate a different relationship—giving her money and telling her to have fun with her friends. He would always give a gift of Mace or pepper spray, to which Paulina would give the recited "Thank you so much, Grandpa," handing it over to Jessica or Aunt Lodi when he left. But he did not impose his will on Paulina; Aunt Lodi made sure of that. Jessica believed that since Aunt Lodi was put in a position to call the shots, her father had no grounds for a defense. Jessica wanted Paulina to experience a healthy relationship with her grandfather, so she guarded the past by not speaking of too many memories. She fiercely hid the fact that her father had killed Paul.

Jessica slid her hand around the back of the passenger seat to touch Paulina's leg. Paulina reached over and grabbed hold of Jessica's hand, squeezing it tight.

Aunt Lodi pulled into the parking lot closest to the river that her father would spend hours at, trying to escape the elements of cement and brick. New green grass had emerged from its hibernation and ran over small dips along the edge of the tree line while squirrels raced around playing an intense game of tag. It was a short walk along a paved path to get to the pavilion where the service would take place. Bob Ripp asked to give a speech and two of their close police officer friends said they would also like to say a few words.

Her mother and Jason arrived early to place a lace tablecloth and pictures on a picnic table while Seth was waiting for Jessica in the parking lot. She told him he didn't have to come the day of the funeral but he insisted, saying that Matt would do that for his family. Matt had called and left a message on her mother's home phone—Jessica could hear the angst in his voice. He said he was going to try to fly to Chicago, but the flights were full and he did not think he would see her for a few more days.

Jessica sat with Aunt Lodi and Paulina on an iron bench that was next to the river while Jason and her mother stood near the pictures saying hello to the small pool of people that had gathered at the edge of the picnic tables. A cold breeze sent a chill down Jessica's body. As she shivered from the frigid air, Aunt Lodi drew her in closer and rubbed her arm for warmth. The sun was weaving in and out of the clouds, making the day feel grimmer than Jessica wanted. She started to lower her head after peeping up at the slight brightness but lit up when she saw Marilee and her family walking toward her. She had met Marilee's husband, David, last night. He was tall and trim with a caring tone and talkative, which made Jessica wonder how he and Marilee ever got a word in edgewise with each other. Marilee's children were also with her: Sophia, who was eight years old, branded with Marilee's looks, and her boys, Michael and Curtis, ages seven and five respectively, who looked a lot like her husband, but Jessica could also see Eddie in them. And the Ripp confidence coursed through all Marilee's children.

Marilee proceeded toward Jessica as her family walked under the pavilion to say hello to the rest of the Ripp clan. Bob was getting ready to say a few words and two men, one with deep creases on his face, the other wearing his bravado, lumbered up beside him.

"Hello," Marilee whispered.

Everyone on the bench greeted her with smiles and a hug. When Jessica wrapped her arms around Marilee, she whispered that they needed to talk about something important.

Jessica nodded, but Marilee broke the hug and grabbed her hand.

"Jess, we need to talk . . ."

But before she could finish, Marilee's father cleared his throat and asked for everyone to find a place to stand or sit. Jessica was taken aback by the sharp look on Marilee's face. Whatever was on her mind appeared extremely important, but it would have to wait; she would not be disrespectful toward her father or Mr. Ripp on this day. Jessica sat back down with apologetic eyes. Eventually, Marilee walked to Jessica's side of the bench, stood behind her, and rested her hand on the top of Jessica's shoulder.

Jessica never heard Mr. Ripp say so many words in succession. He spoke in a deep voice about how he met her father, two skin and bone towheads in boot camp, and how they counted on each other, in battle, like brothers. That Jim had a deep commitment to his country, and Bob and Jim trusted each other with their lives. And because of their training, they operated a very successful private security business together.

"Jim was a man called to duty; he would never leave a person behind. He was driven by courage, loyalty, and the love of protecting others." Mr. Ripp choked up at the end, but like a specially-trained machine wheeled it back in and finished his speech in fifteen minutes flat. Jessica could not see the people behind her but could hear a few chuckles when Bob mentioned Jim's panache for scaring people, not in a bad way of course. The two police officers, who also served in Vietnam with Bob and Jim, gave their own rugged version of a life together, what Jim taught them, and what they would miss about him. The one theme Jessica kept hearing was his love of the life, being a private gun for hire, or as the men saw him, a one-man paramilitary force. Jim lived to keep people safe; he even died for that invaluable right. But what truly haunted Jessica the most was that her father was addicted to war.

Hearing about her father through their eyes made Jessica come to realize how little of himself he showed her. They told stories about his humorous nature and brought to light parts of his personality he hid from her. *This* thought, not of his death, made her cry. Marilee rubbed Jessica's shoulder gently at first, but then Jessica felt a push ever so slightly. Marilee's hand was starting to feel too forceful on her body, and Jessica wondered what the problem was but did not move her gaze from the men speaking.

As the last policeman concluded his eulogy, everyone got up to say their last good-byes to the pictures on the table. Jessica pushed herself off the bench just as Marilee tried to drive her in a certain direction. She became unbalanced and ended up turning awkwardly and falling slightly back into the bench. As Jessica lifted her head to regain equilibrium, she saw him. The him whose child she carried and raised. The him she was supposed to love now and forever. The him who was dead. *Oh God, Oh God,* kept ringing in her head. Her heart was another matter; it had stopped. Jessica tried to inhale so she would not pass out, but it was too late. Her body met the hard surface of dirt and grass in one blow.

Smudges of familiar faces crowded around her but only one did she see clearly.

He also gathered around, staring at her as if he had seen the resurrection of Christ.

"Mom, are you all right?" Paulina asked. Jessica watched his reaction to those words; he looked from Paulina to Jessica, back and forth, back and forth. His brow furrowed as he searched both their faces. She heard him ask someone if that was her daughter. Yes. She watched his face become confused, anxious, sad. She saw him turn toward Marilee and ask how old she was. Marilee met Jessica's eyes with guilt, then looked away. Seventeen. Paul's face collided into Jessica's stare. He knew.

Seth pulled Jessica up and kept a grip on her until she was steady on her feet again. Everyone thought she was reacting to her father's death; only three knew the truth. Jessica tried as hard as she could to regain a sense of stability, but she could not take her eyes off Paul.

His hair was cut close to his head but remained thick, with the same rich auburn that branded Paulina. Jessica noticed his face was the same as she remembered from their youth, with the only change coming from the lines that surrounded his eyes and the corners of his mouth. It made him look wiser, tougher too, but in a solid way. He stared at her and she could see a small tremor works its way down his throat.

Jessica whispered a thank-you to Seth as he slowly left her alone, then shooed away Jason, Aunt Lodi, and Paulina, not ready for Paul to hear her name out loud. The few gapers who hung on gradually walked away. Marilee stood by her side when Paul finally approached.

"Jessica? That is you?"

She nodded and swallowed a larger tremor in her throat, not quite able to find her voice.

He looked from her to Paulina and after a few seconds back to her. "I haven't seen you in what, seventeen years?"

Jessica felt the blood drain from her face and she tried to say, "I thought you were dead," but the words refused to form. Jessica's knees began to slump, and she reached for Marilee, who twisted her fingers into hers ever so slightly.

Paul stared into her face. "And your daughter. She looks familiar."

Jessica's unblinking eyes filled with tears, and they spilled down her cheek. She wanted to rejoice that Paul was alive, but it was flanked by her father's betrayal.

"She's mine, isn't she?"

Marilee squeezed harder, but Jessica released her fingers, grabbing Marilee's arm, her entire body shaking as she dug into the cotton of Marilee's sleeve.

Paul became restless, shifting back and forth, looking from Jessica to Paulina. Marilee tried to say something, but he put his hand up.

"I need to hear from her. I need her to tell me."

Jessica was now a "her." Her heart sank deeper into the abyss. The truth, as ugly as it was, would have to be revealed. It was not her fault; surely he would see that.

"This is not the right place," Marilee said anyway. "Look around. Do you really want this discussed here?"

Paul's face became more thoughtful despite the red tinge. "Fine. But I want to talk to Jessica *alone.*"

Jessica was gripped by fear, not only about facing Paul but that she would fall down again without someone to hold onto. Marilee parted slowly, showing in her face the courage Jessica needed to summon. Jessica wiped away her tears and did her best to swab her running nose, all the while taking deep breaths to calm her emotions. She knew her shaking hands would reveal her need of wanting to touch his face, desperate to make his presence even more real, so she held them tight together in front of her.

Jessica could hear intentional control in Paul's tone as he repeated his question. Swallowing hard, she lifted her face to take the weight of whatever came her way.

"Yes. She's yours."

Paul's face broke. He stepped back and Jessica could see his chest expanding, his heartbeat quick. Jessica watched as he looked at Paulina with a distant stare. She was talking to Seth and Jason, her long auburn hair being pulled gently by the spring breeze.

Paul concentrated back on Jessica's face. "How could you? She's mine."

Before Jessica could explain, some men walked up—one of them was the off-duty police officer who spoke about her father. He gave Jessica quick words of sympathy and then turned to Paul.

"We're heading up to PJ's. Are you coming?"

Jessica watched Paul compose his face and voice. "I got some shit to do. I'll meet up later."

Eddie walked up and the policeman asked him the same thing. He looked apprehensively at Jessica then at Paul.

"Yeah, after the lunch."

"Fuck that," said one man, wearing a hat with the inscription De Oppresso Liber. "I need a drink."

The men barely smiled as they walked toward the path to take them to the bar. Eddie stood in between Jessica and Paul, asking if they were all right. Jessica could not answer for herself. She kept staring at Paul, who looked like he wanted to take Eddie's head off but then thought otherwise. Abruptly he searched his jacket pockets, pulling out a crumpled wrapper and taking a pen from the front pocket of his T-shirt so he could write on it. He handed it to Jessica.

"I'll be at PJ's later. Call me when you get there. We'll talk then."

Jessica nodded as she looked at the cell phone number and then watched him walk away. Eddie looked at her cautiously. "This is not my business. Marilee sent me over to make sure everything is okay." Eddie paused for a moment. "So is it?"

Jessica half smiled, nodding she was fine, and then walked toward Paulina on wobbly legs.

As Jessica rode with Seth to the restaurant, he asked all the right questions, not prodding too much, but Jessica could not help but be distant. Why did her father lie about killing Paul? Why would he keep Paulina from her father? Jessica then turned on herself, asking why she didn't go back to Chicago with Paulina, especially in those early years. Why did she allow her father to keep her away for so long? Jessica now believed that if Paul had known she had his child, he would have welcomed them with open arms.

Jessica loathed herself for allowing fear to control her. She felt so stupid, so bad, so wrong. Her fingers started pushing into her hands, making lasting marks with her nails. Seth asked her a question about some people at the service.

Jessica stopped hurting herself and spoke as if reciting a fact. "Most are police officers. Not sure about the others. I didn't know most people there."

Seth cracked a laugh. "Could've fooled me."

For the first time since leaving the service, Jessica looked Seth's way. "Well, the Ripps are a big family, a lot like yours."

As Seth got closer to the restaurant, he commented on how happy he would be to get back to the clean air and no traffic of the UP. "I don't know how you ever lived here."

The Freilassen was quiet as smoky smells of meat hung in the air, making even the most grief-stricken attendee crave a piece. The back room held ample space for the lunch, and Jessica spent the first few minutes staring at the large mounted elk on the wall, its eyes black and nondescript. It reminded her of her father's office, a room that even to this day made the pit of her stomach drop.

Marilee's voice pulled her attention back to the present. "I am so sorry you saw Paul that way. I tried to tell you once I figured out you thought he was dead."

"Please don't apologize . . . it's not your fault. But I'm in complete shock."

The girls found a spot at the bar. Marilee ordered a Bloody Mary, Jessica an iced tea, and Marilee filled her in on Paul.

"When you disappeared, he went crazy. He followed me home a few times, thinking he may see you at my house. Mrs. Daley searched me out, asking what happened to you; she even went to your house. I really had no clue what happened, my dad was tight-lipped—you know how that brotherhood is." Jessica grimaced. "My mom said you were alive, but she wouldn't give more details—too loyal to my dad. I felt so bad for Paul; he seemed completely lost. He went over the deep end: fighting in school, openly selling—and it was definitely *not* tamales. I didn't see him much over the summer of our junior year—he was too troubled. But at some point, he changed. I'm not sure how or why. And guess what? He's a police officer. He's on a tactical unit—gangs and drugs. Eddie says he's good, knows his stuff. Oh, and guess who he's . . ." But before Marilee could finish, Paulina walked up with Seth, and their conversation was overtaken with Marilee asking Paulina, "What are you doing and where are you going in life?" Paulina had a lot to say about her last year of high school and plans to venture off to college. As Paulina was answering Marilee's abundant questions, Seth leaned in and asked Jessica how she was holding up. He had gathered from overhearing little details that coming home might be really hard on her.

Jessica tried to loosen her tight smile. "I'm doing the best I can, under the circumstances."

"You should hear your boyfriend. He's frantic to be with you. I told him I have it under control but he doesn't sound assured."

Jessica saw Marilee peek at her when the word "boyfriend" was mentioned. She chuckled when Marilee broke the flow of conversation to ask Paulina about Jessica's boyfriend.

Jessica missed Matt deeply and could summon the feeling of his comforting arms when sorrow paralyzed her. But considering the circumstances, she was glad he was not there. Jessica rationalized that Matt would not let her and Paul have a word alone, something Jessica desperately needed to do.

Aunt Lodi finally edged Jessica into a corner at the restaurant. Jessica had been avoiding her looks since she fell to the ground in the forest preserve and while she was talking with Marilee and others at the restaurant.

"That was Paulina's father? How could that be? He's supposed to be dead!"

"I know. I know," Jessica said, hating herself again.

"Jim didn't kill him," Aunt Lodi said in shock.

Jessica and Aunt Lodi stared at each other for a few seconds.

"Jim didn't kill him," Aunt Lodi repeated, but with a small smile on her face. After a few more minutes, Aunt Lodi asked what Jessica was going to do.

Jessica pursed her lips together for a moment. "He asked me to meet him so we can talk. He knows Paulina's his; all he did was look at her and ask how old she was."

Aunt Lodi shook her head. "Jessica, be careful. Your feelings are falling out of you, and I sense they're not all platonic. You have Matt to think about. And of course Paulina—Matt's the only dad she knows."

Jessica gave careful consideration to what Aunt Lodi was saying, and she could not deny the truth in her words. Paul was her first love, her daughter's father, and seeing him today sparked a feeling Jessica had only felt with him. As the truth of his existence settled inside Jessica, her thoughts were taking a physical turn. She so desperately wanted to reach out and gently stroke his face, touching parts of him that he gave her so many years ago. Jessica knew it was wrong to think that way, but she could not convince her younger self, the fifteen-year-old that fell in love for the first time that the thirty-four-year-old knew better.

People filtered in and out of Jessica's periphery at the restaurant, but her head was sunk into how to excuse her shame and how to explain to Paul her inability to dictate her destiny at sixteen. But how would she explain it at eighteen or twenty-one? Or thirty-four? Would he believe that she thought her father killed him? Believe that she thought he was sunk at the bottom of the Chicago River in cement shoes? And what about Matt? How did he fit into the equation now? Jessica shivered at the thoughts of Matt. She loved him deeply, safely, but Paul inflamed her like no other. And Paulina was his, despite Matt being the only father she had known.

Jessica started feeling nauseous, so she got a ginger ale to calm her stomach and walked to where her mother was standing alone, near a window that overlooked the street.

Jessica approached quietly and asked what she was doing.

Her mother continued to stare out the window, her silhouette doused with a clouded hue. "I was just remembering the last time your father and I were here. We met Bob and Sue. Your father had the venison roast. I had the only fish item on the menu. It was a lovely evening."

Jessica became nervous, unsure how to respond. "That sounds nice."

Her mother turned to her slightly. "Those are the moments I will miss the most. It may be small and insignificant to some, but to me those are memories of a solid life."

Her mother gave Jessica a half smile and walked toward the waitress to pay the bill.

In the parking lot, Jessica thanked Seth for staying with her and circumvented his guilt about driving back to the UP. Despite numerous angles, he finally agreed to leave and unwittingly let Jessica wrestle her demons alone. Of course, the only demons Seth knew of were the ones Matt told him about; Jessica shaded the truth as much as she could. Marilee was another matter because she insisted on going to PJ's with her. Jessica decided that her conversation with Paul needed to happen alone; it was a private matter.

And deep down she still wanted Paul to want her.

"I know you mean well, but I have to handle this on my own."

Marilee looked at Jessica as if she were a child, but relented. "Promise me you'll call afterwards. I need to know what happens."

Jessica agreed, and after lots of hugging and hand-holding, each crouched into their respective vehicles and drove away.

In the car, Paulina was talking a mile a minute, about all the new people she met and how much she loved Jessica's friend Marilee. But Paulina also questioned why she was never exposed to any of the Ripps if they were such good friends. Jessica had planned all the ways to deceive many years back and explained that when she got pregnant and moved to the UP, they were very young and struggled to maintain communication, eventually losing touch all together. But she always missed her friend and knew that one day they would seamlessly ignite their friendship because they had too much history, too many "firsts" together. Jessica also admitted it was more her fault than Marilee's and that she has never been a good pen pal.

"I guess," Paulina said. "But Marilee seems like the type who would be in your life no matter what. It's weird you never talked about her."

Jessica didn't know how to answer and fell silent. Aunt Lodi chimed in about how much easier it is to stay connected today with cell phones and e-mail and that their losing touch was a matter of technology not choice.

When everyone arrived at the Turner home, they once again retreated to their individual sanctuaries. Jessica stood outside her former bedroom to let Paulina know she had a few errands to run and would be back later tonight. Paulina hardly batted an eye as she crawled under the covers on the bed and gave her a sleepy grin.

"I love you very much," Jessica said, lingering in the doorway.

"I know," Paulina muffled, with her head covered by the comforter. "I love you too."

"You're going to meet him?" Aunt Lodi asked after entering the guest bedroom.

Jessica was rummaging around the closet, trying to find something that was not black. "Yes, as soon as I find something to wear."

Aunt Lodi sat down on the edge of the bed and watched Jessica fumble with the hangers, finally stepping back and turning toward Aunt Lodi. "Forget it. Do I look all right?"

"All right for what?"

"Please, I'm just going to talk."

"I want you to call upon the life you have built with Matt and Paulina. I want you to remember how long it took you to build that life. Please don't let a moment of guilt burn all that to the ground."

Jessica summoned all her goodness to shine in front of Aunt Lodi. "I promise I'll do what's best."

"Best for who?" Aunt Lodi retorted.

Pulling into the parking lot of PJ's, heart in throat, Jessica said a prayer. She was hoping God would intervene in a loud way if necessary, possibly with a lightning bolt in between her and Paul if He saw their intentions less than austere. But it also gave her the courage she needed to step out of her truck and face her past in the light of day.

As she walked through the parking lot, she called Paul's cell phone, but it went straight to voice mail. Unsure whether to leave a message, she hung up, hesitated, and then phoned one more time, hanging up again when she heard the voice mail message.

Classic rock songs seeped onto the sidewalk as Jessica passed along the darkened windows of the bar, each step bringing another layer of nervousness, and before entering the doorway spotted Paul. He blocked her entry, looking at her through drunken eyes. "I can't believe you never told me, never told me we had a daughter."

Jessica backed against the bright red door that was being propped open with a brick.

"Don't you know that I'm the assistant coach of my kid's baseball team? And when Lexi needed a parent to be a part of Brownies I stepped up? Don't you know that I'm a stand-up dad and man? My kids know who their daddy is." Paul stumbled forward, looking straight at Jessica. His eyes tightened, and his face was red with sweat collecting in the seams of his forehead. "How the fuck could you not tell me that shit?" he spurted as he fell against the wall next to the door of the bar. "How could you not let me be a part of her life . . . her . . . her . . . I don't even know *our* daughter's name."

Jessica's eyes widened as she stepped away from the door and back onto the sidewalk, afraid he might be so drunk and mad he would hit her. "I am so sorry," she pleaded. "You have no idea how sick I feel about this, how sick this secret has made me."

"I don't give a fuck how sick you feel. You kept someone from her dad. I'm her daddy, *me*," he yelled, pounding both fists against his chest.

Jessica put her hands over her nose and mouth. She expected Paul to be hurt. However she was not prepared for the words he was throwing at her.

"You knew I never had a dad. You knew I said I would *never* leave my children. That they would never feel unloved—they would always know their dad."

Paul's face was contorted; his chest was pumping up and down, and he looked as if he could spit on her at any moment. A piece of her was in shock. This was her first love, the boy who helped open her up, not only emotionally but physically. She lost her virginity to him. The boy she loved with every part of her adolescent being. But staring at his face, feeling the hurt and betrayal oozing from his body, she knew he had lost any love he may have had for her with this secret. Knowing this, along with him being drunk, put her in an uncomfortable position. In an instant, her mind raced and grabbed onto one solution. Jessica turned and ran, ran as fast as she could to her truck around the corner.

She was unsure if Paul would chase her but believed the alcohol would not let him get too far. Quickly starting her truck to speed out of the lot, Jessica glanced to the left, so she could turn onto the busy street and saw two men restraining Paul and mouthing words she assumed had to do with calming him down. Jessica's tears descended, and at times, she could barely see the road. Her heart was aching; she had never felt this kind of ache, even when her mother left her years ago with Aunt Lodi. She now understood what the word *heartache* really meant.

Jessica drove around for hours so the years of pain could drain out. Aunt Lodi would say hours are not long enough, but Jessica knew that despite her running away, she would have to face a sober Paul. She needed a game plan, one that included telling her daughter. She did not want Paulina finding out the truth about her father on the Maury Povich show.

Entering her mother's house unnoticed, Jessica slipped into the guest room without turning on any lights and sat on the chair facing the window. She began taking cleansing breaths to help center her while focusing on the night sky, all dark with barely a hint of stars. *How different from home.* Jessica never realized that the only place that felt like home was the UP. She loved the beauty of the night sky, the stars that connected to each other in never ending brightness. How the moon would shine a path of light from above to guide one on a walk through the woods. And the air—how clean and fresh it smelled. It was almost forgiving in that every day the dew, the rain, the snow, never had the same dull smell. It was as if nature was granting one a new start despite one's old self.

For the next hour, Jessica sat in complete solitude, feeling a mist move through her as if she were part of the landscape. With only the street lamp outside to guide her out of darkness, she went through scenario after scenario, trying to plan the best way to blow up Paulina's world. Jessica clamored into bed only to toss and turn, and woke with a pounding headache, not feeling like she slept at all. Jessica did not want to deal with her mother or Paulina and their questions about where she went last night. The only thing on her waking mind was talking to a sober Paul, trying to convince him she deserved forgiveness. But thoughts of wanting him kept sliding into her mind, finally admitting how attracted she was to him. The only thing that bothered her was that he was not as tall as she remembered. He stood about five foot ten, and she thought it funny that although Matt was not as strikingly handsome as Paul, she liked that he was six foot. His height and size made her feel really safe. She loved when Matt would engulf her in a hug or try to pull her in for a playful kiss. She could not help but smile about this. It really surprised her how much thinking about Matt made her feel happy, made her feel like she was complete. But she could not deny that Paul was occupying most of her thoughts. Even though she and Matt lived together, she never completely gave herself to him—partly out of shame, partly due to loving the memory of Paul.

Jessica abruptly rolled to her side to wipe those thoughts away, putting a pillow on top of her head. She didn't want to think about Matt anymore; she already had enough guilt. Her attention needed to be spent on a plan to make Paul see that this was not her fault and to figure out how to tell Paulina that the father she thought was dead had been resurrected.

To her surprise, everyone was gone when she got up. There was a note on the island in the kitchen stating some "loose ends" needed to be cleared up and that Mom, Paulina, and Jason had left to take care

of them. Aunt Lodi was also gone taking care of some personal business. They would all meet back for dinner together later in the evening.
Jessica's fingers felt like icicles as she touched her cell phone, thought
for a few minutes, then sat at the island and texted Paul.

"Can we please talk? I'm free until late afternoon. Tell me where
to meet." She read it over and over then decided to finish it off by
writing, "I know you hate me, but please give me time to explain." She
fixated on it for five minutes before finally pressing *send*. Jessica put the
phone down quickly and placed her head on the island. It felt cold and
smooth, a nice counter to her prickly, anger-filled world.

An hour later, she received a response: "Meet at noon—6142 W.
Rolling." Jessica started shaking at the thought. She believed that address was his mother's home and was unsure if she still lived there, but
the thought made her start to cry. Despite the horrific way she departed
from Paul, feelings of nostalgia about time spent together, especially in
the basement of that house, were too much to bear. Jessica lay on the
guest bed and cried hard, sobbing tears. She was coming home for the
first time in seventeen years.

Chapter 25

Jessica's wardrobe choices were black, black, and more black. Staring at the ink-like cloth, she started to feel like Johnny Cash, remembering a time long ago listening to his voice being belted out of speakers in Paul's home. Jessica decided on dark jeans and a fitted, black pinstriped short-sleeved shirt she wore to the wake, grabbing a thin silver belt from Paulina's bag to balance the outfit. She felt it important to make the appearance that she was put together, despite how she truly felt inside. Purposefully, Jessica let the natural waves in her hair come out and only put on a little makeup. She pulled out a pair of heels, but then decided she did not want to be taller than Paul, so she traded them in for a lower pair.

Paul's childhood home was two minutes from her mother's. As Jessica rolled to a stop, she noticed the outside had been landscaped and well maintained. The bushes under the window were trimmed and the spring flowers in bloom intertwined with a garden that flourished in the summer. The grass was thick and green, edged to perfection.

Jessica made her way up the flawless concrete stairs but before she rang the bell, the inside door opened. Paul, looking tired and gray, pushed open the screen door with one arm and gave her a slight "hi" as she apprehensively smiled and stepped inside. Jessica was stunned at how clean and modern the living room looked. Before she could comment on how impressed she was on the changes that were made, Paul closed the doors.

"We can talk up here or in the basement. No one's home, so I thought this would be the best place."

Jessica could not help but notice Paul's well-defined body. His tight-fitting tee showed toned arm muscles and that he had a six-pack despite being in his thirties. And his eyes held the same pristine blue pond she swam in long ago, although right now they looked a bit on the bloodshot side.

"It doesn't matter," Jessica said quietly.

"I want to apologize for swearing at you yesterday. I was drunk, but I never should've made it seem like I was gonna hurt you."

"No, I understand . . . about the angry drunk part."

"Did you think I was gonna hurt you? My friends restrained me because they thought I was gonna go after you."

Jessica looked at him deeply and intently. "I didn't think you'd hit me, but you did scare me a little."

Paul nodded. "Well," he said, looking away, "I would never put a hand on you or any other woman." As he finished, he looked back at her. "I would think you'd remember that about me."

Jessica wanted to cry, but she held on tight inside, changing the subject about who still lived there. Paul's mother still resided in the home and an occasional younger brother. It appeared Paul was the only brother to make something of himself. Jessica and Paul found their way to a white leather couch and sat down on opposite ends. Paul's mom inherited the bar she worked at, and it was doing great business. She was dating a "nice" guy and cleaned up her life. Danny, Marcus, and Brian all did time—mostly drug possession and selling, nothing violent. All his siblings had children but only one was married.

"Brian fared the best. I think because his dad tried to be in his life. When he got out of jail, he came back around, like he promised."

"So Brian's married?"

"Yeah, besides me," Paul stated. "He's trying to be a dad."

Jessica couldn't help but notice the family portrait of Paul, his wife, and kids on a bookshelf in the living room. Paul followed Jessica's stare and asked if she would like to see it. Before Jessica could respond, Paul was up and removing the picture from the bookshelf. He looked at it with a big smile and sat back down, not passing it off to Jessica but turned it so she could look at the picture from afar. Jessica's breath hitched when noticing how much his children resembled Paulina: deep blue eyes, auburn hair, and rosy cheeks. She inhaled to get her breathing on track, taking notice that his wife looked a lot like a girl they went to high school with.

"This is Lexi, she's thirteen, Garret's eleven, and Conner is six," Paul said proudly, "and my wife, Alicia, you may remember her from high school."

"Didn't she date Danny?" Jessica asked as her heart started to ache again.

"Yeah, but he didn't know how to treat a girl, and you were gone, so we found each other." He looked away for a minute and then back again. "Quite frankly she took the sting away from you leaving."

Tears filled Jessica's eyes. "I never left because I wanted to." Jessica put her head down and a small tear fell. "When my parents found out I was pregnant, well, actually the night my father found out, they sent me away. My mother packed my bags and I was put in the car headed to my Aunt Lodi's in Michigan. I was led to believe my father killed you," she said with a slight grin. "I think my father believed that he was saving me, keeping me safe from your bad habits. I also think he was embarrassed, his only daughter pregnant at sixteen, under his watch. He couldn't handle that." Jessica looked to see how Paul was reacting but couldn't read his face. They sat in silence for a few minutes until Paul, who started shaking his head slightly, spoke.

"Your dad saved me."

"What?" Jessica said in disbelief.

"Your dad saved me," Paul said, meeting her eyes. "After you left, I ran myself into the ground. I took off with Gary and all we did was get drunk and high. When I came back a few months later, I still got drunk and high, but I started selling coke and fighting. One night, guys in an unmarked picked me up. I had marijuana and coke on me. I thought they were gonna bust me but they drove me around instead. They took me on patrol and talked to me. They did this to me for months: busting me, taking me on patrol, and talking to me. Finally I gave in. I remember the night: it was windy and raining. I could not stop looking at the rain; it felt like I was getting baptized. It was at that moment that I decided I needed to get my life in order. When they dropped me off in front of the house, I stood on the grass in the rain with my arms out and hands up. I looked up at that stormy sky and closed my eyes. I let the rain wash away everything that I had done bad. I even let it wash away you." Jessica was crying softly as she pulled Kleenex from her purse to dab her eyes and nose.

"One of those 'cops' was your dad." Paul paused for a moment. "Your dad could've sent me to jail, but instead he showed me that I could be a man, that I could have a legal career. I'm a cop because of your dad. Your dad thought he was protecting you by sending you away. He didn't know any better. Just like my dad, or Marcus's, or Danny's. They knew they weren't responsible men; no way could they teach us how to be one, so they left for our sake. They gave us the only selfless gift they could."

Jessica soaked in his words. "Are you saying you agree with my father sending me away?"

"You see my daughter Lexi?" Paul pointed to her in the picture. "I have *so* much love and protective feelings for her. If she told me she was pregnant at sixteen and I found out the shithead was selling drugs, had no dad in his life, and didn't know how to be a man, I think I may have done the same thing."

"You make it sound as if you were a loser, someone who belonged in jail."

"Back then I wasn't on the straight and narrow. Don't you remember that about me?"

"I know we were opposites with drugs and stuff, but not in connection. You opened me up. I lost my virginity to you. Do you think I would do that with a loser?"

Jessica felt Paul look at her with love for the first time since they saw each other again. "No. I know you didn't think I was a loser, but *I* didn't think I was good enough to be with you. Being with you made me feel like I *could* be someone, you know, like someone normal. You were the healthiest thing in my life, but your dad gave me something that I craved—a role model. He mentored me without me really knowing why. I always wanted to ask him but I rarely saw him after that. Plus, I had no idea he was your dad. I knew him as Big Jim. Eddie Ripp told me he died but didn't tell me his last name. I figured it out after the funeral."

Jessica paused for a few moments, letting every word become clearer in her head. "So my father, Big Jim, saved you because he mentored you and you're grateful." Jessica gauged her words carefully. "I wish I could be that insightful, but I'm full of anger and shame. I believed you were dead, by the hands of my own father. All these years I have lived my life with your death blanketing every moment. What you're telling me, my father 'saving you,' that's great, but he didn't save me from a life of sadness. He made me believe he killed you."

Jessica and Paul were locked in a stare until Jessica spoke again. "I was wrong to believe you were dead, and even more terrible for not making an effort to come back to Chicago and search for you. And right now I'm so afraid you hate me." Jessica could not hold down the sob. Paul moved in closer, his family picture sliding to the floor. He clasped her hand. "I don't hate you. I could never hate you." He looked at her deeply. "You were my first love, and truthfully, a piece of my heart is still yours." Jessica looked at those eyes, those eyes that drove her crazy at fifteen and were still making her heart jump at thirty-four. Before she could soak in the moment, Paul moved in closer and kissed her softly on the lips. They were wet with tears. When Jessica tasted the saltiness, it baited her desire of wanting him completely again. Paul's lips spoke to her, telling her he needed to take away her pain, to love her in the innocent way he did years ago, when they were young and naïve. Paul took her face gently into his hands. "You are still so beautiful," he sang softly. He leaned in again but this time the kiss was longer. Jessica's heart decided to take her head for a ride. She was sixteen, in Paul's basement, making love to the only boy she ever felt true love for.

Chapter 26

Jessica's and Paul's naked bodies were intertwined when she woke up. She was surprised that she had fallen asleep after they made love. Her body and mind felt light and free, like she was given a reprieve from a life sentence. Looking at Paul's beautiful still face, Jessica smiled, knowing he still loved her and could forgive the secret she unknowingly kept from him all those years. Smelling his freshly showered skin pressed against hers sent pangs of lust throughout her body. She had not felt that way since she was in his arms in high school. Jessica delicately nestled into his body, craving his heat, wanting to penetrate his skin. All she could think about was being with Paul, making love to him again and again, eating take-out naked, and giving each other loving looks as if they were newlyweds on their honeymoon. This thought made beams of light extend from every pore in her body.

The chimes of the clock in the basement rang four times, jerking her back to reality. She needed to return to her mother's house immediately, knowing everyone would be waiting for her to eat dinner. Her head felt burdened, realizing the load of questions that would be knocked into her by Paulina, in public, and Aunt Lodi in private, as to her whereabouts since last night. She didn't feel strong enough to pull off the lie she would now have to make up. And the other looming reality that she was unable to block out: that she lived in Michigan with a man named Matt, and that he was a good and loyal man and this would break his heart. Jessica started to ache over a new shade of shame. *How could I do this to him? How could I betray him like this?* The relief and excitement she felt only minutes ago briskly departed. Jessica lifted Paul's arm and leg off of her. He twitched a little but remained in the same spot. She grabbed her clothing from the far wall it was tossed toward and put it on hastily.

The honeymoon was over.

Jessica held onto her belt and didn't put her shoes on thinking it would be better to tiptoe out the door, as if she'd never been there. Taking one last glance at Paul, Jessica imaged being wrapped up to his naked body and hearing him tell her how beautiful she was again, touching her in all the right places, and kissing her gently all over her body. Tears came to her eyes as she opened the front door and stepped onto the porch, holding her shoes, purse, and belt. After carefully closing the door, she turned to climb down the steps and there he was. She thought her guilty mind was playing a trick on her so she shook her head, only to see the same image. He was parked directly behind her truck. He looked at her for a few seconds then turned away. *This is not happening, this is not happening,* was all Jessica could think. Her body started to tremble and needles poked through her skin. As she walked down the steps, she felt her legs about to give way so she grabbed onto the railing for support, finally making it to the bottom. Jessica walked towards his truck, her hands shaking and breathing labored.

"What are you doing . . . ?"

"What are *you* doing?" Matt asked. His face was tense. "Why are you carrying your shoes and belt?"

"Um." Jessica looked at the items as if they held the answer Matt was looking for. As she continued to go through a Rolodex of lies in her head, she heard a screen door squeak open. There, standing half-naked, was Paul. His bottom half was wrapped in a small blanket from the couch. Jessica's eyes got big. Matt's eyes, however, got small. He looked

Paul's way and then back at Jessica. The look of tension was gone, and his face became flushed as his eyes started to cloud up. He shook his head slowly, as if he also could not believe this was happening.

"Matt," Jessica whispered, tears rushing down her face. She tried to reach into the cab of his truck to touch his shoulder but he waved her off. He started the engine and sped away, making a loud screeching noise. Jessica's water-streaked face looked over as Paul stood on the stairs. He looked confused but stayed on the porch. Despite a strong instinct to run to him for comfort, she turned, got into her truck, and drove off slowly toward her mother's house, leaving Paul standing on the front porch to piece together what just went down.

"Where have you been?" Paulina and her mother asked at the same time in the same tone.

Jessica cringed at their voices. "I met with some old friends."

"What friends? Marilee called here twice," her mother said.

Jessica opened her mouth to respond, but Aunt Lodi jumped in. "Oh, who cares who she met up with. I'm starved. Let's care about a mouth-watering piece of steak."

"What about Matt?" Paulina asked.

Jessica froze upon hearing his name.

"Did he meet up with you?"

Jessica started to feel nauseous. "Meet up with me?"

"Yeah. When he got off the expressway, he saw your truck parked on the side. I was talking to him on his cell and he asked who you were visiting, but I didn't know. He said he was gonna surprise you."

"No, I didn't see him," Jessica said quickly, trying to select lies she could support. "I'll call and see where he's at."

Jessica asked for ten minutes so she could call Matt and use the washroom. As she took a long look in the mirror, she was not surprised by the red-rimmed eyes or the puffy face. An attempt was made to cover up the pain by placing a cold washcloth on her face. However this only caused her to hyperventilate. She finally settled on cover-up and mascara.

Jessica lied, saying she spoke to Matt and he had to get back to the farm; there was a problem with some of the horses. He was sorry and sends his regrets. Aunt Lodi was the only one who gave her a disbelieving look.

They ate dinner at a neighborhood steak house, and the talk mingled around gentle topics because the rawness in everyone was palpable. Jessica ordered a glass of red wine, thinking it would relax the shoulder muscles that now radiated pain up to her earlobes. Jason put his arm on the back of Jessica's chair and pulled closer to her.

"Are you all right? I've never seen you drink before."

Jessica pressed her head slightly against his. "Just need to relax."

The wine was winding around Jessica, making her feel blotted out. She removed herself from all conversation and continued taking big sips of the second glass she ordered. Aunt Lodi gave her a look, but Jessica smiled confidently, making herself appear perfectly in control.

As she threw up the third glass in the stall of the steak house bathroom, Jessica heard a dizzy voice call her a whore and a liar. Of course she would hurt Matt, why would she think otherwise? She hated herself. Hated the fear that chained her to the UP, hated the belief that love and death were one, hated being thirty-four and still so shortsighted.

"Jessica, are you in there?" Aunt Lodi's voice whispered in front of the stall door.

Jessica placed her hands on the sides of the cold metal walls and pulled her head upward. "Yes. I just need a few."

After a minute, Aunt Lodi punched her hand under the door with wet and dry paper towels. Jessica took them without words and concentrated on the shuffle of Aunt Lodi's feet exiting the bathroom.

It took every piece of self-control to keep Jessica from throwing up on the car ride home. Jason held her hand as they made their way up the back steps and in through the patio doors. Her mother gave Jessica a grim look after she turned on the kitchen lights and told her she needed to go to bed.

Jessica turned on her heels with Jason in tow. "Really? Go to bed? Are you trying to cast me away again?"

Her mother's face looked weary. "I can see you need some sleep."

"Yeah, like seventeen years."

Jessica caught sight of Paulina's head jerking up and stopped. This was not the time or place for such exposure.

"Jason, could you help . . . ?"

"Yep, thinking the same thing," Jason said, interrupting Aunt Lodi.

Jason led Jessica upstairs to the guest room but not before Jessica purposefully halted, hanging onto the doorframe of her old bedroom.

"A door. Look, Jason, a door." Jessica opened and closed it over and over as Jason and eventually Paulina looked on. "You're so lucky to have a door," Jessica said to Paulina.

"Come on, crazy lady," Jason said, playfully prying Jessica away from the doorframe and guiding her toward the guest room. Jessica tumbled on top of the guest bed, and Jason pulled the comforter around her sprawling body.

"Thank you," she whispered, eyes closed, head starting to spin.

Around three in the morning, Jessica woke up with the Sahara

Desert in her mouth. She gingerly pushed off the bed and steadied herself before hobbling to the washroom. Feeling completely confined by her clothing, she tore off the garments she whored herself out in and started the shower, opening her mouth wide as water filled up and spilled out. Jessica put her arms out like Paul told her he did when he was on the front lawn of his home, letting the rain wash away her memory. Jessica lifted her face to take the brunt of the shower jet. After an hour, she finally felt clean. She brushed her teeth, gargled with mouthwash, than wrapped her body in a plush white robe. As the birds welcomed the morning sun, Jessica lit the fire pit in the backyard and burned the clothing she had worn, including the shoes and belt.

Jessica breathed in the morning air that mingled with smoke. *Enough,* she thought to herself. *Enough of screwing up my life and the men I love.* Jessica had spent much of her adult life trying to figure out what she needed—safety, to be a loving mom, and forgiveness—but did not question the other side of the coin: what did *she* really want?

Paul was married to Alicia, and they had children together. Jessica did not want his family to break apart because of their choice to make love. She could not bear the thought of living with another unintended consequence. Paul could not be a part of her life because she loved Matt. Matt and the life they created together was where she was supposed to be. Where she wanted to be. It was home.

For the first time in her life, Jessica felt that she was in control of her fate. She would navigate the rough and troubled waters like a wise captain, not a seasick mate. Jessica folded her hands and closed her eyes, thanking God for the blessing he had bestowed upon her: insight.

After Jessica made sure the fire was a smolder, she turned back toward the house and saw her mother standing on the deck, wearing her makeup and outfit for the day.

A surge of anxiousness overcame Jessica, but she moved it aside, ready to conquer without regret.

"I needed to do some cleansing," Jessica said before her mother had a chance to speak.

"Seventeen years' worth?" her mother stated rather than asked.

Their eyes met and after a few seconds, her mother looked past her.

"Did you put the fire out?"

Jessica continued to stare at her mother. "Yes."

Her mother stood like a wax figure and then finally whispered, "Thank you," and turned to enter the house.

Jessica decided to send Paul a text asking to meet today. As she lay underneath the covers almost asleep, her phone vibrated.

"Can we meet in Ponybrook? A diner called Pop's . . . 11:00 a.m.?"

It had been a long time, but Jessica remembered that Ponybrook was a rural town about fifty miles from the city. Her father belonged to a gun club there.

She texted "yes" then drifted off into sound slumber.

Around eight o'clock, Jessica got out of bed to start her day. After taking another shower and lathering nourishing lotion on her body, she proceeded to the kitchen to delight in a homemade breakfast.

"Boy, you're awfully happy this morning," Jason commented.

Paulina started laughing. "I guess it's because I have a door."

Jessica smiled with the knowledge that the chains that bound her for so long had finally broken off.

After breakfast, in the basement bedroom, Jessica delivered the news to Aunt Lodi about what she and Paul did, and that Matt also knew. Aunt Lodi was sitting cross-legged on the bed and became very still before she spoke.

"I'm not sure what hurts more, thinking about how Matt is taking this or what's going to happen to Paulina. You have definitively affected the only person she calls 'Dad.'"

Shame was knocking on Jessica's door again, but she would not let it enter. "I love Matt. You have to believe me. I fell into the past but I won't make that mistake again. I'm meeting with Paul in a few hours to find out what he wants to do about Paulina."

Aunt Lodi looked at her deeply, and Jessica felt raw with Aunt Lodi's eyes set on her face. "I was right, all those years back—you really do have two loves."

Around midmorning, Paulina and Aunt Lodi packed up their vehicles to return to the UP, each eager to get back to a life they abruptly left. Jessica was desperate to do the same but knew she needed to write the ending on a novel called Paul.

Jessica texted Matt but got no response. She finally left a voice message begging him to not tell Paulina anything until they talked, expressing how much regret she had for her actions and beseeching a second chance. Then she called Marilee.

"I need a big favor. I'll tell you everything later. For right now, can you be my alibi?"

Before Jessica left for Ponybrook, Aunt Lodi took her aside and said she had spoken to Matt. Aunt Lodi explained that she was honest with Matt and told him that Paulina's father was alive, that he was the man standing on the porch steps. "Matt agreed to not disrupt Paulina's world until you guys figure out the next step."

"Did it sound like he hates me?" Jessica asked.

"Nope," Aunt Lodi said. "It's pain."

Chapter 27

As Jessica drove in silence to Ponybrook, she was relieved once the towering buildings and tightly packed dwellings passed in the rearview mirror; the city felt visually aggressive. The longer she traveled, her true and trusted companion recharged her senses; layers of brown and green grass, masses of budding trees, and tracts of farmland were an unexpected gift—one that boosted her desire for closure with Paul.

Jessica navigated to Pop's and pulled into the gravel parking lot that was filled with trucks that reflected a farming community, and before getting out of her vehicle, Jessica once again relied on prayer to give her the strength and courage to do the right thing. As she walked toward the diner, she spotted Paul sitting next to the window running from the floor to the ceiling. He also caught sight of her and gave an apprehensive smile.

Jessica made her way toward his table, saying, "Hi," as she slid into the booth across from him.

"Hey," Paul said, then paused for a moment. "I figured we shouldn't be alone again."

Despite her new confidence, Jessica started to blush.

"Plus I don't want to get spotted together. Alicia's upset you're back."

Jessica's eye widened. "You told her?"

"Yeah."

"Everything?"

"No. Only about your dad. And our kid. But not about the other," said Paul.

The silence barrier grew until a waitress asked if she'd like something. "Just an iced tea. Thanks."

Paul adjusted himself in his seat. "Jessica . . ."

"No, wait," she said. "Can I talk first?"

He nodded.

Jessica took a deep breath and blew it out slowly before she started. "Paul, you were my first love. And while I'll always carry a part of your love in my heart, most of my heart belongs to someone else now."

"Yeah, I think we met."

Jessica scrunched her face, feeling shameful again. "His name's Matt. We've been together many years. Truthfully, I'm unsure where we stand right now, but I'm going to do whatever it takes to get him back. And he's the only father Paulina knows."

"Paulina," Paul said with a small smile.

Jessica lifted her eyes to meet his.

"Is Matt a good dad?" Paul asked.

"Matt's the best dad." Jessica stopped herself from sharing all the ways Matt was the best, not wanting to hurt Paul more deeply.

They sat in silence while the waitress placed the iced tea with a straw on the table and then left.

"Does Paulina love him like a dad?"

"Yes. She loves him very much."

Paul stared into Jessica's eyes but had a look of intense thought.

"And what about you? Are you happy?"

Jessica wanted to pull away but could feel how important it was for her to be present in the moment.

"Yes, very much."

The waitress came back to refill Paul's coffee and asked if they needed anything else. Once she left, Paul looked back at Jessica.

"Remember when I told you about my dad and the other dads after him giving me a selfless gift?"

Jessica nodded, remembering how unsettling those words sounded to her.

"This hurts me, really bad, but I think me coming forward as her dad would bring a lot more pain to a lot more people than it's worth. I've worked too hard for too many years to destroy my marriage and my family."

Jessica could not believe what she was hearing; he was stepping aside so Paulina's world would not shake. Jessica reached out and touched Paul's hand. "Are you sure?"

Paul looked at her carefully and twisted his hand around so they were holding onto each other.

"Yeah. I think it's the right thing to do," he said, with tears building in his eyes. "But promise me, if she's in trouble—needs a blood transfusion or a kidney, promise you'll call me. I need to know you'll do that."

"Of course," Jessica said, exhaling and feeling extricated.

Jessica let her hand discover Paul's calluses, the sharp edges around his cuticles, even the silver wedding band with an inscription on the sides. "Is Alicia upset you have another child?"

"In a way. But not so much with me, more with you. She doesn't get the whole 'under your father's control.'" Paul rubbed the side of Jessica's thumb, tracing it the way he did in high school. "She's feeling nervous about you."

"Why?" Jessica asked.

"History and facts. If you had stayed, I would be married to you."

Jessica gave him a look, one that said hello and good-bye at the same time. She could feel tears coming from behind.

"Thank you, Paul," Jessica said, and then raked her fingertips along the palm of his hand until they fell from his fingers. As she collected her purse and got ready to yank herself out of the booth, Paul reached toward her.

"Jessica, I will always love you now and forever."

Jessica moved from the booth, not wanting to fall into his words, and wiped a tear from her eye. "Thank you for the gift," she said quickly and walked out of the diner.

Pulling herself into her truck, she paused a moment to look at Paul through the diner window. He was looking straight ahead then turned toward her fixed eyes. They shared one last flicker of love, and she drove away.

Jessica rolled down the windows of her truck to let the spring air carry away her sadness. Her heart was feeling pity for two lovers that were permanently divided seventeen years ago. No matter how much love they felt for each other, or the inward hell they lived through, they could not move forward together, so they needed to move forward apart.

When Jessica got closer to the city, she zipped up her windows and called Matt once again, leaving a message. "I am begging you to call me. Paulina is on her way home, and I need to talk to you. Please call me back."

Before pulling into her mother's driveway, Aunt Lodi called and said Matt had just called her. "Honey, I know this might be hard for you, but he doesn't want to speak to you right now."

Jessica felt sick to her stomach again.

"We talked it over and think we should tell Paulina I threw out my back with all the stress, and you're staying with me until I get better."

"Okay," Jessica said slowly. "So that explains why I'm not living at home."

"Matt packed up some of your belongings and drove it out to my place. He's not ready to see you yet."

After hanging up the phone, Jessica sat in her mother's driveway fishing for a way out. She would drive to Aunt Lodi's tomorrow and devise a plan to get Matt back. How she would accomplish this was still a blur, but knowing that Matt packed her belongings and shipped them to Aunt Lodi's felt like the banishment she experienced at the hands of her parents seventeen years earlier.

Jessica walked over to Marilee's home after she got off work. Marilee and Eddie both lived within walking distance of their parents' home. Jessica sat on the back deck underneath the shadow of arching trees, drinking iced tea and scrambling to tell Marilee all the sordid details of the last twenty-four hours before her family came home from work and school.

"So Paul said he would be married to you instead of Alicia if he knew you had his kid?"

"Yes. And there would always be a piece of him that loves me 'now and forever.'"

Marilee took a gulp of her Diet Coke. "Whoa, what did you say?"

Jessica closed her eyes for a second and took in the smells of the yard. She slowly opened them while blowing out the air from her lungs. "Many years back those words would have meant everything to me. But the only person I want to hear those words from now is Matt."

Marilee smiled lovingly. "Tell me about him."

"Oh look, there's that cute boy Matt. Remember him?" Aunt Lodi asked as Jessica pushed Paulina's stroller through the draft horse barn at the UP state fair. Jason, now ten, was gobbling cotton candy and pulling off little pieces for Paulina, who was now three. Jessica's return to the state fair had been Aunt Lodi's idea, trying to pry Jessica out of the beehive she hid herself in. Jessica was attending college, but had no social life to speak of because she rejected all invites from classmates. Eventually, their efforts faded away.

"Yes, I remember," Jessica whispered. "But don't say one word to him."

"It's good to see you again, Matt," Aunt Lodi said, ignoring Jessica's eyes.

Matt looked at them cautiously and then grinned. "The folks from Chicago."

As Aunt Lodi engaged him in conversation, Jessica found herself trying to hide but having nowhere to go. Paulina was starting to make a fuss about the lack of motion so Jessica picked her up and tried to distract her by looking at the beautiful horse, Moses. Jessica recalled their last encounter and felt drawn to him again.

"You can come on in and touch him," Matt said.

Jessica walked into the stall, quietly talking to Paulina so she would not become frightened by the horse's size. But truthfully, Paulina rarely withdrew from new experiences, which only reinforced how strong Paul's DNA was not only in her looks, but also in her personality.

Jessica could feel Matt's eyes on them. "Who's the cutie?"

"This is Paulina . . . my daughter," she said, trying not to sound defensive. Sometimes people would judge Jessica because of her teenage mother status.

Matt smiled at Paulina. "Well hello. You want to see Moses?"

Jessica watched Paulina size Matt up, and then she finally gave him a toothy grin and said yes. Jessica held her up to Moses so she could reach out and touch his body. Paulina stroked his shoulder blade for less than a minute and then started pounding her fists on him, yelling,

"Come on horsey, Go, Go, Go." Jessica pulled away and gently scolded while Matt laughed.

"I know," Aunt Lodi said, "feisty."

"Looks like she's more like Dad than Mom," Matt said.

Matt's accurate assessment caught Jessica by surprise, and she could not help but give him a small smile. Jessica took special care in how she interacted with men, never wanting their attention, never wanting to love another man again.

"Hey babe," said a blond girl who walked toward Matt with a welcoming smile. She looked like the same girl Jessica had remembered during their first meeting many years back.

Matt leaned over and gave her a kiss, pulling away slowly. Jessica started to place Paulina back into her stroller, but she started screeching and arching her back, making it impossible for Jessica to place her in easily. As Jessica wrestled with her, a swell of incompetence rushed through her but was quickly pushed back by Matt's voice.

"Now stop giving your mom trouble, little one," he said as he approached Paulina's stroller. Paulina stopped squirming to look up at him, and Jessica took advantage of the moment and quickly snapped the straps.

"Good girl. You just made your mom happy," Matt said and then looked at the blond girl, who was laughing at him.

"You are too much," she said, walking over and grabbing his hand.

Aunt Lodi thanked them and then asked when they were getting married. Jessica swung her head and looked at the girl's ring finger. On it was a thin gold band with a small round diamond.

"As soon as she graduates from veterinary school," Matt said. "In two years."

"Well congratulations, and veterinary school—how wonderful," Aunt Lodi said as Jessica gave a weak smile and started pushing Paulina away from all that happiness. It was just too hard to be around young love.

Jessica, Paulina, Aunt Lodi, and Jason continued to attend the state fair yearly, making it a point to visit with Moses and Matt, along with his wife, Anne. Matt and Anne were friendly greeters, making Jessica and everyone feel like extended family members. When Matt and Anne got married, Aunt Lodi gave them a small wedding gift and Jessica tried hard not to make her body feel like stone as Matt gave them each a hug. Matt and Anne were at the state fair one more time after that, then they vanished for two years. That second year Aunt Lodi inquired as to their whereabouts and they were told, by Matt's brother Seth, that Anne had cancer. Matt and Anne had moved to Minnesota to be closer to the Mayo Clinic where she was being treated.

Matt returned to the state fair, alone, when Jessica was twenty-five and Paulina eight. Aunt Lodi approached him as if he were an injured animal, and Jessica watched as tears built up in the corner of his eyes. Without even asking what had happened, Aunt Lodi said, "I'm so sorry, Matt," and reached for his hand. He took hold of it and nodded, looking from her face to the ground, over and over again, his other hand wiping away tears that fell softly from his eyes.

"She's in a better place. No more suffering," he repeated a few times.

Jessica tried not to look at Matt's face because she felt herself sliding back into a terrible undercurrent of sadness, one that she worked very hard in the last few years to swim away from. But his tears and the pain in his voice, his hunched over body, it all reminded Jessica of the grief she felt for Paul.

Before she could turn the valve to "off," tears streaked down Jessica's face. Matt looked up, let go of Aunt Lodi's hand, and walked toward her.

"You know this pain, don't you?" Matt said, looking deeply into her eyes.

Jessica looked up at him and, before she could stop herself, nodded and stepped closer where they quickly embraced each other in their sorrow.

It was Aunt Lodi who suggested they take a walk to clear away some of the air. It had become stagnant with pain.

Matt guided Jessica to a remote part of the fairgrounds, where RVs and campers were parked for the weeklong event. He led her to a small clearing past the RVs, under a few white pines, and they sat on a bed of soft needles. Matt shared the details of watching Anne battle the disease, how each new treatment was met with joy and hope, but with each failure came a piece of her life: first the hair, then the weight, then the light in her eyes. He sat next to Anne as she withered away, and he felt much of his own heart wither away too. Jessica shared that her one and only true love had died at the hands of her father. That she felt responsible for his death and was reminded of Paul every day because of Paulina. Matt's face turned from anguish to shock.

"Your own father killed the father of your daughter? How could that be?"

"My father's very powerful."

"Shouldn't you call the authorities?" Matt asked.

"No . . . my father is the authorities."

Matt continued to stare at her and Jessica was starting to feel like she was under a microscope, on a petri dish of insanity. She quickly asked Matt another question to change the topic of her nightmare back to his.

They talked for over an hour, and the sun was starting to fade past the horizon as a whisper of a breeze blew. In the distance, a man's voice came over the loudspeaker announcing the start of the demolition car derby in the grandstand, and the draft horse pull contest that would be starting in the horse arena in thirty minutes.

"Are you staying to watch?" Matt asked.

"Yes. I have Paulina hooked on it now. I think she's a groupie, like me."

Matt laughed for the first time since they spoke. "Groupie, huh? Now that's something I've never heard about in draft horse pulling." He slowly lifted himself off the ground, reaching his arm out so Jessica would have a steady hand to grab onto in order to pull herself up.

"Thank you," she said, and then bent over to wipe pine needles from her jeans.

"Thank you too, Jessica. I really needed someone else to talk to. My family and Anne's family are great, but they keep looking at me like I'm broken. I'm tired of being looked at like damaged property."

Jessica felt the same way although for her it was all internal. She gave him a nod, and they walked in comfortable silence until they reached the draft horse barn. Matt shared that he claimed Moses once he realized how much better care he took of him than his brother and confided that without Moses, he probably would not have a contending team.

At the end of the night, Jessica surprised herself with the excitement she felt because Matt's team won, even beating two of his older brothers.

"Aren't you going to say good-bye to Matt?" Aunt Lodi asked as they were making their way off the metal risers to leave the arena.

"No, we'll see him next year," Jessica said.

"But I want to say good-bye to Moses," Paulina said.

Jason looked at them and quirked his eye. "Man, you guys love horses. I just don't get it."

Jessica looked toward the back, which led to an enclosed dirt arena outside where many men had gathered their teams. Some talked and others loaded their horses onto stock trailers to drive back home. Jessica could see Matt, and who she believed were some of his brothers, and his father, who did not compete this year. They were talking with a group of overweight men, who wore caps on their heads and sleeveless shirts.

"Next year," Jessica said, and the four of them stepped out of the stuffy arena and into the cool night air.

Later that night, after saying good night to Paulina and Jason, Aunt Lodi mentioned she was surprised by Jessica's out of character response to Matt's grief.

"I don't know what came over me," Jessica said. "One minute I'm listening to him, the next I'm in his arms. My tears came up so fast that I couldn't control them."

"Controlling tears is not what you should be practicing anyway. How do you expect to heal when you're still smothering your feelings?"

Jessica had no answers for that. In fact, she was searching for an answer as to why she would allow herself to be in Matt's arms in the first place. She was also searching on how to erase the reality that it felt really calming.

When the state fair came around the following year, Jessica's plan was to avoid Matt, fearing her body would give away that she wanted to be closer to him than any man since Paul. That was a feeling and action she was not willing to take a risk on. But Aunt Lodi would not have it.

"I know what you're trying to do, and it's not going to work. I won't let you deny something that can bring you *and* Paulina some true happiness."

Matt was talking to a group of men when Jessica, Aunt Lodi, Paulina, and Jason walked up to his stall.

"Hey there," Matt said. "It's good to see all of you."

Everyone greeted Matt, but Jessica lost her ability to speak. She had planned on saying hello and making small talk, then walking away, but she felt a warmth flow through her veins and even a small knot form in her gut. Matt was likeable. In fact, Matt made her think about things that she had only reserved for Paul.

"Jessica," Matt said. "It's really good to see you again."

Jessica grinned with embarrassment and then said hello.

"You look great, Matt. I mean really, you have a spark of life in those eyes of yours again," Aunt Lodi remarked.

Matt thanked her and told them about his life now. That he had spent the last year throwing his time back into his farm and the horses, and partnered with a charity in Anne's honor.

"I have to move forward," Matt said. "Anne would want me to."

Jessica noticed that Matt sent those words towards where she was standing. As Jessica looked up, she became engaged in Matt's eyes, struggling to pull away even after Aunt Lodi suggested they take another walk.

"I'd like that. What about you, Jessica?" Matt asked.

Jessica hesitated and looked at Paulina, afraid that she would see how transparent her feelings were for Matt. Even though Paulina knew nothing about Paul, Jessica felt a sense of loyalty towards his memory because of Paulina.

"Go, Mom," Paulina said, while Jason gave a smirk that reminded her of when he would get into trouble by their mother for misbehaving when their father was gone. Jessica finally relented.

They walked and talked for two hours, and Jessica realized how much she missed the attention of a man. And Matt felt so strong to her. She loved his size and that he was in good shape but not like a weight lifter; his muscles were more natural because of his profession.

Matt took her for ice cream, and they sat on a picnic table eating while many balding men and a few chubby women stopped to chat with him.

"You're a popular guy," Jessica said while they caught a brief break from the steady stream of people.

"That's what you get when you've been in a small town your whole life. And I've been coming here since I was a baby. Many of those old timers knew me when I was holding a bottle."

Jessica found solace in that thought, and her body started to let its guard down. Her muscles, including her heart, relaxed and she felt, for a fleeting moment, carefree.

As they were walking back to the horse barn, Matt asked if he could call her sometime.

"I like your company. And you understand how I feel about everything, you know, with Anne."

Jessica was on uneven ground, scared to say yes but afraid to say no. Remembering Aunt Lodi's words, she finally decided to push herself to take a chance.

"Okay," she said with a tight smile.

When they returned to the barn, they exchanged information, Matt placing it directly into his phone.

Before Jessica left to join the others on the risers to watch the competition, Matt thanked her again for being such a good listener and added, with some redness on his ears, "You make me feel joyful again."

Matt called her two days later, and they talked on the phone for two hours, and a week after that, three. After spending two months talking, Matt finally asked Jessica on a date. Beads of perspiration gathered along her hairline, and she could not cool down the flames of heat that tore through her body after hearing those words.

"Uh," was the only response she could muster.

"I really like you. I think this is the most I've talked to anyone in my whole life."

Jessica laughed and started to feel the fire getting doused by comfort.

"All right, Matt. I think it would be good for me too," she finally said.

Matt picked her up on a Saturday evening and took her to dinner at Murphy's Pub. Jessica had never gone, even though most of her former college classmates hung out there. Matt's farm was in the opposite direction of the pub and Aunt Lodi's, but he insisted on picking Jessica up.

Jessica's room was strewn with clothes and shoes that had been tried on again and again. Looking at Aunt Lodi, Jessica finally said, "I don't think I can do this. Look at me, I'm a mess."

"You're just nervous, and that's to be expected. But you owe it to yourself to give his company a try. Come on," Aunt Lodi said, placing her hands on Jessica's shoulders and leading her away from the mirror and toward the bathroom. "Your clothes are perfect; now let's fix that hair of yours, maybe a little makeup, and off you go."

Matt, holding a fist of flowers, was met at the door by Paulina and Aunt Lodi.

"These are for you," he said, giving some to each of the girls.

"Thank you so much, Matt," Aunt Lodi gushed, and Paulina gave him a big smile and said this was the first time getting flowers from a boy.

"I think one day we'll have to scare the boys away from you," Matt said to Paulina, giving Aunt Lodi a quick wink.

Aunt Lodi opened her mouth to say something, but the sound of heels clicking on the wooden stairs made her turn her head. Jessica was dressed in dark jeans with a black cap sleeve top that had lace running through the overlay and her golden hair falling around her face in loose curls. Matt's mouth dropped open, and Jessica took some pride in that.

When she reached the bottom of the stairs, she looked at Matt, whose mouth was still hanging open, and gave a cautious grin. Aunt Lodi finally broke the silence. "Well, don't you look gorgeous? Doesn't she, Matt?"

"Yes, ma'am," he finally said.

After a few more seconds of heavy silence, Matt shook his head. "I'm so sorry to be just standing here staring at you, but, well, you look so beautiful."

Jessica's cheeks colored as she said, "Thanks."

"Usually I see you at the fair and you don't look like this . . . not that 'this' is a bad thing, I mean . . . well . . ."

"I think it's time for you guys to get going," Aunt Lodi said as she pushed them both toward the door. "Now don't worry about the time. Paulina and I will be just fine. You two go and have yourselves a *great* night."

And Jessica did have a great night. Matt was easy to be around; he nourished her spirit because of his simple ways and he made her feel safe.

They walked the marina after dinner, even though it was dark and slightly chilly. Jessica was thankful she had brought a sweater, and Matt helped her put it on. While they walked, Jessica found herself being drawn toward his body, wanting her shoulder to push up against his, aching for some warmth.

"Can I hold your hand?" Matt asked after they had been walking for a few minutes.

Jessica looked up at his face, at those brown eyes that looked inviting in the light from the lamp above, and nodded yes.

This was the first time she had willingly placed her hand in another man's since Paul. There was an ache in her chest and her gut, but the touch felt liberating because it brought an instant rush of happiness. Happiness that only male companionship could bring, that only Matt could bring.

After dating a year, Matt asked for her and Paulina to move in with him. Jessica was thankful he did not ask for marriage, even though he had peppered her with questions about what her father's reaction would be to their relationship. Jessica skated around the edges, finally admitting that her father knew nothing about him yet.

"Why?" Matt asked.

"I don't talk to him like that. You know, about us. I use distractions in my relationship with him, specifically Paulina."

After a few minutes of silence, Matt finally spoke. "Are you sure that he killed Paul?"

"If you're asking if I saw a dead body? No. But I don't need a body to know, in my heart, what was done."

"Jessica, I hope you don't take this the wrong way, but I'm not sure I want to meet your dad."

Jessica nodded and savored in the truth. "Aunt Lodi's going to tell him about you and about us moving in together. Coming from her is our safest bet."

Matt's eye widened. "Can you tell me when, so I can arm myself, you know, have my shotgun next to the bed?"

Jessica smirked, but behind it were wounds that all too often seeped out from under the flimsy bandages she placed on herself. After a few minutes, Matt squeezed her hand and Jessica returned the pressure.

"I'm sorry about Paul. I know how much you loved him."

Jessica lifted her eyes. "And I'm sorry about Anne. You also lost your love."

Matt smiled gently and then wrapped his other hand around their hands.

"I think Paul and Anne are together looking down on us with smiles." Then he drew their wrapped hands toward his mouth and placed a tender kiss on them.

"Jess, he sounds wonderful," Marilee said after staying silent for well over fifteen minutes.

Jessica grinned, trying not to let the image of Matt outside of Paul's home ravage her.

"You know, I made a lot of mistakes, but I really regret not telling you about what Paul and I were doing in high school. Sometimes I think if I had told you, things wouldn't have gone as far as they did with him."

"You were lonely, and in love. I don't blame you one bit. And your parents' shipping you off was not your fault."

A ripple of gratitude ran through Jessica. "After all these years of not seeing each other, you still are the best friend I've ever had."

Marilee held up her can of Diet Coke. "Cheers, my BFF, to new beginnings together."

They clinked their drinks, and Jessica asked how to get Matt back. Marilee gave her ideas, even grabbing her laptop and searching "how to reclaim your man," but in the end, Jessica decided it would occur to her and her alone, when the time was right.

The girls made plans for Marilee to visit Jessica the following week, which was her spring break from school. The hugs were relentless, but Jessica finally pulled away, ready to return to her mother's home.

On her walk back, Jessica looked up at the maple, elm, and white oak trees that had smiled upon her when she was birthed from her insulated youth freshman year. In the quiet of the late afternoon, Jessica stepped onto the front porch of the house she grew up in, with the sun lowering itself behind, and felt home.

Chapter 28

Saying good-bye to her mother was harder than Jessica envisioned. It always left a hollow feeling when Jason said good-bye after a visit to the UP, but her mother did not cause that type of reaction. Jessica had filled her mommy void with love from Aunt Lodi and Matt's family, and had accepted the fact that her mother's family ethos reflected an unspoken boundary that kept everyone at a distance.

Her mother was sitting on the wicker love seat on the front porch as Jessica placed her duffel bag into her truck. She walked toward her mother, smoothing her hand over the white paint on the wooden railing.

"You know, this was the first time I've been back since I was sent to Aunt Lodi's."

"I know," her mother stated matter-of-factly. "You've been missed."

After many minutes of silence, Jessica spoke up. "I always wondered about that picture by your nightstand, the one in a silver frame."

"What have you wondered?"

"Who's in the picture?"

"My father is holding me on my baptism, and his mother took the picture."

"Oh. Where's your mother?"

"She died giving birth to me," her mother said and then looked out onto the street at a passing car.

"I'm sorry," said Jessica, feeling her eyes start to tear.

Her mother shrugged, and Jessica detected a slight remove from the conversation.

"Who raised you then?" Jessica asked.

Her mother kept her eyes on the street. "My grandmother. Sometimes my father, but he was much too busy working. I'm afraid I didn't have very good mothering."

She fixed her eyes sternly on Jessica. "My grandmother never wanted my father to marry my mother and resented my presence. Of course, I'm reading into it, but that's how I saw it."

Jessica felt empathy, imagining her mother as a baby and toddler not getting the love and affection she needed to thrive.

"When I met your father, he was so strong and solid. I felt I didn't have to worry about a thing when he was around; he could provide me with what I needed."

"Love?" Jessica blurted.

"Yes, love. But in his way. Your father had been through a lot; we both had."

"What did Dad go through?"

Her mother's face lifted up and gestured toward Jessica's truck. "You have to go back to find that answer out. Talk to Lodi."

Damn, Jessica thought, *so close.* This was the first time her mother had expounded on the past, and Jessica was grateful for the long drive back so she could let the words and image fully sink in. Certain events could never be unstitched from her heart, but Jessica felt moved to soften their mother-daughter relationship, knowing how limited her mother's parental qualities were because of the way she was raised. Jessica decided, in an absurd way, to be a loving parent toward her mother's limited qualities.

Jessica loped up the steps and, to her mother's surprise, bent down to fully embrace her. After a few uncomfortable seconds, her mother pulled her arm around Jessica's waist and patted it.

"I hope you'll be coming back to this home more often," she said. Jessica released her mother and smiled. "That would be nice."

The drive to the UP was filled with new songs that engulfed Jessica's truck. She visualized how she could earn Matt's trust back by creating scenes in her mind of the words, the looks, and the touch they would exchange in order to share a life together again. Her insides were like high beams with a blazing focus on her future; Matt had to be in it.

After five hours on the road, Jessica pulled into the cheese store Matt loved on the outskirts of town. It was a small building that was painted yellow with a huge wooden slab of holey cheese on the roof. Matt loved the mustard dips for pretzels and, of course, the beef sticks and cheese curds. He would munch on them in front of the television, especially when the Green Bay Packers' season was in full swing. The act of purchasing the items sent pangs of loneliness through Jessica's heart, and the only thoughts that rolled through her mind when she paid the cashier were, *please let me be forgiven.*

Aunt Lodi's grass and gravel driveway felt extra rough as she rolled over it and parked. Jessica felt a flash of contentment seeing Aunt Lodi step onto the front porch to greet her with hugs and kisses, but Aunt Lodi's face, a mix of sympathy and disappointment, slammed the situation back into focus.

Once Jessica got settled into her former bedroom, unpacking all the items Matt brought over, she searched through the suitcase for any note, any evidence that Matt still loved her. All she found was a tarnished penny and a tiny seashell. The last time the suitcase had been used was when she, Matt, and Paulina had toured a college campus by Lake Superior. They took a walk on the beach and collected a few shells to bring back home.

Jessica placed the shell and penny on the dresser and climbed on top of the bed, setting her eyes on the objects as if they held the answer to her woes.

The rest of the night, she pumped Aunt Lodi for information about Matt.

"How did he look when he dropped off the suitcase? Did he sound mad? Did he say anything specific?"

"For Christ's sake, Jessica, I already told you everything I may have seen, thought I saw, and what I saw."

"Sorry. I'm just trying to figure this out."

"I know," Aunt Lodi said, then reached for her hand from across the dinner table. "He said when he's ready to talk he'll call you. It's your turn for patience."

Jessica texted Paulina that night, being extra cautious that nothing in her text would bring about suspicion. Paulina texted back that she was worried Matt was sick because he was not himself. Jessica swallowed hard and agreed he may have a cold but to not worry about it because everything will be fine. Paulina ended the text asking when Jessica was coming home; maybe her return would help Matt feel better.

During the next couple of days, Jessica purposefully filled her daytime hours with so much activity that at night she would crash into bed, hoping to sleep through without self-torment. It didn't work. Her brain and body would move back and forth wrestling as if she were in the ring with two guys called guilt and shame. She returned to her normal work schedule, jumping at the chance for overtime, begging Jean to give her one of her shifts, just so she would not have to think.

Not wanting to fall into a pattern of secrecy, Jessica had a heart-to-heart with Jean the day after her return to the UP.

"Oh my," Jean said after Jessica shared her story. "Well, you sure know how to make life interesting."

Jessica tried to smile, but it turned into a frown. "Do you believe I love Matt and the life we created?"

"Yes. Yes, I do." Jean looked down at her folded hands set in front of her on the kitchen table. "I suppose you needed to know where you belonged. Although, I would not have taken it quite so far."

Jessica nodded in agreement. "Thanks for listening and not hating me."

"Oh sure," Jean said. "I may not agree with what you did, but I am your friend."

After a wet embrace, Jean reached over for some Kleenex on the counter. "Now how are we going to get Matt back?"

Jessica was unsure how to proceed forward, so Jean suggested a heartfelt letter, maybe with a song attached.

Every night in bed, Jessica searched for a song that expressed the lyrical unity she could not convey in person. After another session of interrupted sleep, Jessica decided one song would not express her feelings properly; she would gather many. Grabbing her laptop off the floor, she started searching for love songs. *This is it. This is the song,* Jessica announced one after another in the darkness of her bedroom as she continuously pressed the repeat button, listening to the songs with her eyes closed, wrapped under the warmth of her covers until the alarm went off.

During breakfast, with Aunt Lodi still in heavy sleep, Jessica sketched out a rough draft of a letter with the love songs from last night singing the overture. The songs made her feel quite empty at times, but Jessica partnered with the lyrics and her thoughts flowed onto the paper beneath her hand.

At work that day, Jessica thought she saw Matt's truck sitting idle in the parking lot of the pharmacy. Jessica's heart banged with hope and her netted mind started to untangle, but as she approached the door to go outside, the truck pulled away.

Later that night Paulina made an unexpected visit to Aunt Lodi's. As soon as she was spotted pulling into the driveway, they ran to take their places in the makeshift hospital ward. Aunt Lodi was in bed with rotations of ice and heat packs while Jessica tended to her needs.

They sat around Aunt Lodi's bed, gobbling up apple slices and laughing about old stories. Paulina begged Jessica to find her old blankie in Aunt Lodi's storage closet.

"That thing was a choking hazard," Aunt Lodi recalled. "Remember how torn up it was? We found it had wrapped around your neck one night, and we said 'That's it for blankie.'"

"I loved blankie," Paulina announced. "And you guys tried to replace it with that teddy bear, but I wouldn't have it."

"Yeah, remember when Matt and I were dating and he babysat Paulina one night?" asked Jessica.

"That's right. After he left, we looked in on you and you had it wrapped around your body," Aunt Lodi said.

Jessica reached over and poked at Paulina to tickle her in the stomach. "You made him believe that blankie was something you slept with every night, even though it was in a box in the storage closet."

The girls laughed and Aunt Lodi pretended that laughing hurt but still did it anyway. After a few minutes of Paulina begging, Jessica finally got up to get a flashlight and search the storage closet for blankie. Jessica could hear Aunt Lodi and Paulina laughing from the bedroom about some other stunt Paulina pulled on Matt. As Jessica read the scribble of writing on the boxes, she lifted her eyes to one in the very corner of the top shelf. It was not like the others; it had a weathered, older look to it. Jessica stood on her tiptoes and tapped it with an out-reached finger. It was heavy and slipped back a little. Jessica decided to pull a stool from the bathroom so she could reach it, even though she had glanced at another box with the words Paulina's Blankie on it.

On the stool, Jessica was now eye level with the box.

"Did you find it yet?" yelled Paulina from the bedroom. "I need my blankie."

"Almost," Jessica yelled back.

Holding the flashlight in her left hand, she dusted the top of the box with her right one and aimed light at the writing on the lid. "From Jim" was written in black faded ink. Jessica started to quiver, almost afraid she may not want to uncover the contents of the box. Her mind was a flurry of the past her father made her believe—maybe old bones of Ermaline and Walker. Jessica lifted the lid slightly and shined the light in. The box contained Mace, pepper spray, old sticks that had been whittled into daggers, even a rustic butter knife. Jessica lowered the lid quickly upon hearing footsteps and jumped off the stool just as Paulina stepped into the storage room. Jessica grabbed and with one motion threw the box with "Blankie" written on it at Paulina.

"Hey, what are you trying to do, take my head off?"

"Sorry. You scared me," Jessica said, out of breath.

Paulina stared at her for a second and then turned her attention back to the memories of her youth.

In bed that night, waiting until Aunt Lodi was snoring, Jessica found herself excavating the contents of the old box. She had sneaked into the closet, seized the box, and brought it to her bedroom, locking the door behind.

After laying a bath towel on her bed, she proceeded to remove the weapons, one by one, placing them in the order for which she believed they were given. The Mace and pepper spray were easy because of the dates on the canister; the sticks were another matter. While studying one after another Jessica came to the conclusion, as with anyone who practiced a skill, her father became more proficient at making the tips of his daggers and knives pointy, so that some were quite dangerous if jammed into the right fleshy part on the body. She placed the hand-made weapons in order of proficiency. The older pieces were quite battle scarred, uneven and notched out in some spots, and hardly had the ability to do harm. But ones made with acquired skill were so intricately carved that on one she believed her father's initials were etched into the hind-quarters of a bear on the handle, the blade smooth and long. Jessica studied it with her eyes and hands, turning it over and over, holding it to feel the power of its lethality and to hypothesize why it was made.

Chapter 29

In the morning, Jessica drove into town to go to the post office and send Matt's letter and CD with the love songs burned on it. She knew Paulina would never see it because she ignored the mail unless she thought something was coming for her.

After stopping at a local coffee shop, Jessica drove to her favorite spot on the marina to watch the water wrinkle against the sand. Dangling her legs over the wooden slabs, she rested her head on the tall post that held the pier in place. The sun was milling around the horizon with a crisp breeze whisking through Jessica's semi-wet hair. The word she attached to herself was melancholy. Sometimes she and Matt would come to this spot with sandwiches in hand and have a lunch date, usually on a day Paulina was in school. Matt would surprise her at work, and they would take her break on the pier. Jessica's memories whirled around their moments together but the wood dagger in her hand from last night crept into her thoughts. Now that the lid was lifted off the box, the knives, daggers, and Mace were not going to slip away so casually. Jessica started thinking about why her father made those and gifted them to Aunt Lodi. In fact, why did he give her gifts that only had to do with safety and protection?

After sipping on coffee, Jessica came to the conclusion that she would have to ask Aunt Lodi straight out. Hadn't her mother said to talk to Aunt Lodi about her father's past anyway? Jessica stared at the seagulls basking in the morning warmth on the beach, living on the margins of nature, wishing her life could be that still and calm. But it wasn't, and as much as she wanted to live that way, Jessica knew she had to unearth the entire truth. She decided to drive back and unveil the cache of weapons to Aunt Lodi, hoping it would finally bring answers to her father's past.

When Jessica returned, Aunt Lodi was in the back of the house, tending to her vegetable garden.

"Good morning. You were up and out early today," Aunt Lodi said, shading the sun from her eyes as she knelt on her rubber mat.

"I mailed the letter to Matt."

"Well, that's good. I guess all we can do is keep praying on that."

"Yes," Jessica said, feeling distracted by how to start the conversation about the box. "Aunt Lodi."

"Uh-huh," she said, as she returned to the task in front of her.

Jessica milled around in her head for a few seconds, imaging the seagulls in their calmness. "I have to know something about Dad."

"Uh-huh," Aunt Lodi said, sounding like she was not paying full attention.

"I have to know why he would give you Mace and pepper spray and knives he carved from sticks."

Aunt Lodi's hands stopped moving, and she slowly pulled back onto her knees, turning to look at Jessica, not shading the sun anymore. "How do you know about that?"

"I found the box in the storage room. I looked through it last night."

Aunt Lodi stared at Jessica's face for a long moment.

"Dad's dead. Don't you think it's time I knew the truth?"

Aunt Lodi's face looked burdened, but she pulled her lips apart. "I'll tell you the truth. Jim may rest easier if you know."

Aunt Lodi told Jessica to give her a minute to change and she would meet her in the truck. They would have to take a road trip . . . to hell.

Jessica's nerves were jumping as she followed the directions Aunt Lodi dictated. At first, they drove on the highway north for about an hour, and then angled onto a county road for about another thirty minutes, finally turning on a very narrow path with overgrown bushes and weeds. The trees hovered over, blocking out much of the sunshine. Jessica rolled her window down slightly, taking in the banging sounds of wood hitting metal, and bugs in every form jumped or flew past as the truck crushed their homes.

"There. Over there." Aunt Lodi pointed to a burned-out trailer and a few yards away, a slim building that looked like an old outhouse.

Jessica pulled the truck over to what seemed like the lowest lying weeds and parked, finally looking over at Aunt Lodi. She was pale and said, "I feel sick to my stomach."

Jessica started feeling guilty about pushing the issue, not wanting to see Aunt Lodi in pain.

"Are you all right?"

Aunt Lodi pulled her hands away from her mouth, folded them, and placed them on her lips, mumbling a prayer. After a minute, she took a deep breath in and let it out loudly.

"I can do this. It will be good for me . . . for Jim . . . if you know the truth."

Jessica felt like she was in a movie, the moment felt so surreal. She started looking around at the setting. The burned-out trailer was in ruins, charred and taken over by the woods. Moss, fern, and other green inhabitants covered the side that had been left intact, while large yellow and brown weeds had struck a partnership around the top. The tall slender building had the look of weathered wood, faded by the elements, but surprisingly the door was still there, hanging from one rusted hinge.

Jessica looked back at Aunt Lodi to see what she wanted to do.

"I'm not ready to get out yet," Aunt Lodi said, staring straight ahead.

Jessica reached over to grab her hand, but Aunt Lodi pulled away. "I need a minute. Actually, don't touch me at all here."

Jessica pulled back, stunned, but respected her wishes, feeling like a toddler and keeping her hands to herself.

"I have not been back here since 1963, when that trailer burned."

"Were you in there when it burned?" Jessica whispered.

"No," Aunt Lodi said, pausing for a minute. "But Ermaline and Walker were."

Jessica's eyes widened, those names were finally going to have a story attached.

"Ermaline was our momma's sister and Walker was her husband. Our parents didn't like Walker, so we never spent much time together. Every now and then Ermaline would drive to the farm to visit with Momma but that was it. My parents knew nothing about wills, never entertained the thought that they may die before us. When they were killed, the state gave us to Ermaline, the only living relative. I was older than Jim, so I knew a little more about what was going on, and I was on guard around them, knowing there was a reason Momma and Daddy didn't spend time with them. Well, I soon found out. Walker was mean when he was sober, nice when he was buzzed, and too nice when he was drunk."

The pit of Jessica's stomach caved, knowing where this story was going.

"He hurt you," Jessica stated.

Aunt Lodi nodded her head. "For years I was at his call. Of course, Ermaline had no idea. She worked long hours and Walker was on disability and home all day. I would find loads of reasons to stay away, but this is where I would always have to come back to. And as you can see, we were isolated, so unless I got a ride on the school bus, I was stuck here.

"Of course we did run away once, but didn't get far, and Ermaline convinced the county sheriff we were having adjustment problems to our new home. I was afraid to tell the truth. I thought I was the one doing something wrong, the one who people would look at as dirty. Jim asked me why I didn't tell the sheriff what Walker was doing. I said it was because they would know I was a whore—because that's what Walker told me I was. I just didn't know."

Tears started streaking down Aunt Lodi's face, and she let them drop onto her lap. "Jim was only seven when we came here. The abuse started a few months later. Those weapons you found, the sticks and daggers, he made those so I could fight Walker off. Walker didn't hide what he was doing; Jim saw what was happening. When Jim was eight, he took a butter knife from the drawer and stabbed Walker with it. Walker threw him in the outhouse, locking him in there until Ermaline came home, but she ended up pulling a double shift and didn't return until the next day. Jim stayed in that God-awful building all night until Walker let him out, right before Ermaline got home. If you look inside the outhouse, you'll see carvings Jim made on the walls, carvings of him killing Walker."

Jessica looked over at the outhouse. The door was held in place by a rusted piece of metal at the top of the left side and the small roof was completely peeled off. She watched a bird fly in and out of the structure, seemingly calling it home.

Aunt Lodi made no attempts to plug up her nose or eyes as she cried without inhibition.

"They had a Rottweiler chained from a stake in the ground over there. Walker would put the dog by the outhouse so Jim couldn't escape when he was thrown in there for attacking Walker on many different occasions. We were so scared of that dog."

"The only thing that kept me and Jim alive in that first year was our love for each other and our horses. Ermaline agreed to board the two horses that were ours from the farm—Buttercup and Lightning. We would trek two miles up the road and stay for hours, sometimes falling asleep in their stalls, until woken by the farmer and shooed on back to hell. Jim and I would race through the trees, up the creek, and back through the pines; that's the only time in our life after our parents' death we truly felt safe and free. But all good things must end when you are living with evil."

Jessica, who had been staring at the wreckage, turned her face toward Aunt Lodi again, wishing to eradicate some of the pain.

"Remember the picture with me and Jim on the horses?"

"The one on his nightstand," Jessica said.

Aunt Lodi smiled. "We were so happy that day because we got our horses back. And please forgive me, God please forgive us, but we were also happy because Ermaline and Walker were dead."

"Around when I turned thirteen and Jim nine, Ermaline said she ran out of money to care for our horses. She sold them to another farmer in the area. Walker laughed when she told us at supper, and Ermaline threw a piece of cornbread at him. I tried not to, but my tears just started falling onto the table. Jim—he sat there with a look of hate. Ermaline apologized but said it had to be done, and then left the trailer to go to work. I had to clean up the cornbread that was scattered all over the floor while Jim got smacked around by Walker for having that look of hate on his face. I think Walker was starting to get a little scared of Jim, thinking maybe one day, he really would succeed at killing him."

Aunt Lodi broke off her speech and rubbed her temples in a slow circular motion as Jessica found her stomach retching and felt embarrassed by her apparent lack of grit.

"There was a country vet named Norbert Olson. He used to care for our animals on the farm. He was kind to my parents, and they always thought highly of him. Every once in a while, we would see him in town since he had a clinic there. He would ask how we were being treated, and we always put on a strong face saying fine, but I think he could tell that was not so. When I was fifteen, he asked if I wanted a job, helping in the clinic. I jumped at the chance but *only* if Jim could come too. We spent all of our time in that clinic, and Mr. Olson figured something wasn't right when we asked to stay there on Sundays, too. He never questioned us directly, but I could see in his expression he sensed something was amiss. He said we could stay in the apartment above the clinic as long as we kept it clean. Of course Walker was outraged, since I was not at his call anymore, and tried to put a stop to it, saying Mr. Olson must be doing something 'funny' to me. Mr. Olson took a drive out to see Walker when Ermaline was at work. I'm not sure what happened, but when he came back, he had a box with our clothing and a few other items from the trailer and said we could call this place home if we wished.

"Ermaline was fine with it, as long as she got her budget money from the state. At that time that's the money the government gave orphaned kids. Mr. Olson told her she could keep it, and from then on, I raised Jim above the clinic. Mr. Olson helped us of course. We would ride out to farms to help him care for animals, receiving dinners and canned food as payment. Along the way, we searched for our horses, believing that one day we would happen upon the farm they were at and Mr. Olson would get them back for us.

"I graduated high school and got a job at the local market as a cashier until Jim graduated. But Jim started getting into trouble in high school, drinking and fighting with a bunch of guys, the 'going-nowhere bunch,' I called them. Jim said he was going to hang out the summer after graduation then get a job in the fall. Well, I saw where that was headed so I said no. I'm the one who convinced him to join the Army, the only place I thought that could save him from himself. But in order to join the Army, you had to have a birth certificate and the only people we knew to have that information were Ermaline and Walker. We could have gone to the court building and requested a new birth certificate, but Jim pumped our heads up, feeding our egos, wanting to show them that we were in control of our lives. So we went to reclaim *all* of our personal items: pictures and other things that were rightfully ours. I had not been out to their place in seven years, and let me tell you, I actually had to pull over so I could throw up on the side of the road. Jim coped by cracking his knuckles and sipping on a flask of Johnnie Walker. By this time Jim was well over six feet, and I was worried about his anger; he really had a lot of hatred toward Walker and I was afraid he might hurt him."

Aunt Lodi's tears slowed down until they came like a casual drip from a faucet.

"The first Rottweiler had been replaced by another vicious-looking dog that barked endlessly until Ermaline opened the trailer door and told it to shut up. She then turned to us saying how happy she was to see us and called to Walker, 'the prodigals have returned home.' I never thought of that place as 'home.'

"I barely made it through the door when the stench from Walker's too many drinks hit me hard. He grabbed me and said how much he missed me, and before I could step away from his grasp, Jim went ballistic. He pushed Walker so hard that Walker flew into the small stove where some food was cooking. Walker's sleeve ignited and as Ermaline struggled to push him down and put the fire out, a towel in the kitchen also went up in flames. Before we knew it, part of the kitchen had been surrounded by fire. I was frozen for a minute, but Jim pulled me into their back bedroom and started searching for our stuff. He yelled for me to help him but all I could think was these two were about to get burned up, and even though they had done wrong, they should be saved. But I couldn't move into action. Jim grabbed a small metal box and rushed me out the rear door. By that time, the kitchen and living room were now ablaze, and while maybe we could have pulled them out, we didn't. I don't remember hearing them scream; in fact, I barely remember hearing anything but that dog barking like he was the one burning. Jim and I looked on as the heat and brimstone and everything that I envisioned hell to look like overtook the place, wiping out all physical reminders of Ermaline and Walker. When we finally got into the car, I looked at Jim and said, 'I think our nightmare is over' and started to cry. Actually, we both cried and hung onto each other in the front seat, with the blaze casting sparks of light until Jim said we needed to get away before the place blew."

Aunt Lodi gave Jessica a small smile as she leaned her head against the headrest.

"Mr. Olson broke the news, and me and Jim played shocked and saddened, asking if anyone knew what happened. After a while it was ruled an accident, knowing that Walker's blood alcohol was so high he could have ignited the fire with one blow of his breath. That metal box contained our birth certificates, a few old pictures from the farm, and the sales receipt for our horses. We burned the other contents, their personal stuff, and set off to get our horses back. Unfortunately, the farmer who originally purchased them had passed away, and they were sold at auction. We could have gone to the auction house to get that information. Jim was ready for us to take a road trip and chase them down, but I thought it would be in Jim's best interest to go into the Army. I was afraid that what happened to Ermaline and Walker would prove to be a memory that would be hard to shake without Johnny Walker. Jim disagreed, but in the end, like always, he did what I asked him to do. I told him I would find them and we would go together and reclaim them, money in hand. So Jim left for boot camp and I, the one who was afraid of Jim falling into the trap of Johnny Walker, fell into a different trap—the '60s.

"I had spent from age eleven until twenty-two taking care of and raising not only myself but also Jim. I never realized that without that anchor, I was like a stormy sea. Plus the memories, all those terrible memories, had no place to go because I kept them sunk real low. But trust me, secrets make you sick."

Jessica could not help but say, "I know."

Aunt Lodi turned toward Jessica. "I know you do. But the secrets I'm talking about are the kind that you will do whatever it takes to forget. And that's what I tried to do. I was everywhere and nowhere for a while, finally ending up in San Francisco during the Summer of Love. I sent Jim letters, staying places long enough to get a response back, but nothing came. I thought he was dead and believed I didn't have much to live for either."

For the first time since Jessica and Aunt Lodi became engaged in the story, Aunt Lodi chuckled. "He tracked me down in a friend's rented room on Haight Street. I thought I got a hold of some bad stuff and kept saying 'No, you're not Jim. You're the devil.'"

Jessica had visions of hippies strewn through the streets of Haight-Ashbury while her father, in fatigues, stormed the place, making the hippies walk around him as he strode down the sidewalk on a mission to save his sister.

"He brought me to Chicago where he set up residence and

introduced me to his girlfriend, Katherine. Oh, I wish you could have seen your mother's face when she set eyes on me. I wore flowers in my hair because I was addicted to that song and felt like flowers were some magical beings that could transform the hate I had for myself into something sweeter, at least to those looking at me from the outside. After smoking too much hash in the apartment and cooking with it, your mother had a fit when she realized she ate one of my 'special' brownies. Jim then pushed me into rehab. But I wasn't an addict; I was suppressing memories of abuse and needed someone to talk to. So that's what rehab did for me—allowed me a safe place to confront the past without falling into a state of self-induced amnesia.

"I came out of rehab and quickly realized a big city like Chicago made my skin crawl—too many people on top of each other. I could not stand to be in close proximity to anyone but Jim. So, with his blessing, I returned to the UP and set up my life where I live right now. Jim helped me buy the property—he gave me a place to call home."

Jessica sat motionless while the picture of her father saving Aunt Lodi settled into her head.

"War was not good for your father but at the same time it was. He had all the makings of a killing machine from living here, but I figured better to kill for your country rather than incur a death sentence in Michigan. Sometimes I regretted pushing him into the Army, but that was the best solution I had to offer at the time."

They sat in silence for a while until Aunt Lodi spoke again. "I think he saved Paul because he saw himself in him, knowing that without me or Mr. Olson, he would have been on that track too."

Jessica nodded in agreement, and while her head was still absorbing all that was shared, she felt angry for not knowing this information when her father was alive.

"Why didn't he want me to know all this?" Jessica finally asked.

Aunt Lodi looked past her and toward the charred remains. "He didn't want to remember it. He surely didn't want you exposed to it."

"But it would have explained a lot about why he did certain things. I would have understood him better."

"Those were his wishes; this is his story."

"And yours."

"Yes. We are braided by experience—survival really."

The sun was fading over the edge of the tree line to the west as a sharp breeze started shaking the vegetation.

"How did you get the horses back?"

"Once I settled up here, Jim came in the winter to help me with some things. We started talking about the horses and decided to find them. It took us a week, but we located them on a farm, about twenty minutes from my home. After all those years, I knew they remembered us because Buttercup nuzzled her nose in the nape of my neck like she did when we were together long ago. The owner—her name was Ingrid—said she never saw her do that before. Ingrid's the one who took the picture of us on that sunny winter day. I made it a point to go there once a week to ride Buttercup, and Ingrid was great about it. The horses passed away when you were a little girl. I don't think you remember, but we took you to Ingrid's and you fed them carrot sticks. Your dad lifted you up so you could reach your small hands up to meet their mouths. It was so heartwarming."

Jessica smiled at the thought of her father holding her in a loving embrace while she met the horse that helped save her father and aunt from such distress.

"Where's Mr. Olson?"

"He passed many years back, but we always shared time together and your dad would do the same when he was in town. I'm not sure if me or Jim would have turned out this way if Mr. Olson had not helped us."

Jessica started thinking that the layers of a person could not be defined until you unearthed his or her past. And that while you will never forget the pain, and will be forever changed because of it, you can start living again. Slowly, very slowly, the heaviness Jessica encountered when thinking about her father started lifting away, believing now that her father really tried to be the best dad he could under the circumstances.

"Jessica, I'm ready to go home now," Aunt Lodi said. "I really do have closure."

Jessica gave Aunt Lodi a loving smile, which was returned, and she gently turned the ignition to move them forward, leaving the past to only be remembered by the land.

The drive back to Aunt Lodi's was quiet. Jessica paying attention to the sounds her tires made on different pavements while her mind wandered toward Matt, wondering how he would respond to her letter, and to her father and Aunt Lodi's past.

When they returned home, Aunt Lodi said she was going to take a shower and would love some hot tea. Jessica blended chamomile and rose petals together and poured hot water into a large mug, placing it on the end table in the living room, along with the TV remotes and burning sage. They sat together on the couch watching a comedy, just like the old days, but this time Aunt Lodi was cradled under Jessica's outstretched arm.

Chapter 30

Night after night Jessica's pillow was damp, as she pictured her father as a young boy, being smacked around, witnessing untold acts being done to his sister. Images of the harshness her father had to endure, knowing he was a man divided between a permanent war zone and true belonging, made Jessica feel pity for him and her heart soften toward his plight. She wrestled with the history between them, wishing he were still alive so that she could mend their relationship. But maybe Aunt Lodi was right; he never wanted her exposed to his story, never wanted her to experience the trauma of his youth. Never unleashing childhood memories to protect Jessica from the dark side he was capable of igniting at the flick of a flame.

Jessica was thankful for the daylight hours because it distracted her from endless thoughts and gave her time to prepare for Marilee's visit. It was Marilee's spring break from school, and she would arrive on Wednesday and leave Saturday. Jessica was so excited about having her best friend back in her life. Although their relationship was different now—Jessica felt more in control of her decisions, unlike in high school, and believed Marilee got that message when she was home dealing with her father's death and Paul. But Jessica was clear on how much she missed having a girlfriend, one in which she could confide in about everything. While Jean was a good friend, their age difference made Jessica sometimes feel like her daughter.

As Marilee drove up Aunt Lodi's driveway, Jessica ran out to greet her.

"Oh, Jess, this is so beautiful," Marilee said after getting out of the car and looking around as the trees moved to the song of the breeze.

"I know. I wish you could see the farm—it's even more breathtaking."

Marilee cocked her head to the side and gave a faint smile. "Any news on that front?"

"No," Jessica said, turning to look in the distance. "I sent him the letter and CD but nothing yet. I think we're going on a week. Don't you think that's a really long time not to talk to someone? I know I was completely wrong, but to cut me out like this feels like a punishment."

Marilee nodded. "Have you thought about driving out there?"

"Yes," Jessica said quickly. "But then I get cold feet. What if he kicks me off the property? Or if his family's there, I would feel so embarrassed."

"I could go with you."

Jessica felt an inch taller with those words. "Maybe. Let me think about it."

Once Marilee unpacked and got settled into the room Jessica's father would occupy on his visits, they drove to town so Marilee could see the sights: two blocks of independent businesses and a marina. It was creeping up on dinnertime, so they grabbed a bite in a quaint restaurant—an old Victorian home that overlooked Lake Michigan. During dinner, they shared equally about the past, the missed years, and the present, barely pausing to eat or drink.

After dinner, the girls walked through the historic downtown district which ran parallel to the marina, and Jessica introduced Marilee to many of the business owners. Marilee halted in front of Murphy's Pub.

"Look. They have karaoke tomorrow night. Oh, we have to go," Marilee said.

Jessica felt uneasy, recalling the last time she had been there.

"What? Why do you have that look on your face?"

"It's just the last time I was here I drank too much and said lots of things I shouldn't have," Jessica said.

"Well, you won't have to worry about that. I have heard and seen it all," Marilee said, laughing as she put her arm over Jessica's shoulders. "You're in good hands with me."

Jessica couldn't help but believe Marilee's assurances, finally relenting on karaoke and Marilee's idea of inviting Jean and Aunt Lodi to join in the festivities too.

"It's always a good time when you have a bunch of ladies singing off pitch," Marilee stated.

Jessica made the calls as she drove them back to Aunt Lodi's. She also, at Marilee's prodding, called Matt, leaving a message on his voice mail stating she hoped he got her letter and CD and that she missed him so bad her heart ached daily. Her last words on the voice mail were asking for the gift of forgiveness.

Marilee's eyes filled with tears when Jessica hung up. "That was beautiful."

Right before pulling off the county road and onto Aunt Lodi's property, Jessica's phone rang. It was Paulina, asking again when she was coming home. It was easy to switch the subject, telling her Marilee was in town and they would discuss it when she left. After a few moments, Jessica handed the phone to Marilee.

"Paulina wants to say hi."

After some brief chatter, Marilee hung up. "So we have a riding date with your daughter tomorrow, on the farm."

"What?" Jessica said, slamming the brakes of her truck on Aunt Lodi's driveway.

"I couldn't say no. That would look suspicious. She asked for us to be there at three o'clock."

"*Us?*"

"What could I say?"

"Maybe that you're allergic to horses. Something. How do you expect me to show my face when Matt has left me in silence?"

Out of Jessica's periphery, she could see Marilee looking at her. "Can you drop me off and I'll say you had to go back to Lodi, then see if Paulina can give me a ride back?"

A stern look is what Jessica gave Marilee before opening the car door.

"Fine. I'll drop you off and then have Paulina bring you back. But she cannot stay at Aunt Lodi's since we're going to Murphy's, and Aunt Lodi is supposed to be in bed."

"I'll handle everything. Don't worry, okay, everything will work out." Marilee smiled.

The next day, the girls decided to drive two hours to hike to a cluster of waterfalls in Wisconsin. It was a gorgeous spring day, with the temperature hovering above sixty-eight degrees and not a cloud in the sky. Marilee continued to marvel at nature, commenting on the way the pine trees grew, looking through the rows of tree trunks into the cave of the woods. Jessica gave a lesson on the trees that grew in the UP. She pointed out the differences between the red, white, and jack pines and identified most hardwoods, such as the paper birch, sugar maple, and ironwood.

"How do you know all this?" Marilee asked.

"When you live with a farmer and nature lover, you tend to pick up on things, even when you're not paying attention."

Backpacks loaded with food and other supplies, the girls trekked their way upriver with Jessica pointing out the cottonwood, silver maple, and box elder trees that loved living by the water. Jessica ran her hand across the bark of the cottonwood, looking up at the buds just forming. The leaves each year on these trees were almost like friends.

"I love trees," Jessica stated to Marilee. "It's strange, but I always felt a connection to them. Even when I lived in Chicago, I always felt the trees were looking out for me."

Marilee stopped for a minute to pull out a canister of water. After a big swallow, she said, "I get it," looking up the tree Jessica had her hands planted on. "They have some sort of quality, I agree."

"When I was younger, I remember running through the woods with Jason and feeling free. And the trees were my protectors. Kinda like angels."

"A dose of protection without the Mace."

Jessica laughed out loud, something that surprised her, finally being able to make light of the Mace that was her father's idea of protection.

They continued toward the tumbling sounds of water, eventually climbing the multiple rock formations to find a place they could sit on without falling into the rapids. Marilee took a load of pictures while Jessica closed her eyes and tipped her face toward the sun, taking cleansing breaths, thanking God for the beauty of nature, and again asking for Matt's forgiveness.

"Are you still with me?"

Jessica's eyes jerked opened as she set her focus on Marilee, who was sitting only inches away from her face. "Oh, sorry. I was just praying. You know, thankful for all we have and asking for a small gift."

Marilee nodded. "You're a strong believer still."

"Oh yes. Sometimes prayers were the only thing that got me through many lonely days and nights in my home. You guys were always the same way—church every Sunday."

"You know us Catholics—church every Sunday or guilt. But seriously, my parents were really good at laying a solid foundation for us to follow, and I have followed it, with my kids, every Sunday. But we don't prepare those huge breakfasts like we used to, unless we go to Mom and Dad's."

After exploring the area and resting to eat lunch, the girls headed back toward the farm so Jessica could drop Marilee off for her horseback riding adventure.

Jessica's palms started to sweat as her heart tap-danced the closer she got to the driveway. It was as if nervousness was brimming from all areas of her body, including her toes, which were unexpectedly cramping up. Jessica took intentional breaths to get back into the rhythm of ease, daydreaming of Matt seeing her and letting the burden of the past fall away.

"I'll let you off on the side of the road, so all you have to do is walk up that driveway."

Marilee smiled as Jessica pulled the truck over, making a cloud of dust on the gravel road. "Thank you, my dear," Marilee said as she slid out of the truck. "I'll be back in what, two hours?"

"Sure," Jessica said, stretching her neck to see if she could spot Matt. "Actually it will be more like three."

"Sounds great."

Jessica watched Marilee hike up the draw in the hill and then glide down, eventually out of sight. After one more glance around the property line, Jessica pulled onto the road and headed back to Aunt Lodi's house. She hated the stretch of silence Matt was exposing her to, and she had to remember how to be patient. But with no end in sight, Jessica started contemplating telling Paulina the truth, believing Paulina would finally question why she'd stayed away for so long and why Matt didn't go to Aunt Lodi's to visit. Although Jessica lied a few times, telling Paulina about visiting the farm when she was at school, riding the horses, and helping Matt with his lengthy to-do list, Jessica would always call Matt and leave a message, asking him to back up her lie so that Paulina didn't question their lack of togetherness. But backing up lies was not the way Jessica wanted to run their relationship; after her cathartic experience at her mother's home, all she wanted was to be on her new path of freedom from within. Lies were not welcome.

Jessica filled her idle time with a nap, shower, and rereading a section of the newspaper she did not pay close attention to in the morning, realizing that Marilee enjoyed noise, preferably her own, early in the morning before coffee.

Aunt Lodi returned from work, drank some tea, and then changed her clothes, excited about spending time out with the "girls."

"Tell me when Paulina gets here so I can hunch over a little when I walk."

Those words were still floating in the air when Marilee stepped onto the front porch, without Paulina.

"She was running a little late—has a date with Jake."

"Oh," Jessica said, feeling left out of the daily details of her daughter's world.

"Jessica, I had a great time," Marilee gushed, moving Jessica back into the now. "The land you live on is gorgeous. I was in awe at all the colors from one section to the next. It was like a quilt, you know, a section of green over here, then a section of brown, then yellow. Loved it! Although I think I really do have an allergy to horses. I sneezed about twenty times while we were riding and I gotta be frank, my ass is hurting so bad and I can barely pull my legs together. I feel so bow-legged."

Jessica laughed out loud.

"Don't get me wrong, it was awesome, but my body's not so sure."

Jessica held her tongue, letting Marilee roll out her experiences in sequence, before asking about Matt. By this time, the girls had made their way to the guest room and Marilee sprawled on top of the bed, looking like she was about to make a snow angel in the comforter.

"There are muscles in my butt I didn't know existed," Marilee said.

Jessica heard her best friend's moans but could only concentrate on one thing.

"Matt?" Jessica said, again trying to push away the nervousness.

Marilee's face changed when Matt was mentioned, and she slowly sat up on her elbows.

"Well I met him, I mean Paulina introduced us. I tried to chat but he was too busy with farm stuff."

"Did he seem disinterested in talking to you?"

Marilee was silent for a few seconds. "Yeah, a little. He was working hard, you could tell by the dirt and stuff on his overalls, but he also seemed distant, not really wanting to take our conversation deeper."

Jessica frowned as she took on the weight of what felt like another rejection.

"But I chased him down anyway."

Jessica turned to look at Marilee, who had a huge smile on her face.

"So he finally did talk to me. I was able to get away from Paulina for a few minutes, but he really was not interested in talking about you.

Lisa Maggiore

He never came right out and said that, but I could see how uncomfortable he was with me just mentioning you and our history together. He seemed bothered with me telling him how much he means to you and that what happened in Chicago was two people who never got closure."

Jessica mulled over what Marilee was saying. "Did he seem upset that you knew all this information?"

"I wouldn't say upset, just unsure."

The guest room became darker by each minute passing as the sun was now beneath the windowsill and sending a cold shiver in its path.

"Jess," Marilee said as she gently rolled over onto her side slowly sitting up. "I can tell he loves you. I'm just not sure he knows what he's supposed to do next."

Chapter 31

As the dark of night poured onto the streets of the historic district, Jessica, Marilee, Aunt Lodi, and Jean took their places at a corner table in Murphy's Pub. The pub was packed with a mixed group of twentysomethings and beyond, eagerly awaiting to hear who was the next person willing to be made a fool. Jessica ordered a glass of wine, feeling nervous, remembering how she took advantage of its warmth the last time it was in her hand. Aunt Lodi whispered in her ear to not order a second, reminding her of last week's drama. The loneliness was hard to shake, but Jessica had learned and was not willing to sacrifice herself again for the sake of coping.

Aunt Lodi and Jean excused themselves to say hi to some people they knew while Jessica and Marilee winced at a man butchering a Springsteen song. Marilee grabbed the binder of songs and started flipping through the pages, trying to find the perfect one they could sing to.

"You don't really think I'm going up there, do you?" Jessica said.

"Hey, we're all in this together."

Jessica tried not to show her hesitation, afraid of ruining Marilee's fun.

"Oh my God, remember this one?" Marilee exclaimed as she happened upon the pages with all eighties music.

Jessica didn't feel the same nostalgia as Marilee about eighties music. Due to her lack of exposure to entertainment while growing up, the only artists that she had a history with were Prince and Johnny Cash, and both of those had Paul attached.

Marilee continued to talk in her trademark loud voice about all the songs they had to choose from while Jessica pulled away, not sure if this was where she was meant to be. She tried not to allow her depression to eclipse the moment. She knew better but it was hard to push against the wave of sorrow that had Matt's face attached. The fact that he did not want to speak about her with Marilee was not too surprising—Matt was a private man. But that he seemed so disinterested in talking about her was hard to swallow. Jessica reminded herself that time can heal some wounds, but she also felt that she may have to let go, unable to take back what she did, unable to control what happened next.

"Hey, did you hear me? What do you think about this song?" Marilee's voice brought Jessica back to reality.

"Oh, let's see," she said, faking excitement.

As the evening progressed and they listened to one choppy song after another, cheering loudly for the worst singers, Marilee finally persuaded them to get up and sing. It was last call, which meant they were the last song to perform that night. Dragging her body onto the dance floor, Jessica hated how vulnerable she felt in front of everyone and stood halfway behind Aunt Lodi, trying to hide herself from direct light. After their rendition of "Respect" by Aretha Franklin was complete, Jessica bounded off the floor and tucked herself back into the corner seat. Jean and Aunt Lodi were all smiles because they were so proud that they had enough nerve to actually get up there and sing, both firsts for them. They clinked their glasses in celebration and went to the bar to get more water before heading home. Marilee turned toward Jessica with an expression of joy, but it vanished after setting her eyes on Jessica's face.

"What's wrong?"

Jessica put her hands over her eyes that were now collecting tears and tried to wipe them before they fell. "I'm sorry. I don't want to spoil your night."

"This isn't my night—it's everyone's."

"I know. I just can't get my mind past what you said about Matt. I just feel so lost and alone right now."

"I'm sorry, Jess," Marilee said, pulling the chair next to hers to rub the middle of her back. "Look, if you and Matt break up, you'll learn from it and move on, right? You've been through worse and look how you overcame it. You're a strong woman. You'll find a way to make it."

Jessica never thought of herself as a strong woman and was surprised by the way the words pumped a brief amount of adrenaline through her veins, but the thought of Matt leaving her left her wide open. The tears were coming at a faster pace, so she told Marilee she needed a few minutes alone and excused herself to the restroom.

Jessica tried to look chipper as she waited for a few girls who were putting on lipstick and fixing their hair to leave. Once they did, she cupped her hands underneath the sink and placed cool water on her face, not caring about the mascara streaks running down it. She heard a faint husky voice start singing on and off through the bathroom doors as she started falling apart. Marilee's words, because of a short supply of faith at the moment, left her feeling hopeless. As Jessica ripped paper towels from the dispenser in an attempt to wipe the blackness from her face, she was again drawn to that husky voice, standing completely still so she could make out the music that sounded so familiar. After a few seconds, she realized she was hearing "The Beautiful Ones" by Prince. Jessica placed the towels back on her face, rubbing a little harder and wondering who was singing that song here.

The voice faltered but then sounded stronger, almost pulsating through the wood. Jessica realized she recognized the voice. At that moment, the bathroom door swung open and Aunt Lodi stepped in. "Do you hear that?"

Jessica nodded, feeling love awaken in her soul.

"Well, get out there."

Jessica followed Aunt Lodi as they walked back into the dining room area. Patrons and acquaintances surrounded the dance floor while Marilee and Jean were standing by the karaoke table, holding onto each other, amazed at what they were seeing.

Jessica peeked from behind Aunt Lodi, not sure how she should be reacting, then moved to Aunt Lodi's side so she could be in full view.

The words she knew well and the image she dreamt of over and over during her teenage years while lying next to her pile of pillows was actually happening. A boy was singing this song to her because he loved her so much and he did not want to lose her to another.

He looked awkward, microphone in hand, singing toward where Jessica was standing, but needing to look at the words in order to sing them properly. Jessica was drawn to how attractive he looked in his dark wash jeans and plaid shirt, how tall his frame was, and how his voice made her feel comforted.

He continued to send the song Jessica's way, pouring his heart and sweat into the concert, increasing the pitch as best he could without faltering.

Jessica and Aunt Lodi held hands while he asked Jessica who she wanted: *him or me?* "Because I want you."

Not caring who was staring at them, Jessica brought herself to stand inches from his body. Every ounce of her felt like she was whole, not because of his love, but in coming full circle in understanding that love and loss were a part of life, but so was love and forgiveness.

He inflated his pitch, adding a few fist pumps and then reaching his arm out toward her to accentuate the last part of the song's intensity. Jessica, who normally hated this type of attention, braved the onslaught of stares from those around them and continued to set her sights on Matt.

He pushed his body to perform things it had never been asked to do before, and Jessica was so grateful for his performance. Her face shone as he spun around and then launched forward to sing the end as strong and memorable as it could be. This was out of character for him but so admirable. Matt grabbed the microphone with both hands when he screamed the last lines, then fell to his knees as the song ended.

The whoops and hollers from the crowd overtook Jessica, and on instinct she advanced toward Matt, who had quickly risen from the floor. She walked straight into his chest, placing her lips on his with such fervor that it made her heart lurch upward. Matt returned the gesture, and they kissed while the crowd continued to whistle and cheer, Jessica soaking in the heat from the lights above them.

Epilogue

Jessica shivered beneath the alpaca cape wrapped around her shoulders. She'd thought about wearing something warmer but didn't want to ruin the dress underneath with the weight of the wool.

With Jessica planted on Moses's back, they walked through the crisp snow, taking deep breaths, letting her mind wander and fall at will. Blowing out air from her lungs, Jessica stared at the path of white it made, focusing her energy on being a worthwhile human being, one that anyone could love, even herself. For the first time in her life, she felt at home from within.

Snow had fallen the night before, leaving a path of pristine whiteness covering the birch, beech, and white pine trees. Deer and small animal tracks could be seen from Jessica's standpoint, and she tilted her head to the side to admire nature's beauty. From above she heard the call of the crow and sparrow, and she kept a sharp eye out for the grouse, which on her many rides through the woods had scared her with its explosion of flight from just a few yards away.

Jessica leaned forward and placed the right side of her face on Moses's warm neck, loving the way muscles and hair felt next to her skin and appreciating the subtle fragrance of sweat and the outdoors with leather from the saddle mixed in. A smell she loved the first time she got a whiff.

Gently, she pulled her head from Moses's skin and said a prayer, thanking God for bringing her safely to this day.

Their journey would end just past the balsam fir and white spruce, where a slight clearing revealed the top of a hill that overlooked a valley. On a summer day, the valley would be an array of patchwork to indicate which fields were growing which crops. Today it was an expansive field of white, looking regal and wise as it lay out in front of her like a blank canvas.

Jessica had asked to make the journey alone, something that most everyone found alarming, except for Matt. He understood even before she explained that she needed to be with her inner self before stepping in front of him and others on this day.

They picked winter because of the picture of her father and Aunt Lodi, on horseback in the snowy woods, feeling one with the universe. That image made Jessica believe that surely her father would know that today was a day he helped create—one that took a long time for her to appreciate, but one that she wanted to share with his spirit. To be as close to his spirit as she imagined she could be here on earth.

And to also thank Paul, who gave a selfless gift to Paulina and in so doing gave Jessica the freedom to commit to love. She'd written him a thank-you letter and burned it the night before. Watching the smoke billow from the woodpile into the night air, listening to the crackle and hiss from the logs, believing that Paul's gesture of goodness would be rewarded one day, but probably not by her own hands.

The people on horseback were in sight even before the clearing. Most rode their own horses while a few guests from Chicago rode some of Matt's that were good followers. Her mother decided to take Matt up on his offer and rode in a sleigh drawn by one of his Belgians along with Aunt Lodi.

Matt's family, including his mother, Irene, were hedged next to him in a neat array of brown, gold, and amber horses, facing toward the woods. Jessica popped out from the tall trunks of pine and crept to the edge of the clearing along a small trail that had been made by the guests. Moses lifted his head and nodded a few times, letting out rankles of hot breath and appeared to be calling attention to the people who gathered together that they had arrived.

Jessica set her sights on her good friends, Marilee and Jean, who both looked freezing cold but breathtakingly beautiful, and with her eyes and smile said hello. Jessica's face also acknowledged that without them separately running interference with Matt, this day may not have been possible.

She then turned her sights on Jason, who more and more resembled their father but with the lightheartedness of Aunt Lodi, and strode toward him, pulling up beside and leaning over to kiss him on the cheek. He met her affection by reaching over to give her a hug, one that almost caused her to slip from Moses.

Aunt Lodi and her mother were next in line to receive the life touch that kept them connected as a family. As Jessica unwrapped her arms from her mother, she saw tears trickle down the side of her cheekbone. Her mother quickly wiped them away with her leather glove.

"They are happy ones," her mother announced.

Jessica giggled from within, watching Aunt Lodi try to tuck her mother into the fold of her arm.

Finally, Jessica found Matt. His face was tender and soft with pink tinges from the cold gathered around the tip of his nose and cheeks. He sat tall in his saddle and, with his black wool coat, looked like a cowboy waiting for his girl.

Small smiles crept up their faces, finally becoming huge ones.

Pastor Erickson was standing in the middle of the semicircle, Bible in hand, and asked if they were ready to commence.

Paulina got off her horse and walked over to Moses, holding onto his reins as Jessica carefully dismounted, not wanting to rip any part of her wedding dress. Paulina handed her a bouquet of red roses tied together with a piece of the wedding dress Jessica's mother wore many years ago. Before leaving her side, Jessica embraced Paulina and kissed her on the lips. Their hands remained clasped, eyes reflecting their bond of a shared childhood, before Jessica set her free and glided over toward Matt.

Jessica smoothed her hand around the arm that Matt was holding out for her, and they strode a few steps together before stopping in front of the pastor. Jessica looked up at Matt and grinned, pulling up her ivory and lace skirt, revealing her pearl-colored cowgirl boots.

"I match," she whispered, showing him her ensemble.

"Me too," he whispered back, showing off his black tux and matching shiny cowboy boots.

After the ceremony, people gathered at their home for a reception. They had close to seventy-five people, including Mr. and Mrs. Ripp and Eddie and his family.

Jessica's mother helped coordinate the reception, hiring caterers, flowers, and a photographer. She'd come a week earlier to help Jessica decorate the house and the heated outbuilding that would serve as the dance floor.

Paulina was in charge of music and had a playlist of songs that Marilee had requested. Paulina sneaked a few choices of her own and danced away the night with Jake at her side.

Well into the evening, with the party getting louder, Jessica and Matt found themselves in the barn, kissing on a pile of hay.

"Do you think anyone knows we're gone?" Jessica laughed, pulling away. "What kind of bride and groom are we?"

"The kind that likes to kiss," Matt said and met her lips again with his.

After many minutes, they took deep breaths and Matt told her he had something for her.

Jessica looked stunned. "But we said no presents."

"I know," he said, as he made his way to a dark part of the barn. "But I thought it would be important for you to have this."

Jessica made herself more comfortable on the hay pile while listening to the faint sounds of music and laughter from the house.

"I hope your brother doesn't go and shoot off his gun again. My mother nearly hit the ceiling when he did that yesterday."

Jessica could hear Matt's laughter from the back of the barn and could not keep her eyes off him as he walked back into the soft light with a wrapped package the size of a shoebox in hand.

"What is this?" Jessica asked slyly as he slid down next to her and placed it in her lap. He wrapped his arm around her shoulder and told her to open it and find out.

Jessica attended to it as if it were fragile, admiring the pink gift wrap that had small hearts with lace attached. She removed the tape then gently pulled the box out of its paper cave.

Jessica ran her hand over the white leather and traced with her manicured fingertips the engraved gold lettering "Childhood Memories." Jessica looked at Matt, puzzled, but at his prodding pulled off the top of the box. Inside were neatly stacked black-and-white pictures, and under those, some color pictures that had faded with time.

"What is this?" Jessica asked slowly, but before Matt could answer she knew. These were the only pictures of her father's history.

Matt had spent two months gathering photos from Aunt Lodi and her mother. Having some restored and labeled so that Jessica could have a more complete past with her father.

"Look at this one," Matt said, riffling through and grabbing hold of a black-and-white shot of a toddler riding a sheep. "That was your dad at a state fair. He won first prize for staying on the longest."

Overwhelmed by feelings of gratitude, Jessica placed the box between her legs and cupped her hands around Matt's face. "Thank you," she said and kissed him passionately. After the heated moment, she pulled away. "I feel terrible. I have no gift for you."

"Your gift was marrying me," Matt said.

Jessica sat for a few seconds until the thought that was rolling in her head finally came into focus.

"Actually I would like to give you a gift," she said with a shy smile.

Matt looked at her and grinned. "Oh yeah? What might that be?"

Jessica met his gaze. "A boy. Someday soon."

Matt blinked and lay back in the hay. After a few seconds, he yelled, "Well, what are we waiting for?" and rolled on top of Jessica as she shrieked in delight.

ACKNOWLEDGEMENTS

Huge Thank You to all my Beta Readers: Kathy Branigan, Amanda Bryant, Kerri Sandberg, Debbie Rosier, and Sabine Willems. You gave tough, honest and valuable feedback which helped polish this story into a gem and I am forever grateful.

Thank you to Sarah Skarda at myshortpockets.com for book cover design. It looks awesome doesn't it?!?! Sarah captured the heart of this story with just a few tries!

And of course, to the editors, proofreaders and eBook formatter: Jennifer McCartney, Michele Moore, JW Manus & Lisanne Kaufmann for their valuable time and effort in making this story the very BEST it can be. I know that sounds like an Army commercial but that's the truth.

And to my daughter, Angelica, who loved the story before it had a chance to blossom into what you just read. Thank you for reading it first and sharing with me the "awesome" parts and the parts that "made me cry."

And of course, to my husband Sam, who read and read and read again and ALWAYS found something that could be improved. Thank you for reading when you didn't always want to and thank you for your honesty, although sometimes brutal, and thank you for being a little bit of Paul and a little bit of Matt. I would love to watch you sing a song to me one day!

ABOUT THE AUTHOR

Lisa Maggiore is the author of a children's picture book, *Ava the Monster Slayer: A Warrior Who Wears Glasses* and a fiction short story, *Pinterest Saved My Marriage*. Lisa is currently working on other writing projects and practicing her storytelling skills during Live Lit performances. Lisa resides in Chicago with her husband and four children. Lisa loves to travel, watch da Bears during the NFL season and be silly with her family.

Check out all that's happening with her writing career on:
Website: lisamaggiore.com
Twitter: @MaggioreBooks
Facebook: Lisa Maggiore Books

Enter your email to join my enewsletter and you can choose a FREE gift: *Ava the Monster Slayer Activity Book* OR *Ava's Birth*, the true short story of how I delivered my daughter while my husband drove 55 m.p.h on the expressway and a prostitute and homeless drug addicts saved her life. You'll be kept up to date about giveaways and free stuff (I like to give cool stuff.) You can unsubscribe at any time.
http://eepurl.com/bDDaB5

Please leave an honest review. Reviews take only a few seconds and can make an enormous difference. Without your reviews, my hard work might go unnoticed. I appreciate your support and I thank you!

CPSIA information can be obtained
at www.ICGtesting.com
Printed in the USA
FFOW04n1952161216
30366FF

9 780986 271800